MURDER

ON THE

INTERSTATE

MURDER

ON THE

INTERSTATE

A Logan & Cafferty
Mystery/Suspense Novel

Jean Henry Mead

First edition April 2011
Second edition August 2011

Cover design by Bill Mead

ISBN: 978-1-931415-32-3

Other novels in the Logan & Cafferty series
by Jean Henry Mead:

A Village Shattered
Diary of Murder

Dedication:

For my friend, Jean Mathisen Haugen
and in memory of her husband, Ron.

Acknowledgements

I'm grateful to Chemist Dick Ayers for his willingness to share his expertise about chemical spills, especially sulfuric acid. And to my Scottish friend Bill Kirton for alerting me to his expertise. Thanks also to Dave Matula of White's Mountain Motors for his information about Hummers in flood waters, and to the truck drivers I talked with and listened to on my CB radio while driving my motorhome along northern Arizona's Interstate 40 when it was under massive road construction. I came to appreciate the problems truckers face en route to deliver their goods as well as the important role they play in our commerce.

I appreciate my blog team partner Ben Small's articles about the problems Arizona faces with illegal immigration and the resultant increased crime rates, including drug trafficking, murder and home invasions. I was shocked to watch hidden camera videos shot on the U.S-Mexican border, which showed heavy traffic of Mexican nationals and known terrorists crossing into this country. It's my sincerest hope that our government takes a more supportive role in helping our border states combat the problems they face with illegal immigration, instead of adding to their woes by taking them to court.

~Jean Henry Mead

Chapter 1

Lulled by a lack of traffic and the steady beat of rain, Dana was in danger of nodding off when a convertible roared past, followed by a late model pickup. The heavy downpour obscured her view, but they appeared to be coupled like boxcars. Why they were driving that dangerously close, and why so fast in the rain?

An I-40 highway sign signaled an approaching curve so she clicked off the cruise control and slowed to forty-five. Their taillights had vanished and she glanced in both side mirrors. The earlier truck traffic had also disappeared and no headlights were visible in either direction. Darkness was closing in on her.

Sarah groaned from the passenger seat, apparently still asleep. *Must be the anchovies.* Her friend had insisted on stopping for a pizza at a Kingman roadside cafe. Dana groped for the Tums. As she rounded the curve, she noticed two sets of brake lights not far ahead. The motorhome swayed as she stepped into her own brakes and skidded on the pavement. Road signs had warned of animal crossings. The convertible appeared to have swerved to avoid hitting a deer and had gone off the mountain road. Dana pulled onto the shoulder as the pickup following the convertible screeched back onto the pavement. Why didn't the pickup driver stop to help?

Bolting upright in the passenger seat, Sarah said, "What happened?" Her words were thick with sleep.

"We're about to find out."

Headlights angled upward from somewhere off the road, illuminating a huge digger pine. Was it the convertible? Dana opened her door and climbed down. The steps were slick with rain and she nearly lost her balance. She heard the passenger door slam as she started down the embankment. Chilled and miserably wet, she slipped and landed in a bed of pine needles. Why hadn't she grabbed the flashlight?

Dana glanced up at her friend, who stood shivering on the shoulder. "Sarah," she yelled, "Call 911 and hurry."

The smell of gasoline was strong, despite the heavy rain. The convertible had missed several pine trees but a boulder had stopped its forward motion. Both doors were locked. Peering through the driver's window, she could see nothing more than shattered glass, a dime-sized hole centering the web design. She then heard several backfires and a ping of metal as though the convertible had been struck with a rock. Realizing it was a gunshot, she dropped to her knees in the mud.

Sarah!

Slipping and clawing her way up the slope, she crawled onto the shoulder. A pickup was parked behind the RV. The driver had a nervous foot. A moment later another set of headlights emerged from the curve down the road. Tires squealed as the pickup roared off. As it passed, the RV's headlights caught a dark red truck, which appeared to be a newer model.

When Dana glanced in the passenger window, Sarah was crouched between the seats, the cell phone clutched in her hand. She took her time unlocking the passenger door.

"Are you all right?"

"I'm not sure." Sarah patted her chest, breathing heavily.

"What happened?"

"He shot up the motorhome."

"Did he shoot at you?"

"I don't think he saw me. He only seemed interested in wounding Matilda."

Dana hated the name Sarah had christened the RV, but that was the least of her worries. Grabbing a flashlight, she climbed back down the steps. A quick inspection revealed inside tires still inflated but the outer ones in the back were flat. She heard an engine shift down and was caught in the glare of headlights. Signaling with her flashlight, she was relieved when the big truck slowed and pulled in behind the motorhome. The driver seemed to be endlessly checking the gauges before leaving the cab. Once on the ground, a warm, plump hand gripped hers in greeting.

"The name's McCurdy," a husky voice said. "Everybody calls me Big Ruby."

At nearly six feet, she was Dana's height although almost twice her girth.

"I'm Dana Logan. There's a Mercedes convertible down the embankment. Gasoline is leaking and both the doors are locked."

"Lead the way."

Rain had slackened and the area still reeked of gasoline. She signaled Sarah to stay in the coach.

"Ruptured gas tank," Ruby said. "That low slung buggy must of hit a rock." She tried both doors before resorting to her knife that she pulled from a sheath on her belt. Slicing the canvas top, she reached inside the car to unlock the door. Her flashlight illuminated the interior where a young woman was slumped across the steering wheel. Her long blond hair was stained with blood and she didn't appear to be breathing. The vintage car had no airbags.

Ruby felt for a pulse. Lifting the woman as though she were a child, she pulled her from the car and carried her some distance before settling her gently on the ground. The flashlight spotted a wound on the left side of the woman's head. Her wide blue eyes then disappeared under Ruby's windbreaker.

"I'm afraid we're too late."

"She's so young," Dana's pizza threatened to return from her stomach. "And so small."

"We'd better find some I.D."

Dana hurried back to retrieve the woman's purse. Shivering in wet clothing and the cool mountain air, she returned to Ruby and the body.

"The pickup driver had to have killed her," Dana said. "He then came back to disable the motorhome. My friend and I are lucky to be alive."

"Tell me about the pickup." Ruby started back up the slope.

"Dark red or burgundy. A Dodge Ram, fairly new."

"You get the license number?"

"I'm afraid not."

"We'll catch the bastard. I'll call the sheriff on the way."

"There's no cell service here."

"No trucker's without a CB."

***

Dana took the passenger seat after Sarah crawled into the sleeper. As rain drummed the windshield, she wondered aloud whether animals would find the body before the police arrived.

"Not likely," Ruby said, "The smell of gasoline should keep the critters away." She picked up her microphone to determine whether anyone was in the area. It was several minutes before someone answered her call.

"What's your twenty, lady?"

"West of Flag. How 'bout you?"

"East of Albuquerque. You've got one helluva power booster," a male voice said, "or we're talkin' some damn good skip." The volume rose and fell as though the other driver were out to sea.

Ruby swore beneath her breath. "Friggin' weather acts like a damn snow blower. Sucks up radio signals and spews 'em across the country." She glanced at her passengers and apologized for her language.

"No problem," Dana said. "I've heard worse on TV."

"You meet a lotta nice drivers out here on the road, but some of 'em are always talkin' trash. It gets lonely on long hauls. If you're out here long enough, you start to sound the same."

Just a matter of fitting in, Dana thought as she squinted through the windshield. There was no sign of the pickup.

Ruby tried her cell phone and reported only static. She returned to the CB. Keying the mike, she said, "Breaker, one nine. This is Big Ruby askin' for some help. Anybody out there got your ears on?" She adjusted the squelch when no one answered.

Dana sighed. "Maybe we should have stayed with the body."

"And let that so-and-so get clean away?"

"Yes, you're right." *I couldn't leave Sarah there alone.*

"Tell me again about the pickup. Did you get a good look at the driver?"

"No, but Sarah might have." She turned to determine whether Sarah was listening from the sleeper.

"A dark red Dodge Ram." Sarah said. "I remember the name on the tailgate. It looked like a young man's truck."

"Was it jacked up?" Ruby asked.

"Don't think so."

"Notice any dings or rust spots?"

"It looked shiny new."

"Rain shines up most trucks." Ruby patted the dash. "Even Old Bertha."

Bertha was barreling down the highway much too fast for prevailing road conditions. Dana hoped Ruby was a competent driver.

"What about bumper stickers?"

Dana closed her eyes and tried to remember what she'd seen.

"One said something about a Las Vegas casino," Sarah said, "but I don't remember which one."

"Nevada license plate?"

"I didn't notice."

Dana cringed. Some sleuths they were. She consoled herself with the fact that they'd been taken by surprise. If the murder hadn't happened, she might have fallen asleep at the wheel. The motorhome would have run off the road like the Mercedes.

She knew that convertibles have a low center of gravity, but the high profile RV probably would have overturned and killed them both. She shuddered, remembering the young woman with a bullet in her head. No one deserved to die that way.

Ruby said, "It'll come back to you. It's surprising how much we remember the next day."

Truckers were like bartenders, roadside psychologists who seemed to know more about human nature than their high-priced counterparts.

"I wonder if the killer went back."

"I doubt it." Big Ruby picked up her phone. They had reached the top of the grade where cell service might be available. "A lotta people coulda stopped there by now."

While the trucker punched in some numbers, Dana held her breath, hoping the call had gone through. She listened intently as Ruby reported the murder to a 911 dispatcher.

"No, I can't return to the crime scene. I gotta load of produce that'll spoil. In case you didn't know, drivers foot the bill if the lettuce wilts before it gets to market."

Closing the phone she said, "I'll drop you off in Flag. Somebody there can take tires back to your rig."

"What about the killer?"

"Soon as the rain lets up, I'll warn the other drivers to keep a lookout."

"But how will they know it's him? Or if it's a man, for that matter?"

"You're right. Plenty of women drive pickup trucks in Northern Arizona. Quite a few of 'em Hopis and Navajos. There's more than a few dark red pickup trucks."

Sarah startled her by gripping her seat back. "I forgot to tell you, Dana, I got a look at the driver when he grabbed his gun from his glove compartment."

"Why didn't you say something sooner?"

"I was too busy thanking my lucky stars he didn't shoot me too."

"What's he look like?"

"Dark hair with a thin beard that runs along his jaw line. Connects with his hair."

"Long or short hair?"

"It was slicked back but I didn't see a pony tail."

Dashboard lights illuminated Ruby's grin. In profile she resembled a queen-sized Sarah, although her hair was darker. "Most people wouldn't remember anything but the gun."

"We're amateur sleuths," Sarah said.

Dana groaned inwardly. She'd hoped Sarah wouldn't tell anyone about the murders they'd solved, but nodded confirmation when Ruby glanced at her. The driver shook her head in disbelief.

"Dana captured a killer single-handed."

Ruby laughed. "Are you two traveling Jane Marples?"

"I'm only sixty," Sarah said. "Dana does facial exercises so she looks much younger. But we're the same age."

Sarah's main spring had snapped. If she didn't calm down, she'd be hyperventilating.

"Tell me about the cases you solved." Ruby reached to adjust the wipers.

By the time Dana filled her in on all the murders, the rain had stopped and they were taking a Flagstaff exit. The road curved down to a large truck stop and they pulled into the nearest fuel lane.

"All out for Flag." Ruby grinned as she descended from her truck. Her bright red hair was dazzling in the overhead lights.

"She's no spring chicken either," Sarah muttered as they prepared to leave Old Bertha.

Dana reached for the handle, reversed directions and swung down to the step, comparing the dismount to that of the motorhome. She could drive this rig as well, with a few instructions from Ruby.

Sarah's short legs flailed in mid-air when she groped for the lower step. Dana reached to help her down. Groaning and stretching on solid ground, they offered to buy their benefactor a cup of coffee. Ruby agreed, but before she could hook Bertha up to a diesel pump, Sarah stopped mid-stride and gasped.

"It's him."

"Who?"

"The man with the gun."

Chapter 2

"Where?" Dana craned her neck to scan the service area.

"Getting in his truck." Sarah nodded toward a lighted area beyond the café.

Dana glanced at the dark red Dodge. It appeared to be the same truck, but she could not be certain. "Don't stare, Sarah. Keep walking."

The truck door slammed and a dark-haired man glanced into his rearview mirror. The pickup backed slowly and pulled into an exit lane. He was too far away to read his license number.

"No lights on the license plate holder," Ruby observed.

Obviously excited, Sarah said, "What'll we do?"

Ruby rolled her big brown eyes. "Follow him, of course. Good thing Bertha's not hooked up yet. We've still got half a tank of fuel."

Dana told them to wait. Someone had to go back for the motorhome.

"I'm the only one who can identify him," Sarah said. "I'll ride with Ruby. We'll meet you down the road after we report his license number."

Ruby pulled a small notepad from her shirt pocket and wrote down her cell number. "Call as soon as you're on the road. I'll drop Sarah at a motel after we nail the creep."

"Get in touch with the police as soon as you write down the number." Dana was well aware of Sarah's excitement. Like a bloodhound with the scent, she wouldn't give up until the suspect was caught.

She hurried into the truck stop store as Ruby pulled from the lot. Retrieving her cell phone from her purse, she called emergency road service before inquiring about new tires. While she waited for the service truck, she punched in 911. She was told a deputy was on his way to the murder scene. Ruby had reported the nearest mile marker, and he couldn't miss a thirty-six foot motorhome parked along the road.

Dana glanced down at her clothing caked with mud. No wonder people were staring. She headed for the restroom to make herself presentable. After cleaning her clothes as best she could, she combed her shoulder length auburn hair. People said she resembled the actress Geena Davis but tonight she looked like the Wicked Witch of the West.

Half an hour later they left the truck stop, headed west toward Ashfork. The new tires had cost a small fortune but Dana didn't complain. *They* could have been killed instead of the tires. No more driving after dark, if they had to spend their nights in Walmart parking lots.

The crime scene resembled a carnival, complete with flashing lights. The woman's body had been removed to an ambulance, which appeared ready to leave. As soon as the wrecker came to a stop, a sheriff's deputy walked over to question her. He accompanied her to the motorhome where she retrieved the victim's purse. Dana watched as the young officer rifled through the soft leather handbag.

While she waited, she asked the dead woman's name.

"I can't tell you that."

"I could have searched the purse on my own."

He hesitated. "All right, but this is confidential." The deputy withdrew a wallet and pulled the driver's license. "Her name was Lori Murphy, age twenty-seven. That's all I can tell you."

"Was she married?" Dana asked.

"Why?"

"The killer could have been her husband."

"That's a possibility, but he probably would have killed her at home."

"Not if she had a head start."

He appraised her for a moment before dropping the wallet back in the purse.

"Where's she from?"

"If you looked at the car, ma'am, you'd have seen the Arizona plates."

"I'm aware of that."

"Interstate 40 is a heavily traveled truck route. It was probably a random shooting."

"Random killers don't return to finish off the job. Not with people standing around who can identify them."

"And how would you know that?"

"I read a lot of mystery novels."

He flashed his light in her face. "Can you identify the pickup driver?"

She shook her head, telling him that her friend Sarah could identify the killer.

Too much time had elapsed and she needed to call Ruby's cell number. "My friends may have already spotted the killer and are in need of police assistance." She told him about Ruby McCurdy and that Sarah was riding with her.

"Two women chasing a killer in a produce truck?"

"I'm afraid so, officer."

"You expect me to believe—"

"Call my friend, Sheriff Walter Grayson. He's an old friend who helped us solve a serial murder case." Dana didn't tell him that Walter was in love with her.

"Murder case?"

"That's right."

"You need to come down to the sheriff's office to file a report."

"But I can't leave Sarah stranded."

"I'm afraid she will have to wait. As soon as the RV's ready to roll, you can follow me back to the station. . . By the way, you could have driven into Flagstaff on the inner tires."

I wonder why Ruby didn't tell me that.

***

Several miles east of Flag, construction barriers necked the highway down to two lanes. Light rain resumed and traffic slowed to the speed of a centipede. Every trucker in Arizona must have been waiting at the truck stop to pull out ahead of them. Ruby's CB chatter was getting on Sarah's nerves.

"Listen up," Ruby said every few moments. "There's a bad dude driving a dark red Dodge. Late model four-wheel drive. He's not far ahead. Keep your eyes peeled 'cause he killed a young lady west of Flag. This guy's armed and definitely dangerous."

"What are you?" a baritone voice drawled. "One of them bounty hunters?"

"Makes you wonder, don't it?" Ruby put the mike aside and reached for a pack of gum.

A new voice filled Bertha's cab. "Breaker one-nine for Big Ruby."

"Go ahead, Breaker."

"This is Johnny Reb. There's a red Dodge four-wheeler ahead a me. Describe the driver, will ya?"

"Hold on, Johnny Reb. There's somebody here who saw him." She handed the mike to Sarah.

"Ever used one of these?"

When she admitted she hadn't, Ruby said, "Press the button and talk in the slotted side."

For once in her life, Sarah was speechless. With Ruby's urging, she said, "Dark hair and a thin beard all the way to his sideburns. He might have a pony tail."

"Can't hear ya, lady. Speak up."

Sarah yelled into the mike.

"We can hear ya now." An unfamiliar voice laughed as he turned up his radio. Rock music briefly filled Bertha's cab.

Ruby retrieved the mike. "You morons give us truckers a bad name."

"Aren't they going to help?" Sarah peered through the windshield to scan the endless lane of traffic.

"Come back, Johnny Reb. What's your twenty?"

"I'll let you know when I see a mile marker."

"How far are you from Flag, and can you still see the Dodge?"

"'Bout fifteen miles out and right on his tail."

"You s'pose he's got a CB?"

"No antenna that I can see."

"Good. What're you driving? I'll call it into the highway patrol."

"New Peterbilt," he said with obvious pride. "Its bright royal blue with white striping along the cab."

"Who're you with?"

"Independent bull hauler. John Reb Trucking."

"Are you loaded or deadheading it home?"

"Made my last drop in Flag. I can keep up with him, if necessary."

"Great. By the way, how far does this construction mess go?"

"From here, looks like all the way to the White House."

Ruby sighed. "Guess I'll be eating this produce myself. I'll never make it to St. Louis in time."

"Wish I could help, but it's bumper to bumper far as I can see. I don't know how the cops are gonna nab this guy."

"How about writing down his license number, Johnny?"

"Will do. Hold on."

When he came back on the air, he said, "Must be the creep, all right. There's mud caked on the license plate. I can't even tell which state he's from."

"Stay with him, will ya? If you coulda seen the girl he killed, you'd know why we can't let him get away."

"I ain't got nothin' better to do. I'll keep you posted, Ruby."

"Don't forget me," another driver chimed in, followed by several others.

Ruby sighed. "Listen up, gentlemen. Soon as we get the hammer lane back, we'll put him in the cradle and keep him there, you hear?"

"What's in it for us?"

"A cuppa coffee in Winslow."

"Ah, Ruby, you can do better than that."

Wipers thumped hypnotically as rain smeared taillights across Bertha's windshield.

"What's the cradle?" Sarah asked.

"You ever watch that movie, 'Smokey and the Bandit?'"

"As a matter of fact, I have."

"You'll be watching a reenactment soon." Ruby picked up her cell phone and punched in 911.

* * *

Dana repeatedly tried to call Ruby's cell while following the deputy into Flagstaff. When she finally had service, Ruby didn't answer her phone. The patrol car's blinkers reminded her where she was going and she followed him down the ramp. Heavy rain still splattered the windshield and lights emitting from a service station streaked across her vision. Her eyelids were heavy and she knew she couldn't drive much longer. Hopefully, a hot cup of coffee was waiting at the station.

After she had filled out the paperwork and produced her I.D., Dana was free to leave. Punching in Ruby's number, she was relieved when the trucker answered her phone.

"Where the hell are you?"

"Just leaving Flagstaff. Please put Sarah on the phone."

A moment later she heard Sarah's voice. "For heaven sakes, how long does it take to buy a new set of tires?"

"I'll tell you when I get there. What's your location?"

"Our twenty is south of Winslow." She was beginning to sound like Ruby.

"Why are you still with her? I thought Ruby had a load of produce to deliver."

"We can't let him get away."

Dana sighed, frustrated. "Has Ruby notified the highway patrol?"

"That she has, and we've got a caravan of trucks for escorts."

"All of them after the killer?"

"I guess so, Dana. Must be a dozen of them."

"Good grief."

"They're placing bets about how far the killer will get before he's captured."

Dana blinked her eyes, blinded by oncoming traffic. "He must know everyone's after him."

"He probably thinks they're all tired of the highway construction."

"He'll have to stop for gas soon."

"That's when we'll nab him," Sarah said.

"It's too dangerous. Leave it up to the police."

"Ten-four."

"Has Ruby had any sleep?"

Sarah lowered her voice. "I don't know, but I saw her taking some pills."

"She must be on Vivarin. I could use some myself."

There was excitement in Sarah's voice when she said, "Here comes the cavalry."

"The police are there?"

"I can see their flashing lights in the side mirror. They're coming up behind us."

"How many of them?"

"It looks like three highway patrol cars that are traveling awfully fast."

"Good, I hope they catch him soon."

"The road's so narrow and the trucks are so wide, I don't know how they can pass."

Dana sighed. "I'm so relieved the chase's coming to an end."

Sarah's scream nearly shattered her soul.

"What's wrong?"

"There's been a terrible wreck."

"What happened, Sarah?"

"An eighteen wheeler swerved out in front of the patrol cars."

Chapter 3

Dana called Sarah's name repeatedly before she came back on the line.

"It's horrible, Dana. Ruby stopped just in time but there are trucks all over the road."

"Stay in your seat. It's too dangerous to leave the truck."

"That's what Ruby said when she was climbing down."

"She knows the ways of the road. You don't."

"I'll have Ruby give you directions when she gets back."

"I'll be there as soon as possible. Promise me you'll stay where you are."

"No problem. I've got an eagle's eye view from here."

Dana thought she heard a sob in Sarah's voice. She then heard the truck door open.

"Ruby's back," she said, handing over the phone.

She then heard Ruby's voice. "This Dana?"

"Yes, what happened?"

"Worst accident I've seen in years. A police cruiser was smashed flat by a new Peterbilt. There's a pileup of trucks blocking the road. But I think I can maneuver past. The killer's getting away."

"What about your produce, Ruby?"

"Too late to worry about that now."

Dana heard the big truck shift into gear. "Why don't you leave the killer to the police?"

"They're too busy tending to the wreck. Besides, Sarah's the only one who can identify him."

"But he might shoot you both."

"Don't worry. I'll follow until he stops for fuel. Then I'll pin him in."

Dana bit her lip. *This is insane.* "Give me directions so I can pick up Sarah."

After Ruby had given her detailed instructions, Dana hung up and slapped her own face. How was she going to catch them if she couldn't stay awake? Rain had resumed and the wipers' rhythmic movements were hypnotizing her. It wasn't long before grooves on the edges of the road jarred her fully awake. What did they call it? Driving by braille?

Her cell phone rang and she reached to retrieve it from the dash.

"Dana?" a familiar voice asked. "Where are you?"

"Walter? Why are you calling?"

"The Flagstaff sheriff's office called me to verify your story."

"My story?"

"About the murdered woman."

"Oh, that story."

"You're a magnet when it comes to murder victims."

"Seems that way, doesn't it?"

"Where are you, Dana? I'll catch the next plane."

"No! I'll catch up with Sarah and hurry on home."

"We didn't spend nearly enough time together while you were here."

Any more time and you would have talked me into marrying you. "It was wonderful seeing you, Walter, and the rest of our friends, but Sarah and I need to get home. That beautiful house my sister left me is sitting empty."

"Couldn't you find someone to house sit while you were gone?"

"We haven't been in Wyoming long enough to make dependable friends, except—"

"Except who?"

Dana hesitated. "One of the murder victims we met not long after we arrived." Walter was jealous and she couldn't tell him about her former relationship with state agent Matt Brown. Why did she attract officers of the law?

"I heard a trucker's chasing down the suspect."

"That's true. And Sarah's with her." Dana filled him in on the pertinent details.

"That settles it. I'll take a leave of absence and—"

"No, you won't. We can handle this on our own."

"Do you have a weapon, Dana?"

"Just Sarah's baseball bat."

"What did you do with your Glock?"

Dana sighed. "I left it at home."

Walter, a San Joaquin Valley sheriff, had helped to solve the murders of her friends at the Valley Retirement Village. During the investigation he had fallen in love with Dana. Walter was so overly protective that she kept him at arm's length while she tried to hang on to his friendship. Her second husband had died two years earlier and she wasn't ready for another permanent relationship.

"I'll call if we get in trouble."

"Sounds like you're already there."

Dana made static sounds before saying, "I'm losing you, Walter. I must be getting out of cell phone range. . . Talk to you later." She hung up without saying goodbye.

She ignored the phone when it rang again. Thinking it might be Sarah, she lifted her cell to peer at the screen. *Walter.* She'd wait to return his call after she picked up Sarah.

***

The eighteen-wheeler listed to the right as it drove into a shallow ditch and passed the accident scene. Someone with a flashlight tried to stop her but Ruby applied pedal to the metal and roared on past.

"That was a patrolman, Ruby. What if he comes after us?"

"He won't. He's too busy controlling traffic."

"You think we'll catch the killer?"

"Depends on who runs out of fuel first."

Sarah sighed and reached for the grab handle. She hoped Dana would find them soon. Riding with Ruby was like taking part in a rodeo. She didn't even slow for the bumps.

"There's a thermos in the sleeper," Ruby said. "Think you can make your way back there?"

Sarah nodded but was afraid she'd wind up in Ruby's lap. The truck was swerving around potholes on the narrow two-lane road. Gripping the seat backs, she maneuvered past the gearshift and into the sleeper.

Where's it all going to end? And how's Ruby going to pin the killer in his truck? She shuddered at the thought of another wrecked vehicle. Grabbing the thermos, she made her way back to the passenger seat.

"Anyone die in the crash?"

"Don't see how the patrolman could have lived through it."

"Then that creep is responsible for the deaths of at least two people."

"That makes him a serial killer in my book," Ruby said. "More'n one trucker was involved in the wreck so there could be more bodies."

How was Dana going to get through that tangled mess?

"Where ya headed now?"

"To our new home in Wyoming. Dana's sister's will left her a mansion about twenty miles from Casper. We were just getting settled when we got a call from a friend who lives in the retirement village. She was seriously ill so we drove back to California."

"How's your friend doing?"

"Much better and we're anxious to get home."

The road narrowed even more as Old Bertha slowed to take a curve. When the road straightened, they noticed a set of taillights ahead.

"Is that him, Ruby?"

"Must be unless somebody pulled on the road ahead of us."

"How far to the next service station?"

"Can't say. This side road is new to me and I've been over most of 'em."

Sarah punched a button on her watch, illuminating the dial. "It's ten minutes past two. How long do you think he'll keep driving?"

"God knows, I don't." Ruby reached for a small, slender box on the dash and offered it to Sarah. "Better have one of these unless you're an insomniac."

Sarah hesitated. She thought of Dana driving alone and more than half asleep. Sighing, she opened the box and selected a pill.

"There's a bottle of water in the side panel." Ruby shifted into high and leaned over the wheel.

"I don't see any taillights." Sarah nearly swallowed the pill before she could wash it down.

"He must have pulled off the road to catch some winks. Keep an eye out for the Dodge."

Sarah swigged water and moved closer to the side window as Ruby shifted down again.

"Keep an eye out for a side road while you're at it."

"There's some headlights headed off to the west," Sarah yelled, excited.

"I see 'em." The truck slowed and Bertha left the two lane road. Sarah's seatbelt tightened as they bumped onto a trail, her head nearly striking the roof of the truck.

"Damned almighty washboard trail," Ruby grumbled as she maneuvered the previously muddied ruts. "Hang on to your hat. This ain't gonna be fun."

Old Bertha took to the trail as though a ship in high seas. Listing first to the right, they were tossed back violently to the left.

"How's that pickup making such good time?" Sarah wondered aloud.

"Must be driving off the trail but I don't see any lights. I hope we didn't pass him."

"There he is, off to your left. Looks like he stopped."

"I see 'im. Let's hope his headlights don't go out before we get there." As Ruby spoke, the headlights did go out but she barreled on in that direction.

"What are you gonna do?"

"Crunch the S.O.B., that's what."

"But, Ruby, he needs to go to trial."

"Says who? You didn't see that poor woman he killed. Looked just like my daughter, Casey."

So that's why Ruby's so determined to catch the killer.

Bertha's headlights illuminated an embankment not far ahead.

"You're not going to try to jump it, are you?"

"Damn straight unless it's fulla water."

The truck slowed and came to a stop. To the right, a dusty dark red pickup was parked. Ruby wasted no time leaving her own truck. Sarah cringed as she watched her jerk the driver's door open, a short, thick club held in her left hand. A moment later she returned.

"Couple of kids necking out here in the boonies," she said.

Sarah hadn't heard it called necking since she was a teenager. "What about the Dodge?"

"They saw it heading south on the two lane."

Sarah bit her lip to keep from crying. "We'll never catch him now."

"I wouldn't be too sure. He has to stop to sleep."

Not if he has his own box of wakeup pills.

***

Dana pulled off the two lane road several miles south of the interstate. Her head slumped forward as soon as the motorhome came to a stop. When her cell rang moments later, she groped to flip it open. Sarah asked her *twenty* and Dana nearly hung up on her.

"I need to sleep badly," she said, refusing to open her burning eyes. "I'll call as soon as I wake up."

"We'll see you later then." Sarah sounded so cheerful that Dana growled her goodbye. She then stumbled back to her bunk in the rear of the coach. Later might mean next week as far as she was concerned.

The sun was peeking over the mountains when she awoke. Reaching for her phone, she punched in Ruby's number. When there was no answer, she tried again. Why didn't Sarah have her own cell phone? Dana slammed hers down on the small dining table and headed for the driver's seat. Although she was hungry, she would eat her breakfast later.

Chapter 4

Dana heard her cell phone ring before she had driven a mile. Why had she left it in the dining nook? By the time she'd pulled over, the ringing stopped. Was it Sarah or Walter? Or some telemarketer who had managed to get her number? She barked her shin on the edge of the couch in her haste to grab the phone. When she read the caller I.D. it was the Flagstaff police department. What in the world did they want?

Her heart rate quickened. Maybe Lori Murphy's killer had been caught and the nightmare was over. But why wasn't Ruby answering her phone? Something must have gone wrong. How was she going to get in touch with them? She should have bought a CB radio for backup.

After rubbing her bruised ankle, she returned to the driver's seat to punch in the call back number. The phone rang several times before someone answered, a dispatcher by the sound of the background noise.

When told who she was, the woman said, "There's a sheriff in Modesto trying to get through to you."

Walter!

"He's flying into Phoenix tomorrow morning and asked that you pick him up."

Dana grabbed a notepad and pen she kept on the dash to write his flight numbers down. Should she try talking him out of coming? No chance of that. Walter Grayson was one stubborn man.

"He said not to call him back because he'll be out of range?"

"Out of range? In California?"

"Said he was part of a search and rescue party looking for hunters lost in the Sierras."

"Then why—?"

The dispatcher laughed. "You know him better than I do, Miz Logan."

Boy, do I ever.

The phone rang a moment after she clicked off with the dispatcher. Sarah, at last.

"We lost him, Dana." There were tears in her voice.

"I know you're disappointed but it's probably for the best. He could have killed you both."

"If you want a lettuce sandwich, you better hurry before the load wilts."

Dana rubbed her palm over the dashboard and sighed. Poor Ruby. It was going to cost her plenty. "Maybe there's an Indian reservation nearby that would like to have the lettuce."

"We passed the corner of the Navajo reservation some time ago and Ruby says there's none nearby. Fort Apache is quite a ways to the east and we don't have enough fuel to get there."

"Did you get any sleep, Sarah?"

"Three hours before sunup."

"Where are you exactly?"

"We're southwest of Winslow on Road 87, headed for the Mongollon Plateau on the road to Strawberry."

"Strawberry?"

"A small town where the killer might be hiding."

"I wonder if there's a service station there."

"I hope so. I'm afraid we're going to have empty fuel tanks." Dana peered at the gas gauge which registered a quarter of a tank.

"If we're lucky we'll make it to Payson."

"Isn't that headed toward Phoenix?"

"It's half way, more or less."

"Good grief, Sarah. What have you gotten us into?"

She heard her friend yawn. She then said, "Don't forget my cousin Tillie who lives in Holbrook."

"You'd call her to bring us gasoline? Enough to make it back to Winslow?"

Sarah laughed. "She owes me, Dana."

"For what?"

"I saved her from being grounded forever when we were teenagers."

"How many years ago was that?"

Sarah hesitated and Dana knew she was counting on her fingers. "Forty-six years."

"I never realized what an optimist you are."

She could hear Ruby's voice yelling in the background. "That's him."

"Are you sure?"

"It's him all right."

"We're turning Bertha around, Dana."

"Good. I'll wait for you along the road."

"The killer passed us on his way back to Winslow."

"What?"

"Ruby's sure it's him."

"I hope we can make it to Winslow in time for fuel."

"I always liked that song." Sarah launched into "Standing on the corner in Winslow, Arizona . . ." in a key that made Dana cringe.

"I used to like it, too," she heard Ruby say before she turned up the radio.

"She doesn't appreciate talent," Sarah whispered into the phone.

"Everyone's a music critic. Don't let it bother you."

"I'm getting tired of the chase."

Dana smiled to herself. "You are?" The music ended and she could hear Ruby talking on her CB.

"She needs her phone to call the highway patrol to report the killer's twenty."

"No offense, Sarah, but I'm tired of trucker lingo."

"Ten-four."

"Very funny. Hand Ruby the phone. I'll turn around and wait for you."

Checking her watch she saw that it was only 8:25. The sky had cleared of storm clouds and the sun blinded her in the side window. Who could have predicted their return trip home would be so adventurous? Dana sank deeper into the seat and fell asleep. She awoke later when she heard the sound of an approaching vehicle. Dark red and speeding.

Dana switched on the engine and placed her foot on the accelerator. The least she could do was record the license number. As soon the Dodge passed by, she pulled back on the road. She couldn't possibly keep up but would try. When they reached Winslow she could report the direction he took.

Her cell phone rang and Sarah's excited voice asked her to follow the Dodge. They were only minutes behind. "Stay with him, Dana. We can't lose him now."

"I thought you were tired of the chase."

"Not when we're this close."

"Tell Ruby I still have him in sight but that won't last much longer. There's no way I can catch up with him."

"Please try."

"If I weren't a lady I'd be swearing."

"You should hear Ruby."

She glanced at the speedometer. She couldn't be doing ninety. Not in the motorhome. Stepping into the brakes she managed to prevent the RV from leaving the road but it listed dangerously to one side. *This can't be happening.*

Her cell phone rang and she resisted the urge to answer. What were they going to ask her to do next? Jump a river?

A scene from the movie, "Speed," scrolled through Dana's mind. She wondered how Sandra Bullock managed to keep the highjacked bus from overturning. Real people don't do things like that, do they? The motorhome had to be more unstable than a large bus. And dangerous at high speeds. She slowed to 65. The Dodge was nowhere in sight.

When the phone rang again, Sarah said, "We're right behind you. Pull over so we can pass. Ruby's got Bertha cranked up to eighty-five." *Thank God they were able to get past the wrecked trucks.*

"Gladly. I wish she'd stop long enough to let you off so we can visit Tillie."

"Tillie can wait. We're going to catch him first."

"Or kill yourselves trying."

Dana pulled over, her hands shaking so badly that she couldn't continue driving. The tractor trailer was already out of sight.

Chapter 5

There was no sign of Bertha or the Dodge. Punching in Ruby's number she waited through five rings before she answered.

"Headed toward Winslow," Ruby's voice boomed. "No sign of him or the patrol."

"Where can I meet you to pick up Sarah?"

"There's a truck stop at the first exit into Winslow. Old Bertha's breathing fumes."

"I hope I can make it. I've only got an eighth of a tank."

"Take 'er easy and you'll be fine. We'll see you there."

Easy for you to say.

She spotted a small cafe off to her right and pulled in for a cup of coffee. Her lack of breakfast was making her grumpy.

Parking the RV next to the building, she entered the cafe and was immediately assailed by various cooking scents. Taking a seat in the first booth, she heard a bell tinkle when the door opened behind her. A young man with dark hair walked past and took a seat in the next booth facing her. Apprehension chilled her as the waitress approached her table.

"What'll it be, hon?"

"Coffee and a cinnamon roll. I'm in a hurry."

The waitress flounced over to the next booth, where the dark-haired man sat staring at Dana. When she stared back he raised his gaze to the waitress.

No, it couldn't be. She was paranoid. The killer was miles ahead with Ruby and Sarah in pursuit. The waitress arrived with her order and Dana attacked her food. When she looked up the man was gone. How strange. Maybe he was the waitress's boyfriend on his way to work.

Dana left the waitress a tip and hurried back to the motorhome. She was surprised to find the door unlocked. She was sure she had locked it but her memory wasn't what it once was. And she'd been preoccupied when she reached the cafe.

Placing her purse on the passenger seat, she cranked up the engine, circled the cafe and pulled back on the road. She could see the town of Winslow ahead. Retrieving her cell phone, she called Ruby's number. Before it rang the phone was jerked from her hand and a cold piece of steel jammed her neck.

A man's voice said, "Thought I wouldn't recognize your RV? It has a distinctive design along with the Wyoming license plate. You don't see many bucking horses on plates in Arizona."

She swallowed the remains of the cinnamon roll which had made its way up her throat.

"W-what do you want?"

"If you don't stop following me, I'll blow your brains into Winslow."

"I'm not—"

"Sure you are. You think I'm blind?"

"I'm just trying to get home. My friend took off with a trucker and I was following them to get her back." Dana cringed. She realized how lame she sounded. And how frightened.

He laughed. "You know, you're not bad for an old broad. If I had more time—"

Gathering courage, she said, "Take my money and credit cards." She gestured toward the keys in the ignition. "Take the motorhome. You must be in need of money to rob someone driving an RV."

"You think I'm a common thief?"

"Isn't that what you're doing? Robbing me?"

When he leaned into her seat, she nearly gagged on a mixture of sweat and cologne.

"Listen, lady, I know you're the one who parked along the road west of Flagstaff. You saw—"

"All I saw was a Mercedes convertible that ran off the road. I didn't see anything else except a pickup that stopped briefly and a trucker who came to help."

"You're lying."

She glanced at him in the rearview mirror. All she could see were his eyes, which had narrowed with disbelief. "I'm telling the truth. I've never seen you before and have no idea who you are."

His voice took on a commanding tone. "Call your friend and arrange a meeting. Tell her you'll meet her on route ninety-nine, two miles south of Winslow-Lindbergh airport. Nothing more." He jammed the gun so hard into her neck that she cried out in pain.

"Keep driving. I'll tell you when to stop."

The tank was nearly empty. She tapped the gauge to bring it to his attention.

"We'll stop at the first station in Winslow. You stay at the wheel and keep your mouth shut."

Dana cringed but said nothing more. Maybe she could alert them ahead of time. "When do you want me to call my friends?"

He pulled the gun from her neck and handed her the phone. "Careful what you say or you'll never make another call."

She nodded and swallowed the remnants of cinnamon. Punching in the numbers with the thumb of her free hand, she held her breath, her heart pounding erratically. Ruby's voice boomed in her ear. "Where are you, Dana?"

"Meet me on the old Winslow Highway two miles south of the airport. I have to stop first to refuel the motorhome but it won't take long." She talked fast so that Ruby had no time to ask questions. She then hung up without saying goodbye. Gasping for breath, she waited for his reaction.

She prayed that Ruby would be suspicious and disregard her request. What would happen when they pulled into the station? She hoped the trucker would know something was wrong. The gun was once again jammed into her neck. If he would only take the passenger seat, she could slam on the brakes before the seatbelt was fastened. She might then have a chance to grab his gun.

"Slow down," he growled, gripping her seat back. "You want to get a ticket?"

Good idea. Would he dare shoot while I'm driving? She searched frantically for a place to crash that wouldn't kill her as well. A road sign said two miles to Winslow. There wasn't much time.

When he grabbed the phone from her, it rang in his hand. Swearing, he threw it against the wall, the parts falling onto the couch. From the corner of her eye she watched him scoop up the pieces and turn to throw them in the trash. It was now or never.

Chapter 6

A ditch ran along the right side of the road. It might be her last chance. Jamming the brakes with both feet, she sharply crimped the wheel. The RV left the road, leaped the embankment and crashed into the opposite bank. It then flipped onto its side. Dishes and other possessions fell from the cupboards and rained down on her passenger.

Dana released her seatbelt and fell into the passenger seat. Blood trickled down the front of her blouse and she wiped it from her lip. Gripping the seat back, she turned to look for the killer, who had crumpled head first into the breakfast nook. She had to leave the RV but knew she couldn't get the main door open. If the crash hadn't broken the killer's neck, it wouldn't be long before he came after her.

Slinging her purse strap over her shoulder, she climbed uphill to the driver's seat and pushed the button to open the driver's window. The engine was still running so she pulled the keys from the ignition and tossed them with her purse from the window.

She heard a groan and knew she didn't have much time. Pulling the handle, she tried to open the driver's door but it was too heavy at its current angle. Struggling to reposition herself, she pulled the handle again and kicked with both feet. The door flew open but fell back, causing stabbing ankle pain. She should have bailed out the window head-first.

"Are you hurt?" someone called from outside the coach.

"Help me!"

A face appeared at the window and a large hand reached to grip her own. "You all right?"

"There's a man in here with a gun. We've got to get away."

Her rescuer, a middle-aged man with huge arms, stuck his head in the window and glanced where she had pointed. Nodding, he pulled Dana through the window and lifted her onto the road.

"Call the police." Dana's breathing was labored. She then noticed a delivery van parked not far from where the RV left the road. Locating her purse, he stooped to retrieve it. He then carried her to his van where she was promptly buckled in.

While he was buckling himself in, she turned to look at the motorhome, which seemed to have been dropped from the sky. Steam poured from the engine but the killer had apparently not yet tried to escape.

"Hurry," she pleaded. "He killed a young woman along the highway."

The driver stomped on the accelerator and the delivery van jerked forward. She thought she heard a bullet strike the van a moment later, but when she glanced in the side mirror she was unable locate the shooter.

"Please drop me off at the truck stop at the first Winslow exit."

"Sure, ma'am. You want to tell me what happened?"

He had saved her life and deserved to be told, so she briefly filled him in.

Taking a phone from his shirt pocket, he handed it to her. Inhaling deeply, she punched in 911. After she told the dispatcher what had happened, she called Ruby's number.

"My gosh, Dana. We thought you'd lost your mind."

When told what happened, Ruby repeated it to Sarah, who then came on the line.

"You all right, Dana?"

"Not too bad, considering."

"You didn't tell him you were meeting us here?"

"Of course not. We'll talk about it as soon as my Good Samaritan delivers me to the truck stop."

Handing back the phone, she took a good look at her benefactor. He turned his head to smile at her, his deep blue eyes crinkling at the corners. "You're a wonder, lady," he said. "If that had happened to my girlfriend, she would have driven him clear to Tucumcari, where he'd have killed her."

"Why Tucumcari?"

He laughed, a deep baritone that echoed through the van. "There's an old joke about taking a woman to Tucumcari, but you're too much of a lady to hear it."

"Thanks." Glancing at a highway sign, Dana said, "One more mile to Winslow. How can I ever repay you?"

He fished in his pocket for a card. "Call me sometime and let me know how this murder case turns out."

"Gladly."

When they pulled into the truck stop, Dana left the van. Circling to the driver's side, she gripped his warm hand in parting. She winced when her swollen lips made contact with his cheek. Sarah and Ruby came running over. Dana told them again about her abduction and the wrecked motorhome.

"That was a gutsy move," Ruby said. "Are you sure you're not hurt."

Dana gingerly touched her lower lip. "I won't be kissing anyone else for a while."

"Speaking of kissing someone, who was that great looking guy who dropped you off?" Sarah wanted to know.

"I don't know." Dana pulled the business card from her purse. "Joseph Brandley, owner of the Brandley Van and Storage Company."

Ruby took the card. "I'll be damned. Brandley's a former weightlifter who competed in the Olympics. You couldn't have picked a better man to rescue you."

Sarah looked worried. "What now?"

"We'll call the police and a wrecker. Then we'll rent a car." Dana turned to Ruby. "What about you? How will you dispose of the lettuce?"

"I'll make some phone calls to see if anyone around here needs it."

"Sorry we got you into this."

Ruby shrugged. "I'll hang out with you two until we find out about the killer. I'd hate to think he's running loose in Winslow... Let's grab a cuppa coffee."

***

Ruby drove them back to the scene of the crash in Old Bertha. A wrecker and the police were already there, but the suspect had escaped.

Ruby frowned. "It appears the motorhome's totaled. Practically new, wasn't it?"

"We bought it seven months ago, but Dana can afford another one. I'm not sure I want one, though."

"I can't say I blame you. If you want to travel, why not buy a rig like mine. Get paid for traveling."

Dana laughed. *I've had enough traveling. I'm ready for the peace and quiet of the Wyoming outback, but that won't happen until the killer's arrested. Whomever he may be. . . .*

Chapter 7

"Good thing Ruby found a couple of supermarkets to take most of the lettuce," Sarah said. "I'd hate to think she lost a whole month's wages."

Dana glanced over at Sarah, who had reclined the rented Hummer's passenger seat. "You know, sometimes being a good Samaritan doesn't work out."

"That's true. I remember a passage from the Gospel of Luke about a man who was traveling from Jerusalem to Jericho when attacked by a gang of bandits. They beat him, stripped him of everything he had, including his clothes. They left him for dead along the road. A priest passed by but didn't stop and neither did a temple assistant. But a Good Samaritan helped him, although he was despised by everyone."

Dana checked her side mirrors. "There've been plenty of good Samaritans throughout history. I've read about people in the Old West who left their doors unlocked while they were away so that travelers would have a place to sleep. And something to eat. It was a matter of survival."

"Too bad there aren't more Samaritans around today."

"You'll be pleased to know that our new home state of Wyoming has a Good Samaritan law."

"I hope we'll never need another one."

Dana glanced again in her rearview mirror. There didn't appear to be anyone following them. *The killer knows we're from Wyoming, and will take the most direct route. Maybe we should stay off the main roads.*

"How far is it to Holbrook?"

Sarah's seat moved forward and she reached for the Atlas. "We just passed by Joseph City. It looks like about twelve miles."

Dana suggested that she read the GPS system manual but Sarah insisted that it was too complicated. She then asked if Sarah's cousin Tillie was expecting them.

"I told her we'd be there for dinner."

Dana sighed. "I hate to think we may be putting her life in danger."

"I hadn't thought of that."

Dana suggested a motel.

"That would hurt Tillie's feelings."

"Not if we tell her why."

Sarah shook her head but said nothing more. She was obviously disappointed.

"Why don't you route us onto secondary roads out of Holbrook instead of visiting the Petrified Forest."

There was that look of disappointment again. Sarah's finger traced a route on the map. "A road goes south to Snowflake and Show Low."

"Strange names in Arizona."

"Or we can head southeast past the Zuni Reservation to St. Johns, then north along the eastern border of the Navajo Reservation."

Dana smiled. "That would be interesting, but what if he catches up with us in the middle of nowhere? I think it's best if we keep going, switching drivers. We can buy an air mattress in Holbrook and put the back seat down to take turns sleeping."

Sarah stared at her in the deepening twilight. "I don't see well at night."

"You can drive during the day. I don't think the killer can keep up with us," Dana said, "especially if we switch to alternative routes that connect back with the interstate."

"Thank heavens for the Atlas."

"Why don't you start mapping our route before we get to Holbrook?"

"Ten-four."

Dana sighed. "Or maybe you'd prefer riding with Ruby. She's seems to have thoroughly indoctrinated you."

Sarah smiled that wicked smile of hers and laughed. "Just tweaking your ears, Dana. Me thinks you take life too seriously."

"Really? *Me* thinks you would be a lot more paranoid if the killer had drilled *your* neck with his gun."

Sarah's brows rose, her smile slowly fading. "I'm sorry. That must have been horrifying. Especially when you drove the motorhome into the ditch."

"I don't know about you, friend, but I've had enough travel to last me for quite a while."

Sarah went back to work mapping alternative routes. Holbrook was only a few miles away and they needed to know which route to take the following morning.

***

Cousin Tillie was nearly a carbon copy of Sarah. Their mothers had been twins and the family resemblance was striking. An inch taller and several pounds heavier, Tillie's curly blond hair and facial features made *them* look like twins.

"We were born in the same month," Tillie said.

Sarah beamed. "Our teachers couldn't tell us apart in grammar school."

"How did you get separated geographically?"

"Tillie married a sailor from Arizona."

Dana smiled. "And you stayed in California."

"Right."

"I think you should tell Tillie about our latest adventure, don't you?"

When Sarah finished, Cousin Tillie was shocked and disappointed their visit would be cut short.

"It's not safe for us to stay," Dana warned.

"But I had all these plans."

"Come visit us in Wyoming. You can stay as long as you like."

Tillie smiled like a Cheshire cat when Sarah described the mansion. Ten of her grandchildren lived nearby. They apparently thought Grandma's house was a race track. Dana cringed. She imagined them running wild in the mansion. There was also Tillie's husband, who appeared to work in a slag mill. She wondered if he ever changed clothes.

Dana caught Sarah's attention and quietly tapped her watch. It was time to find a motel somewhere down the road.

Sarah hugged everyone and said goodbye. She followed Dana to the H2, asking "Couldn't we have stayed a while longer?"

"We need to find an electronics store to buy some cell phones."

"One for me?"

"Survival gear, Sarah. Keep it with you at all times."

The lights of a strip mall loomed ahead and she pulled in front of an electronics store. Forty minutes later they were on their way again in search of a McDonald's.

Sarah checked her side mirror. "Hard to tell if anyone's following."

"A pickup has been with us since we left the electronics store."

"Maybe we should forget the food and head out for the highway."

Dana looked in the rear view mirror. "We can get a good look at him if he follows us into the drive-through lane."

"Should have rented a sports car. They're much faster."

"Remember what happened to the last sports car the killer was following, Sarah?"

The pickup pulled along the curb and waited while they drove to the order window. Dana ordered a cheeseburger and fries although she didn't plan to eat them. When they left the window the Hummer crept down the ramp as Dana watched oncoming traffic. Her right turn signal blinked as the pickup moved closer along the curb. As soon as there was a break in traffic, Dana floorboarded the Hummer and made a *left* turn. Behind them the pickup attempted to negotiate a U turn and they heard a horn and screeching tires.

Dana made another quick left across traffic and then another. Hopefully, the pickup had been unable to follow. When they reached their starting point, the truck was nowhere in sight. They then scooted back into traffic and headed for the interstate.

Dana was breathing hard but Sarah had already taken a bite of cheeseburger. "How can you eat when a killer's after us?"

"I wasn't worried. I knew you'd lose him."

"I'm not so sure. There's a set of headlights behind us."

Chapter 8

Sarah nearly choked on her burger when Dana stomped on the accelerator. Maybe her friend was right. She should have rented a faster car. But the H2 seemed safe—like a tank—and it was definitely more comfortable than a sports car.

"Turn on your pen light, Sarah, and find a side road that eventually heads north."

"What if he follows us and opens fire?" Sarah's voice grew higher with each syllable.

"I have a plan. Hurry, find us the next road."

Dana watched from the corner of her eye as the pen light scanned the map. At last Sarah looked up. "You said we weren't going through the Petrified Forest."

"Not with a killer trailing us."

"The next road goes right through the middle of it."

"You're not serious."

"I am and I doubt we'll make good time in a national park. Dana, I really don't want to become one of those fossils."

The headlights behind them grew larger and brighter, nearly blinding Dana in the Hummer's mirrors. When she increased the Hummer's speed to ninety a series of blinking lights appeared in her rearview mirror.

"We're getting a ticket." Sarah giggled, obviously with relief.

"I hope it's only that. What if the killer stole a police car?"

"You're paranoid, Dana."

"If you're wrong, we're dead."

"If you don't pull over, *the patrolman* will be shooting at us."

Dana hit the turn indicator and pulled off the road. Her heart was racing like a greyhound at the track.

Whoever it was that pulled in behind them was taking his time. Watching in her side mirror, Dana saw the door slowly open and someone of average height leave the car. Rolling down her window, she held her breath. A flashlight blinded her as a woman's voice said, "Do you have any idea how fast you were going?"

"No, officer. I was frightened to death you were the man who tried to kill me this morning."

The patrol woman suppressed a laugh. "I've heard some tall tales but yours is over the top."

"Get in touch with the Flagstaff PD. They'll fill you in."

The officer stepped away, telling Dana to get out of the Hummer. Before herding her back to the patrol car, she spotlighted Sarah, who shielded her eyes.

"That's my friend, Sarah Cafferty. We're on our way home to Wyoming."

The patrol woman motioned her away from the H2, then opened the door and jerked the keys. "Lock your doors and stay put," she told Sarah.

Half an hour later the officer was satisfied the women weren't lunatics escaping the state asylum. "It's a good idea to call a male friend or relative to ride the rest of the trip home with you," she advised.

"Out here in the middle of—?" Dana then remembered Walter. With all that had happened, she'd forgotten they were supposed to pick him up in Phoenix. She didn't want him to come but he might now be their salvation.

"My friend's flying into Phoenix."

"You'll have quite a drive to get there, and I wouldn't advise backtracking very far. You might run into the suspect who was following you."

"What do you advise?"

"Follow me back to Holbrook. Then you can head south on the back roads to Phoenix. Payson is a little over half way."

"That's not too much backtracking."

"Or you can drive through the Petrified Forest and down through the Apache Indian Reservation. I think I'd take my chances with Holbrook."

"Agreed."

"Better get back to your friend before she thinks you're under arrest."

Dana opened the door and hesitated. "About the ticket?"

"I won't add to your trauma. You've had enough for one day."

Dana thanked the officer and resisted the urge to hug her.

***

It was a quarter past eight when they reached the outskirts of Holbrook. The patrol woman stopped a mile down the secondary road that lead southwest to Heber. Closing her door, she walked back to the Hummer.

"Take it easy on this road till you get to the junction. The road gets better there. We're expecting more rain so be prepared." She smiled and saluted Dana before she left.

Dana sat a moment staring at the two lane road. "Looks like we're on our own. We should be in Phoenix by half past midnight. We can get some sleep and meet Walter's plane at 10:30 in the morning."

"How do you feel about him coming? I thought you wanted to put some space between the two of you."

"I do but he took a leave of absence—"

"He must be worried about you."

"It's more than that, Sarah. He wants to get married."

"And you're not ready." Sarah knew how skittish she was about a commitment. Not that she hadn't been happily married to Ed. She was simply enjoying her freedom and a third marriage wasn't in her plans.

Before she pulled back onto the road, she checked her rearview mirrors. The only light was the fading taillights of the departing patrol car. Settling lower into the driver's seat, she inhaled deeply and tried to relax. Route 377 wasn't only narrower than the interstate, it was as dark as the inside of a boot. Clouds covered the moon and more rain was in the forecast. Switching on the radio, she asked Sarah to find a weather station.

A meteorologist forecast a downpour by 11:00 p.m. for northeastern Arizona, with the possibility of some gully washers. He warned about low bridges during the storm.

"Check the map to see if we have to cross any rivers."

Sarah's pen light moved over the map. "None until we get within eighteen miles of Payson. Must be a bridge where the road crosses the Tonto River."

"Better cross your toes that it doesn't start flooding before we get there. I've heard horror stories about people getting washed away in flash floods."

"There's a lake just north of there, Dana. Doesn't look very big but if it overflows—"

"We'll need life jackets."

"Maybe you'd better drive a little faster."

"Didn't you see those deer along the road?"

"No."

If we collide with one, it's liable to come through the windshield." Dana reached to pat the dashboard. "I'm glad we're sitting higher than a regular car. We're also sitting high enough to get through a flood. If it's not too deep."

"I wish there was someone we could call."

"We might be calling the Coast Guard if we're caught in a flood."

"Honestly, Dana. All those comedians out of work and you're making jokes."

"It might help to say a few prayers that we get through to Phoenix."

The first raindrops hit the windshield like large globs of clay—huge drops of water that distorted her vision. A moment later the fall was so heavy that the wipers on high couldn't keep up with the rain. Dana was forced to slow to the speed of a snail.

"I wish we were on higher ground. Does the map say whether we'll be getting into some foothills?"

"Not till we reach the Apache Sitgreaves National Forest, but that's a few miles from Heber."

"How far?" Dana didn't dare glance away from the road.

"How far have we come?"

Dana cursed beneath her breath. She hadn't checked the mileage before they left Holbrook. "Twenty miles," she guessed.

"Then we're not even halfway there."

"Turn off the light. I can't see a thing."

Rain drumming on the roof sounded like the anvil chorus or an army marching with hobnailed boots. It was so loud they had to yell to be heard. The last thing Dana needed was a distraction. She was already driving blind. She wondered whether they should turn back to Holbrook.

Chapter 9

Dana brought the Hummer to a complete stop. "I can't see the road."

"We can't turn around. We might get stuck in the mud."

Dana's palms pounded the wheel in frustration. "We'll have to wait it out. Keep watching your side mirror in case someone's behind us."

"Put the emergency blinkers on."

Dana punched the button on the dash and was greeted by blinking lights. "For all the good that will do. I don't know how anyone can see anything in this downpour."

A clap of thunder sounded like a plane crash, followed by a lengthy display of lightning. Both women shrieked as water cascading down the windshield was illuminated. It looked as though they were trapped in a waterfall. What if the Hummer were struck with lightning? Would it catch fire?

"Sarah," she yelled. "Don't touch anything metal."

Her friend could be seen in the glow of the dash lights unbuckling her seatbelt.

"What are you doing?"

"I'm gonna crawl into the backseat to change clothes. I just irrigated my underwear."

Flipping on an overhead light Sarah wriggled over the console. Reaching over the backseat, she grabbed an over-night bag and unlatched it. A few minutes later the interior of the cab was filled with the scent of perfume.

Dana coughed and waved the scent away. "What's that you're wearing?"

"I'm zipping up my new blue pants suit with the silver concha belt."

"The perfume?"

"Ode to a rain storm."

"Now who's trying to put the comedians out of work?" Dana's throat was sore from yelling. The rain drumming on the roof had only grown louder.

When Sarah returned to her seat, she turned the radio to full volume. Music filled the cab so loud that it could be heard above the rain. The music stopped and a man's voice announced the imminent danger of flash flooding, warning everyone to take shelter.

"Where?" Sarah shouted. "On top of the Hummer?"

Dana reached across the console to place a firm hand on her arm. "We're safe in the Hummer," she said, but didn't believe it herself.

The rain gods must have heard her words because the downpour abruptly reduced itself to a sprinkle. She wasted no time stepping down on the accelerator.

"We're out of here."

Sarah warned about the amount of water on the road. "We're going to hydroplane."

Dana switched the headlights to low beam and carefully drove forward. "Where the hell is the road?"

"Stay between the delineator posts. There's one off to your left."

"I see it. Where's the next one?"

Dana heard a scraping sound and Sarah yelled, "I think you found it." Water splashed the doors when Dana jerked the wheel. "This is almost as bad as that Rocky Mountain blizzard we nearly didn't survive."

Sarah's laugh sounded on the verge of hysteria. "That wasn't even close."

The Hummer picked up speed when the rain stopped entirely. Top speed was ten miles an hour as the amount of water seemed to increase. At this rate they would miss Walter's plane. Plucking her cell phone from her pocket, she handed to Sarah.

"Switch on the overhead light and call 911."

Sarah did as she was told, but reported they were in a no service area. "This is the boondocks, Dana. Nobody knows we're here except the highway patrol woman."

"I hope she realizes what she sent us into."

"Maybe she'll send a rescue boat."

"You're making jokes again, Dana."

Water lapped as high as the windows and the Hummer seemed to sink.

"Stop," Sarah screamed. "We're gonna drown."

Throwing the H2 into reverse, Dana stomped on the gas but the force of water was pushing them sideways. The Hummer broadsided a highway sign, which seemed to be holding them in place, but how long would it hold their weight?

"Dear Lord, please don't let the sign collapse," Sarah wailed, closing her eyes and tenting her fingers.

"Don't move," Dana warned. "Don't even breath."

The Hummer rocked in place, water splashing as high as the hood. Dana gritted her teeth and prayed more fervently than she had ever done before.

They sat immobile for what seemed hours. When Sarah said, "The psychic Sylvia Browne says that if you want something done right away, you should pray to the Mother God, " Dana replied that it was worth a try.

While offering up prayers, they heard the sharp crack of wood. The Hummer moved in a half circle around the fractured post and. Dana gripped the steering wheel, hoping to keep it from turning further. Maybe the water would stay at the vehicle's rear but it had a mind of its own. She could hear Sarah's hysterical crying and knew she would be no help.

The Hummer moved as though in a whirlpool, making Dana dizzy.

Sarah screamed, "My feet are getting wet."

"Mine, too. Don't panic."

"Can the Hummer float?"

"I don't think so, Sarah. It's not water tight."

"Can we crawl out the windows and sit on the roof?"

"What if it capsizes?"

"You're right. It's top heavy."

After what seemed an eternity, the H2 stopped moving. They seemed to be high centered on an embankment. Flood waters had pushed them onto a hump of dry land, but for how long? A moment later they came to rest against a boulder. One headlight smashed on impact and probably a fender, but the right headlamp was still feebly burning. It was a miracle it hadn't shorted out.

"Thank you, Heavenly Mother." Sarah's crying stopped as she hugged herself. "Thank you, thank you, thank—"

"We're not out of danger yet. If it starts raining again, we'll be washed away."

"What can we do, Dana?"

"Pray for all you're worth."

"I'm sorry I ruined your new blue dress at the party."

"It doesn't matter, Sarah. Don't stop praying."

"I asked that the power angels to be sent to help us."

"Good idea. Maybe they'll fly us out of here."

"Honestly, Dana That's sacrilegious."

"Get back on the prayer line and ask for a helicopter." Dana tented her own hands and prayed.

"I'll give up chocolate eclairs and blueberry pie," she heard Sarah promise. If anyone in Heaven knew how she liked sweets, they'd be impressed.

Dana's main concern was her only daughter. How would Kerrie react if she learned of her mother's death? And how long would it take to identify their bodies, if they drowned?

The water continued to roar past and they still had to resort to shouting. "Sarah, I've never seen you in a pool. Can you swim?"

"After seven strokes I'm shark bait."

"I've heard that line before."

"Hans Christian Anderson, I believe," Sarah said.

"I was on the swim team in college but I doubt I can last very long in flood waters."

"I can float like a beached whale."

Dana laughed despite her fear. "Then we have nothing to worry about."

"I hope the Apaches didn't do a rain dance. The storm could last for hours."

"Let's hope they have a 'stop this rain' dance. No one could possibly want this much water."

Sarah resumed her crying. Dana would have to keep her talking until help arrived.

"Try the cell phone. Call 911."

The Hummer's electrical system had completely shorted out so Sarah retrieved her pen light. "Looks like a slight signal." Punching in the emergency number she yelled, "Help!" when someone answered. When told they would have to wait till dawn for rescue, Sarah resumed her crying.

Taking the phone, Dana asked for a rescue helicopter and estimated their location.

"They're already out on rescue missions. I'm sorry, you'll have to wait your turn."

"If your department is doing triage, I'm sure we'd be near the head of the list. If the water gets any deeper, we're going to drown."

"I'll tell the helicopter crews, ma'am. That's all I can do."

"Thank you for that." Dana gave the dispatcher her cell number, hoping it would hold its charge.

"Call if your situation changes. In the meantime, bless you both."

If our situation changes, we'll be drowned. "Don't move, Sarah. We've got to remain stationery until the helicopter gets here."

Hiccupping with fear, Sarah agreed.

For the first time that night, Dana was panic stricken. She knew they didn't stand a chance if the water rose any higher, sending them back into the swirling water. Sleeping would be best but there was no way she could take a nap.

"Let's meditate, Sarah. It'll help us relax."

"I'm so scared I can't remember my mantra."

Dana thought for a moment. "Try Le-hoe. You can use any two-syllable word that has no meaning."

"I'd rather take a big bite of chocolate cake."

"So would I, but TM's a better choice."

There was silence inside the cab although the sound of water was distracting as well as frightening. She hoped Sarah was able to concentrate on her mantra to overcome her fear. Apparently so because moments later she heard her friend's soft snore. Sighing, Dana concentrated on her own mantra although she knew she wouldn't be able to sleep.

Chapter 10

The sound of her cell phone woke Dana from a light doze. Nearly dropping it, she pulled it to her ear.

"Dana Logan?" a male voice asked. Engine noise could be heard in the background.

"Yes."

"This is Captain Garrett. We're hovering in the vicinity where you said you were stranded but unable to locate your car due to the heavy cloud cover."

She listened but could hear nothing but water rushing past.

"Can you turn on your lights?"

"The electrical system has shorted out. I can't even roll down a window."

"It'll be dawn soon. We'll be able to find you then."

"I have a flashlight. Will that help?" Dana reached to retrieve it from the side door panel.

"We might see it if you shine the light upward through your windshield."

She leaned across the steering wheel. "Can you see the beam?"

"No, ma'am but we'll circle the area until we find you."

"Thank you, Captain."

"Dana," Sarah's sleepy voice called. "Is the helicopter here?"

"Not yet and sit still. You're rocking the boat."

"Try shining your light through the rear window," the captain's voice said. "Then rotate the light out each window for five seconds. We're not picking anything up yet. But we'll eventually be able to see it if the sun doesn't come up first."

The sun. How she had wished for it to rise that morning. Now it could hamper their rescue. Dana rotated the light until it came to the passenger window. She then handed it to Sarah. On the count of five Sarah handed it back.

The sun roof. She slid back the cover and shined her flashlight straight up.

"I think I hear something, Dana."

"Wishful thinking, my friend."

"No, there it is again. It's definitely an aircraft of some kind."

Dana resumed flashing the light but closed her eyes to listen. "You're right. It's coming from the passenger side." Handing the flashlight back to Sarah, she retrieved her phone from the dash when it rang. Flipping it open, she said, "Can you see us now?"

"Yes, ma'am. We should be overhead within a couple of minutes."

"Bless you, Captain Garrett. We have a plane to meet in Phoenix this morning."

"I'm afraid we can't help you there but we'll hand you off to Payson."

"Can we rent a car in Payson?" Sarah asked when Dana clicked off the phone.

"Let's hope so. Take the flashlight and look at the map. It might tell us Payson's population."

A moment later, Sarah reported a population of nearly 16,000. Forty-eight percent of the residents were male and fifty-two percent female. The average age was forty-nine so she surmised that it was a retirement community.

"The map tells you that?"

"Special insert."

A thump on the roof startled them. Someone tapped the passenger window, setting off a gasp. "Unless aliens have landed, they're here."

A light shone through Sarah's window, blinding them. "Unlock your doors," a male voice said.

They did as they were told. When Sarah's door opened, water rushed from the cab and a dark figure offered her his hand.

"Is the water going down?" she asked before leaving the Hummer.

"It's fairly dry for several feet, ma'am. You seem to be parked on a sandbar. Are you both all right?"

"Right as rain. How's that for an analogy?"

"Stay here while I grab the basket to haul you up."

"We don't have much luck with rental cars," Sarah said when Dana joined her.

"Do you mean the Hummer destroyed in the Laramie Mountains by drug dealers?"

Dana laughed although she wasn't sure why. "That's the one. Our names'll be on the car rental terrorist list and we'll never be able to rent another."

"Don't forget our two destroyed motorhomes."

The helicopter crewman returned in a wet suit pulling a rescue basket.

"You first, Sarah." She didn't dare leave her behind.

Her friend was helped into the basket as dawn stretched pink across the horizon. Sarah looked over her shoulder, her expression one of terror.

"You'll be fine. Hang on for all you're worth. Someone up there will help you inside."

The young man turned to Dana. "You're lucky to have landed on a sandbar."

"Looks like another few feet and we'd have rolled back in the water."

"You're right about that."

"Someone up there heard our prayers."

He chuckled. "I don't know about your prayers but that flashlight came in handy. I doubt we could have found you until dawn. By then the water could have risen—"

"Your crew must be the power angels my friend was praying about."

Dana watched the basket rise to the open door of the chopper and heard Sarah's wail as she was pulled inside. The basket was then lowered.

"What about our luggage?"

"I'll send it up when you're safely inside."

"Good man," she said. *Now all we have to worry about is finding a rental car, picking up Walter at the airport, and staying ahead of the killer.*

"Your turn, ma'am. Ready?"

"I've never been readier." She glanced at her watch in dim dawn light. If they were lucky, they might make the airport in Phoenix by ten o'clock.

***

The flight to Payson took less than half an hour. Sarah slept most of the way but Dana had the wide eye. Sarah could drive to Phoenix if they found a rental car.

"We're landing at Payson Airport, Miz Logan. You can rent a car or hop a flight from there."

They decided on a charter flight to get them there in time. But once they boarded the small two engine plane, they were told they would land at Phoenix Deer Valley Airport, some fifty-two nautical miles southwest of Payson. There they would board another puddle jumper for the trip to Phoenix International Airport. With the layover at Deer Valley, they would only have eighteen minutes leeway to meet Walter's plane.

Dana groaned. Why was Walter so stubborn? He knew she didn't want him to make the trip from California. He had nearly gotten them killed in the flood. Keeping him at arm's length for the entire trip back to Wyoming was going to take more will power than she currently had. Thank heavens Sarah was along for the ride.

Chapter 11

Their flight from Deer Valley was ten minutes late due to high winds in the area. When they left the commuter plane, Sarah insisted that Dana hurry across the airport to meet Walter's flight while she rounded up their luggage.

Exhausted from lack of sleep, Dana jogged off to the Delta waiting area. Walter was one of the last passengers to leave the plane and appeared as though he'd had little sleep. He also seemed to have lost weight and his hair was a little grayer around the temples. When he smiled, she rushed into his arms although she'd planned to keep their relationship casual.

"It's great to see you, Dana."

Pushing herself from his embrace, she took his hand and started off in the direction of the luggage carousel.

"Hold up," he demanded in that sheriff's voice of his. "What's the rush?" Placing his hands on her shoulders, he turned her around and kissed her passionately.

"Not here," she gasped, pulling away.

"Why not? Plenty of people kiss in airports."

"It's just that—"

"What?"

"Sarah's with me. I don't want her to be uncomfortable."

"About what? That we're in love."

"I never said I love you."

"But you know you do." His face crinkled into a boyish grin.

"I don't know anything of the sort. You'll have to keep your hands to yourself if you're going with us all the way to Wyoming."

"Yes, ma'am." He saluted smartly and followed her to the luggage carousel where he grabbed a large bag.

"By the way, where's Sarah?" He sounded as though he were interrogating her.

"She's at the commuter station." Dana started off with the sheriff at her heels, hearing him grumble, "All the way to Wyoming?"

Sarah was dozing in her seat when they found her, feet propped up on their luggage. She screeched with fright when Dana touched her shoulder.

"It's okay. We're in the Phoenix airport."

Sarah blinked several times before recognizing Walter. Carefully getting to her feet, she gave him a more than friendly kiss. Why hadn't Walter fallen for Sarah? It would have made life so much easier.

They stopped for coffee in an airport cafe where the sheriff continued his questioning. When told about the flash flood, he hung his head. "Thank God you're all right."

"I'm still trying to decide which was worse," Dana said. "Crashing the motorhome or trying to survive the flood."

"Don't worry. I'm here to protect you."

"All the way to Wyoming?"

"All the way to hell and back, if necessary."

"Then let's get started." Dana got to her feet to look for the nearest rental car agency. She spotted a booth down the corridor and headed in that direction.

"Doesn't she ever slow down?" Walter's voice was loud enough for her to hear.

"Never. She's like the EverReady rabbit."

"Why don't we fly instead of drive?"

"Because I'm a white-knuckled flyer. Dana nearly had to hypnotize me to get me on the last puddle jumper. I'd rather walk than fly."

"I guess we'll take the scenic route."

The scenic route? Dana didn't plan to come this way again so they might as well enjoy the scenery and take a hundred pictures. When she arrived at the rental booth, the clerk was engaged in conversation. He raised an index finger to indicate that it would only be a moment longer, but Dana was ready to search for another agency.

When she turned to leave, Walter said, "Slow down before you crumple. *I'll* take care of the paperwork." He pointed to a seating area and told them to relax.

Relax? Dana was wound tighter than a Swiss clock and in dire need of sleep. How could she relax?

"Meditate," Sarah said. "We'll be back on the road soon and you need to get some rest. We have our own officer of the law to escort us home."

And then what? Would they all have to worry about the killer finding them at home? Her name had undoubtedly been listed in the newspaper when she had wrecked the motorhome. The killer had to have seen the Wyoming license plates. She wondered if Walter planned to stay long enough for them to feel safe. And how could she prevent him from pursuing her?

"I rented you a Cadillac Escalade," he said.

"You're a mind reader, Walter."

He swept the baseball cap from his head and bowed. "At your service, my love."

He winced when she gave him the evil eye.

***

The sky had cleared by the time they left the airport with Walter driving. Dana checked her watch. It was half past eleven and they still needed to map their route. The Atlas had been left behind in the disabled Hummer so they would have to buy another.

"No worries, ladies. I've already figured out the route. The GPS system says to take I-seventeen to Flagstaff and I-forty to Albuquerque. We'll then head north on I-twenty-five to Denver and Wyoming."

Sarah beamed and Dana recognized that gleam in her eyes. She had a crush on their chauffeur. Smiling to herself, she decided to let nature take its course. After they had stopped to buy bedding, Dana claimed exhaustion and insisted that Sarah ride in front with Walter, while she took a nap.

"Are you sure, Dana? I thought that you and Walter wanted to get reacquainted."

"We'll do that later. Right now I need some sleep."

Sarah hesitated. "Well, if you're sure."

Dana helped Walter recline the backseat and inflate the air mattress. She then told him not to wake her for anything less than another flash flood. Curling into a fetal position, she was drifting off to sleep when she heard them laughing. She jolted fully awake when she realized that if Sarah married Walter, she would be moving back to California. There had to be a better way.

"Dana?" Walter's voice was soft as though speaking to a child. "Would you mind if we stop by the Flagstaff PD so I can check on the murder investigation?"

"Great idea. You can get information that we can't."

"I wonder if they've arrested the killer," Sarah said.

"Hopefully the perp's been incarcerated. If not, we need his description and the general area where he was last seen. By the way, Dana, did you get a good look at him?"

"Briefly in the café and his eyes in the rearview mirror." "They were dark and evil looking."

"The color?"

"Black or dark brown."

"His eyebrows?"

"Black and heavy. Thick, curly eyelashes. They looked as though he were wearing mascara."

"Mascara?"

Dana laughed. "Not really but thick lashes, the envy of any woman."

"What about his voice?"

"Halfway between baritone and bass."

"Any kind of accent?"

"Sort of southern, but only slightly."

"Anything else you can remember?"

Dana hesitated. "His breathing. It sounded as though he were wheezing."

"An asthmatic, maybe?"

"Could be, or he ran to get into the motorhome before I left the cafe."

"Excitement or fear might cause that kind of reaction." Walter said. "What about age?"

"I got the impression he was in his late twenties, early thirties."

"His height and weight?"

"I only got a brief look at him when I wrecked the motorhome. His legs weren't very long sticking out from the dining nook. He might be five-six."

Dana glanced out the side window and realized they were in traffic. "End of interrogation, Walter. You'd better concentrate on your driving."

She was too tired to sleep. Random incidents of the past few days swirled in her mind like a whirlpool, dragging her deeper into its depths. Why did they have to be involved in the murder? And why would anyone in his right mind chase a beautiful young woman down the rain-slicked interstate? He obviously wasn't in his right mind. A psychotic who had tried to kill her as well. Would he try again and were Sarah and Walter in danger?

Raising herself on an elbow, she asked Walter to check the weather report to see if they were driving into more rain. He scrolled through the stations until he found the weather channel. After the commercials aired, they were advised of party cloudy skies and no further precipitation in the forecast.

"Looks like it's all uphill to Flagstaff."

"Flag," Sarah corrected him. "That's what the truckers call it. At home they call Casper the ghost town."

"That right?"

Dana sighed. From Walter's tone, he wasn't interested in anything Sarah had to say. Dana would have to cool his ardor another way.

Chapter 12

They pulled into Flagstaff not long after two that afternoon. First stop was the police station. The sheriff needed to go in alone so that his visit would seem official. Dana wondered whether the officers would question his reason for inquiring about an out of state murder. She didn't ask and he didn't volunteer how he was going to pull it off.

Sarah turned in the seat to stare at her, remarking that Walter had matured in his job since they'd met him. Dana agreed. It had been quite a transition from training police dogs to taking over as sheriff. Then, to be confronted with all the murders in the Valley Retirement Village during the first few days of his new job.

"It couldn't have been easy."

"What are you going to do about him, Dana?"

"What do you mean?"

"He loves you. You can't keep stringing him along."

"I don't intend to, Sarah. It wasn't my idea for him to come to our rescue."

"But aren't you're glad he did?"

"We'd have been halfway home by now, if he hadn't flown into Phoenix."

Sarah sighed. "He feels bad about the flood."

"That doesn't mean I should marry him."

"Would you have married Matt Brown if he'd lived?"

"Why do I have to marry anyone? Aren't two marriages enough?"

"I still miss my husband."

Dana's voice took on a gentler tone. "I know, Sarah, but aren't you enjoying your freedom?"

Sarah shrugged and admitted she would marry Walter, if he asked her. But only if Dana didn't want him.

"You'd leave me alone in the mansion and move back to California?"

Sarah shook her head. "No, you'd have to move back too."

Dana said she'd started a new life and wasn't about to go back.

"Then Walter will have to relocate."

Swell. The three musketeers. Dana decided to take a nap while Walter was in the station. Thank heavens they were in a dark blue Escalade instead of the burgundy Hummer, in case the killer was still looking for her. Sarah promised to watch for young men with dark hair and curly eyelashes, but fell asleep on the job.

Forty-five minutes later the sheriff reappeared, waking them both. From his expression, his news wasn't good. The police were still looking for the killer, but at least they had a suspect in mind. When they asked who, Walter said he was Mark Stone, the victim's former boyfriend.

"I thought she was married."

"A newlywed, according to her parents."

"So he didn't accept her rejection?"

"Her parents said Stone had been stalking her."

"So that's why they suspect him and not someone else."

"Basically." Walter started the Cadillac.

"Does he fit the description I gave you?"

"Not quite. The waitress at the cafe where you stopped before wrecking the motorhome described him as tall and lanky."

"With dark hair and eyes?"

"She said dark eyes and medium brown hair."

"She's wrong, Walter. I saw him—"

"Witnesses never seem to agree on anything."

Dana agreed that Stone was the logical suspect because he'd been stalking the victim and had reason to kill her. A jilted suitor. She asked if the victim's parents had described Stone.

"They pretty much agree with your description."

"So it must be him."

Walter drove the Escalade onto the highway. "Stone's been missing from his job since the day before the murder. We need to watch for anyone answering his description."

"What about his pickup?" Dana envisioned the dark red Dodge with a Las Vegas bumper sticker. "Do they have a description?"

"I didn't think to ask."

Both women groaned.

Sarah handed him her cell phone, ordering him to call.

He "yes, ma'amed" her and plucked a business card from his pocket. When he clicked off, he said, "Dark red, late model Dodge."

"That's him," Sarah said.

Dana wondered aloud how long Walter's leave was and he answered as long as needed. He wanted to know why she asked.

"Just wondered how long we can enjoy your company."

He stared at her in the rearview mirror, smile lines at the corners of his eyes.

"The three musketeers. Friends to the end."

She heard him groan and noticed him glance in the side mirrors.

"Is someone following?"

"Not sure but there's a dark red vehicle of some kind a block or so behind. It's been there since we left the station."

Sarah complained that she was hungry so they stopped at a Wendy's drive through. The sheriff kept his eyes on the mirrors when they pulled into the order lane. Dana heard him mutter, "Dark red Dodge" to himself a moment later.

"Walter?"

"Drove on past," he said with a sigh of relief. He was obviously not in the mood for confrontation with the killer.

They should have taken the first flight out of Phoenix. The drive was going to be a nightmare with all three of them expecting an attack. Be reasonable, Dana told herself. Stone couldn't have followed them to Phoenix through the flood waters and subsequent flights. That was impossible. Or was it? He'd managed to evade the police, determined to kill witnesses to Lori Murphy's murder. Was he waiting in ambush at the mansion in Wyoming?

Leaning over the back seat, she said, "It might be a good idea to take some scenic side roads."

"Not a bad idea. You have a suggestion?"

"Sarah's our navigator. I'm sure she can find some points of interest."

The Escalade pulled to the side of the road. "Why not change seats and give Sarah some room?"

Sighing, she helped him deflate the mattress and pull up the back seat. She then switched places with her friend. *He'd better keep his hands on the wheel.*

"I'd like to see Arizona in my rearview mirror," he said. "Less chance of being followed."

"I'm worried that Stone's already in Wyoming. With the county number on the RV license, it would be easy to track us down."

"I'm afraid you'll have to spend some of that fortune your sister left you to hire a couple of armed guards."

Dana shook her head and grimaced. "We tried that after my sister was murdered. It didn't work out too well."

"No worries. I'll be there to protect you."

"For how long, Walter? And what about your job? You can't stay forever."

"I can resign and find a job in Wyoming."

Dana groaned inwardly. The sheriff was relentless. She was aware of him watching her from the corner of his eye. "Is the red Dodge still back there?"

"Must have turned off. No sign of him since leaving the fast food place."

Dana suggested they drive through Las Vegas instead of Albuquerque so they could avoid Interstate 40 construction. The Escalade pulled off the road again and he punched in data in the GPS system.

"That means going west through Kingman. I wish you'd said something sooner. We'll have to backtrack a ways."

"At least it'll confuse anyone who might be following."

"True, but it's pretty hard to disguise the Escalade. I doubt you've been followed. Unless the guy is a magician, there's no way he could have followed you here."

There was that hint of sarcasm in his tone that she hated. "So you think I'm paranoid?"

"I didn't say that. Believe me, I understand what you've gone through."

"I don't think you do." She jerked her arm away when he reached across the console to comfort her. "I have been stalked by a killer but I've never had to crash a motorhome to escape from one. And then the flash flood."

Sarah leaned from the backseat to hug her. "My fault. We should have taken a plane."

"That would have been even worse. He could have planted a bomb."

Walter appeared concerned. "A doctor should take a look at you, Dana. You could be suffering from shock."

"Oh, you think? What about Sarah? She's the excitable one." Dana bit her tongue. She knew she'd hurt Sarah's feelings. Opening the door, she slammed it and walked down the roadway. A moment later she felt his arms around her. Pulling her close he stroked her hair and murmured something she couldn't understand.

Holding her at arm's length, he said, "Vegas awaits. I can't think of a better place to take your mind off your worries. And Sarah will enjoy herself there."

"She *is* a slot machine junkie."

"Then it's settled." Taking her hand, he led her back to the SUV.

Sarah was ecstatic when told of the change in plans. "Las Vegas is one of my favorite places."

The sheriff frowned. "Why didn't you go that way to begin with."

"Cousin Tilly. If I hadn't insisted on visiting her, we wouldn't be in this mess."

"We're going to leave the mess behind, ladies. The GPS is routing us through Vegas, Salt Lake City and Wyoming. That's country I've never seen. I'm sure it's beautiful."

"You're right," Dana said. "We should enjoy the rest of the trip."

"Good girl." He reached to pat her shoulder.

"Remember our discussion in the airport, Walter?"

"Vaguely."

"Let's keep this trip on a friends only basis. . . The three musketeers."

Sighing, he turned the key in the ignition. "If that's the way you want it. By the way, which musketeer am I?"

"Actually, you should be D'Artagnan. He guarded his friends Athos, Porthos and Aramis."

"So now I'm not even one of the musketeers?"

Sarah leaned to pat his shoulder. "You're better than that, dear. If you were a fictional character, you'd be Rhett Butler."

Dana groaned. *Oh, my word, Sarah. You have got it bad.*

Chapter 13

When they reached the area where the murder had occurred, Dana told him to take the next overpass and drive down the eastbound lanes toward Flagstaff.

"Are you sure this is where it happened?" Walter said when Dana told him to stop.

"No, but it looks familiar."

She left the Escalade and walked along the embankment to search for some sign of the accident. A car door closed and she heard footsteps on the pavement behind her.

"Hold up, Dana. What are you looking for?"

"Evidence the police may have missed in the dark."

"They must have come back the following morning."

"A deputy probably accompanied the wrecker that came to get the convertible, but. I doubt deputies did more than a preliminary search of the area."

He smiled. "You're probably right."

Sarah joined them. "Isn't that the boulder that stopped the convertible?" She pointed to a huge rock backed by tall pine trees.

"Looks like it."

Dana made her way down the embankment. Walter and Sarah were close behind. Before they reached the boulder, she noticed tire tracks in the dead grass and the lingering odor of gas. Kneeling, she ran her hand along the boulder at bumper height. She noticed scarring in the rock and a few chips scattered at its base.

"This is it, unless Stone had a habit of shooting travelers along the highway."

"Now what?" Sarah stood with hands on both hips.

"Look around to see what we can find."

Sarah climbed back up the embankment to look for evidence the killer might have left behind. "

"Be careful, Sarah. Those trucks come flying by."

Walter reached to pick something up from the grass. He unfolded a wad of paper and straightened to read it. "Looks like a betting sheet from Vegas."

"Lori Murphy was a gambler?"

"It's old by the looks of it, Dana."

"It was raining that night, which could account for its appearance."

Sarah called from the shoulder, waving something in her hand. "I found a bullet holder."

Walter laughed. "It's probably a shell casing. Let's have a look."

"Go ahead. I'll search down here."

Moving slowly, she nudged the well-trampled grass with the toes of her shoes, wishing she had gloves. Something small and shiny caught her attention and Dana stooped to retrieve a gold-colored key. Turning it over in her hand, she noticed the letters USPS engraved in the round metal. A post office box key? But from where? Had the key fallen from Lori Murphy's purse when Dana retrieved it from her car? Or had someone else lost it? It seemed unlikely that anyone would be hiking along the sloped terrain this far from Flagstaff.

"Find something?" Walter yelled from the road.

"Yes, and I think we'll be returning to Flagstaff."

He shook his head. "You've got to be kidding."

Dana turned back to search for more clues. Half an hour later, she decided to return to the Escalade. Her friends were already seated inside and laughing about something. She hoped it wasn't her.

"What's all this malarkey about returning to Flagstaff?" Walter asked as he started the Cadillac.

She showed him the key saying they needed to locate the post office box.

"How many are there in Arizona, Dana? You're asking us to find the proverbial needle."

"We'll look up Lori Murphy on a people locater so we'll know where she lived. That will narrow down the search. I brought my laptop along."

"Sure it didn't get water logged in the flood?"

"If it did, I'll buy another."

"Okay, Miz Money Tree. We'll head back to town. You should turn that key over to the police."

Dana smiled for the first time in days. "You're no fun, Walter Grayson. If I can't find the post office box, I'll turn the key in to the authorities. Satisfied?"

"Yes, ma'am. Whatever you say."

"That's my Dana," Sarah said, laughing. "Always on the front line."

"Look who's talking, Sarah Snoop Dog. Chasing a killer in a produce truck."

***

They found a nice motel just off the main street. After dinner the women settled into their room. Dana booted up her computer and typed in Lori Murphy's name when the people locater website came on screen. A list of nearly fifty women appeared in the state of Arizona.

"How will we know which is the right one?"

Dana scrolled down the page, looking at ages. "Lori Murphy was only twenty-seven but everyone here is older. The youngest listed is thirty-three."

Sarah leaned to survey the screen. "Maybe she lived with her parents until she got married, so she's not listed separately."

"But we don't know who they are."

"Walter can find out."

"True. Let's see if we can find the killer." Dana typed in the name, prompting a list of fifty-eight Mark Stones. "The youngest is twenty-nine but we don't know his age. Or which town either of them is from. Maybe we can find a newspaper article about Lori's death. Or a police report on Mark Stone."

"Try both Flagstaff and Phoenix."

Dana typed in "Flagstaff newspaper" and *The Daily Sun* appeared. She then clicked on "archives" and the date of the murder, June 20. A row of news stories appeared and she scrolled to a short article written the day following the murder. Lori Murphy's parents weren't mentioned so she typed in subsequent dates until she found the obituary. The murder victim was survived by her parents, Robert and Mary Schmidt of Scottsdale, and her husband James, also of Scottsdale.

"That's the Phoenix area. So what were Lori and Mark doing racing along Interstate forty toward Flagstaff?"

"Good question, Sarah. If we find the right Schmidts, we can call and ask them."

"I'm glad they're not Smiths. It could take a month to find them."

A number of Robert Schmidts were listed in Scottsdale so she cross referenced the addresses with those of the Mary Schmidts.

"This is getting expensive."

"Your sister Georgi would approve of how you've been spending her money."

"I hope you're right. . . Bingo. Here's the address. Grab a notepad and write it down. No phone number's listed so I'll call information."

The Schmidts' number was unlisted. Maybe they could reach the widower. She clicked back to the people locater. She found three James Murphys in the right age group and called each one. All had living wives.

"Try Phoenix."

Dana found a long list of James Murphys, quite a few the right age unless Lori had married an older man. She was able to call two of them before Walter knocked at their door.

"What are you gals up to?" He leaned against the door jamb, arms folded across his massive chest.

"Calling James Murphys." Sarah invited him in.

Annoyed that he was there, Dana turned her back and punched in another number from her list.

"Who's James—?"

She heard Sarah whisper and tuned them both out.

When a man's voice came on the line, Dana introduced herself before questioning him. When she hung up, she said "Wrong James Murphy. He was real smart aleck who was determined to string me along. He must be well acquainted with the case because he knew a lot of details."

"Then how do you know he wasn't the husband?"

"He just laughed when I asked about the relationship between his wife and Mark Stone."

Sarah frowned. "Do you think that's appropriate to ask a grieving husband?"

"*If* he's actually grieving."

"They were newlyweds, Dana. I don't think you should have asked."

"Maybe you're right."

"You might ask for Lori's parent's phone number."

"If I can find the right James Murphy."

"Why do you think the victim and perp were driving across northern Arizona, so far from home?" Walter asked.

"Good question. It's one I plan to ask."

"You should leave it to the police."

"No offense, Sheriff Grayson, but I remember when *you* needed our help to solve the retirement village murders."

He said nothing more.

Sarah leaned over Dana's shoulder to stare at the list. "How many more Murphys do you plan to call?"

"At least a dozen."

She picked up her cell, and punched in another set of numbers. She clicked off several moments later. "Another wrong number. He wouldn't even tell me if he knows the right James Murphy."

Sarah sighed. "Now what, Sherlock?"

"We have the Schmidt's address. Tomorrow we'll drive to Scottsdale."

"What if they refuse to talk to us?"

"I'll call Kerrie. Have her fly in and interview them."

Sarah smiled. "It'll be good to see your daughter again."

"It's been months."

"Kerrie's a smart gal," Walter said. "And beautiful like her mother."

Dana picked up the phone, ignoring him.

One of the Murphy's phones rang at least ten times and the others were wrong numbers. She circled the *no answers* as well their addresses. She would try again the following day.

The phone rang at six the following morning. Fumbling for the receiver, Dana dropped it on the floor. She could hear Walter's voice yelling, "What happened?"

Rubbing the remnants of sleep from her eyes, she apologized and asked why he'd called so early. He said he wanted to have breakfast with her before he left town.

"You're leaving?" She swung her legs over the side of the bed.

"It tears me apart to leave you but I got a call late last night from Lieutenant Calvy. There's been a triple murder-suicide near Modesto. I've got to fly out this morning."

Dana smiled, relieved that he was leaving although shocked at the reason. "That's terrible. Of course you need to go. We'll meet you at the café in fifteen minutes."

Sarah groaned from the adjacent bed. "Why is Walter leaving?"

"I'll tell you while we're getting dressed. Hurry, we're meeting him for breakfast."

Walter was drinking his second cup of coffee when they joined him. He briefly filled them in on the murders and insisted they tell the police what they knew. "Be careful" were his parting words before he boarded the plane for Phoenix, with a connecting flight to Sacramento.

"Looks like we're on our own." Sarah brushed a tear from the corner of her eye.

"He'll be back. We need to get packed and on our way to Scottsdale."

"Are you sure, Dana? I think we should follow Walter's advice and turn our evidence over to the police."

"What's happened to Sarah the senior sleuth? Are you giving up already?"

Sarah snorted. "I know why Ruby risked her load of lettuce to catch the killer but why is it so important to you?"

"He planned to kill all of us on that lonely highway. Remember? I had to wreck our motorhome to stop him."

"You risked your life. Wasn't that enough?"

"No. I'm madder than hell that he's getting away with it."

"But the police—" Sarah sputtered.

"They have other cases on their calendar. We need to investigate before this case is cold. And Mark Stone kills someone else."

A light seemed to come alive in Sarah's eyes. "All right. Let's go."

The drive to Scottsdale took the better part of two hours and traffic down the mountain was heavy. Both women gasped more than once when, sandwiched between large trucks, they had to keep up with speeding vehicles.

"Crazy drivers," Sarah muttered, gripping the arms of her seat as Dana navigated another mountain curve.

"No turning back now. And definitely no U-turns."

"I wish Walter was with us."

"If I hear his name again, I'll pull off on the shoulder and let you walk." Sarah was getting on her nerves.

Her friend was silent for the remainder of the trip.

They refueled on the outskirts of Phoenix. Sarah tried unsuccessfully to plot their course on the GPS system, so they stopped to buy an area map. She then traced a route to the Schmidt's residence, a large white colonial with a carefully groomed lawn.

"Looks like money, Dana."

"It sure does. I hope we don't have to push past a butler and other servants."

Sarah reached to open her door and Dana followed suit. She had been thinking of questions to ask during the trip down the mountain and wished she had written them down. Dana's main concerns were the relationships between the Schmidts, their daughter, her husband and Mark Stone. Had Stone and Murphy known each other? The other nagging question was the reason both Lori and Mark were speeding along Interstate 40 in the rain.

Dana pushed the doorbell and waited. A moment later a handsome young man answered the door. Blond like Lori Murphy, he wasn't much taller than the petite victim and seemed intimidated by Dana's height.

"We'd like to speak with Robert or Mary Schmidt."

His eyes narrowed. "For what reason?"

Dana told him she had nearly been killed by Mark Stone and would like to ask the Schmidts a few questions about their daughter's death. When he said that wasn't possible and tried to close the door, Dana stopped him by stepping across the threshold.

"You don't understand. He kidnapped me and I had to wreck my motorhome to escape."

He obviously didn't believe her and called for backup. A moment later a large, middle-aged man with white-streaked black hair confronted Dana and eased her back onto the porch.

Dana glared back at him. "I just want a few minutes of their time."

"The Schmidts aren't here. Call for an appointment."

"I don't have their phone number. Would you—?"

The door closed in her face.

"Well!" Sarah huffed. "How rude is that?"

"It's time to call in the cavalry."

When seated again in the Escalade, Dana punched in her daughter's number.

***

Kerrie Compton sat alone at her desk. The rest of the staff had gone to Carlo's Cantina for lunch. She'd begged off because she was expecting a call from an East Coast news service. Her job as staff writer for City Magazine left her little time for socializing. Rubbing her weary eyes, she realized she had not heard from her mother lately and decided to give her a call. Before she could punch in the number, her cell phone rang. Her mother sounded stressed.

"Are you home? How was the trip?"

"You're not going to believe this, dear, but we're in the middle of another murder investigation."

"Where are you, Mom?"

"Phoenix. I had to wreck the motorhome and—"

"You're joking."

"I wish I were."

Kerrie caught her breath. "Are you both all right?"

"We're fine but I think the killer's stalking us."

"What killer, Mom? You're not making sense."

"Long story, dear." She then filled her in on the murder as well as subsequent events.

"A flash flood? You could have drowned. I can't leave you two alone for five minutes without you getting in trouble."

"I know, dear. I was just telling Sarah that we're murder magnets."

"They haven't caught the killer?"

"No, and he may have followed us here."

Kerrie surveyed her appointment calendar. "I have some sick leave coming. I'll fly down tomorrow."

Dana worried that her daughter would jeopardize her job but was assured it wouldn't be a problem. Kerrie would bring her work with her. "Try not to get involved in any more murders before I get there," she said.

Dana hung up smiling. "Kerrie's coming."

"Good. Maybe she can talk some sense into you."

"I thought you were all for solving the murder."

Sarah made a wry face. "We've been lucky so far but our luck might run out."

"I don't plan on a shootout with Mark Stone at the OK Corral. I just want to check out some questions I have about the case. The police should have arrested the killer by now. I don't think they're trying hard enough."

"I'm sure they'd disagree."

"Either you're with me or you can watch TV in a hotel room. Kerrie will be here tomorrow. She's a genius when it comes to investigations."

"I'm well aware of her journalism background, Dana, but you're putting her life in danger as well as our own."

Dana reminded her that they had survived two other murder investigations. What made this one any different?

"First the murder attempt in the motorhome, then the flood. Third time's a charm, they say."

"Kerrie makes three of us, which nullifies your theory."

Sarah grinned. "I like the way you think, my friend. I'm with you all the way."

"Could have fooled me."

"Let's get a room and rethink our strategy. But first we need to reconnoiter James Murphy's house, if he's home."

Chapter 14

James Murphy's modest home was located on a busy street. No parking was available so they circled the block several times. They finally agreed that Sarah would go to the door and ask for Lori. She'd say she was an out of state relative who had come for a visit. Dana dropped her off on the corner, three houses from the Murphy home. When Dana again circled the block, Sarah was waiting for her on the curb.

Sarah appeared disappointed, "Nobody's home or just not answering the door."

"He's probably at work. We'll try again tonight."

"I don't think Lori Murphy lived here."

"I wondered the same thing. A beautiful young woman from an affluent family would hardly settle for a bungalow in a less than desirable neighborhood."

"Unless she was terribly in love."

"You're such a romantic, Sarah. I would think that the wedding gift from her parents would have been a down payment on a nicer home."

"Maybe they didn't approve of her husband."

"That's a possibility. Like the heiress who married her chauffeur."

"We need to talk to her parents."

Dana's phone rang. It was Kerrie asking to be picked up the following morning at the Phoenix Airport.

"We'll be there with bells on."

"Not cowbells, I hope."

Dana laughed. "You're not referring to my new home in Wyoming, are you?"

"Of course not, Mom, unless you're grazing cattle on the grounds of the mansion."

"You can't graze cattle on five acres, dear. I don't think your Aunt Georgi had that in mind when they built the mansion."

"I'm sure my former uncle would have planted pot on the property if he could have gotten away with it. What's happening with him now, by the way?"

"He's currently serving a life sentence for the murder of his teenage mistress."

"That poor misguided kid. They should have hanged my dear former uncle by his—"

"There wasn't much left after I shot him, dear."

Kerrie laughed. "How could I forget. He deserves much worse than a life sentence."

"At least he's off the streets and not ruining lives."

"You should be proud of yourself, Mom. If you and Sarah hadn't solved Aunt Georgi's murder and taken down the drug ring, a lot more lives would have gone down the tubes."

"That's why I'm determined to solve this murder case, Kerrie. A beautiful young woman died needlessly. It got personal when he tried to kill me as well."

"I'll do whatever I can to help, Mom."

"I'm counting on your investigative skills to help us track him down."

"I think my skills are highly overrated but at least I can offer moral support."

"I can't wait to see you. What's your flight number and carrier?"

Kerrie gave her the information and waited while she wrote it down. Smiling, Dana turned to Sarah whose brows had lifted in anticipation.

"Kerrie's flying in tomorrow morning. Let's stop for lunch before we return to the hotel. We've got a lot more investigating to do."

An hour later, Dana booted her laptop and searched for newspaper articles about the Schmidt-Murphy wedding. Guessing at the date, she scrolled through the archives of Scottsdale's *East Valley Tribune*. When she didn't find a notice, she backtracked a year and worked forward. Two hours later she turned the search over to Sarah.

Sarah appeared worried. "I'm nervous staying in Stone's home territory."

"I doubt he's hanging around. My instincts tell me he's camped out in the mansion, waiting for us."

"I wonder how long he'll wait."

"Who knows? I think I'll call our former bodyguard and ask him to check things out."

"Jeff Mailey? That gorgeous hunk."

"I thought you were in love with Walter."

"It doesn't hurt to have a spare."

"You're incorrigible," Dana said, smiling. "Get back to work."

She had dozed off when Sarah shrieked, "I found them."

A half page society article featured the bride and groom. Dana leaned closer to the screen, drawn to the photograph. James Murphy looked uncannily familiar. A few inches taller than his petite bride, he was dark haired and dark-eyed. His narrow beard stretched from his chin to his sideburns, causing a chill to run down Dana's spine. James Murphy looked enough like Mark Stone to be his brother.

"Is that James Murphy or Mark Stone?"

"Oh my gosh, you're right. They do look alike."

"But which one is in the photograph?"

Were the two men related? If they were, it could explain the intense rivalry. But murder? Why not kill each other instead of the bride? Had Lori infuriated one of them enough to kill her? Or did he feel she was better off dead than living with his rival? There were so many questions and no answers.

Sarah read the accompanying article aloud. The young couple had plans to honeymoon in Fiji. That didn't sound as though Murphy was a pauper. Lori's parents could have paid for the honeymoon. They had to find a way to talk to them as soon as possible. Had the Schmidts actually left town to grieve or were they hiding at home? Kerrie was their only hope but could she talk her way inside?

"See if you can find out anything about the Robert Schmidts, Sarah. We need to learn where they hang out. They're probably high on the social register and attend charity events. There's a good possibility they play golf."

"You mean crash a social party or bean them with a golf ball?"

"An art gallery would be nice. With my luck I'd send one of them to the hospital with my back swing. Not the best way for an introduction."

Sarah scrolled through the society pages. A few moments later she announced a library event scheduled for the following day. Mary Schmidt was listed as the coordinator for the Friends of the Library celebration.

"I wouldn't think that she'd attend a celebration this soon after her daughter's death." Dana said.

"If she wants to get on with her life, she will."

"That's true. Duty calls."

Sarah wrote down the address and time the library opened. She then retrieved their map and charted a course for the following morning. The library opened at ten but Kerrie's plane was scheduled to arrive in Phoenix at 10:44. The three of them would attend the library event together. Hopefully, Mary Schmidt would put in an appearance while they were there. They would have to approach her carefully. Kerrie was so much more artful at interrogation than she and Sarah were. Her journalism background had served them well during more than one investigation.

Smiling, Dana unpacked her clothes. They were going to spend some time in Scottsdale. At least until Lori's killer was in jail. But which man had committed the murder? And why would Murphy murder his beautiful bride? Jealousy? Had Lori gone to Las Vegas to meet her former lover? Or had Mark Stone decided that if he couldn't have her, no one would. How had he lured her to Vegas? Lori's mother was the key to unlocking the mystery.

"What should we wear to the library?" Sarah, the clothes horse.

"I think we should dress conservatively if we want Mary Schmidt to take us seriously. We'll come back here so that Kerrie can change clothes. I hope that she brings something other than jeans and T-shirts to wear."

"Why don't you call her?"

Dana placed the call but Kerrie wasn't answering. She left a message. Mother and daughter were the same size but she doubted Kerrie would wear one of her dresses. Kerrie's closet was filled with the latest styles while Dana's clothing hadn't been updated in ages. Maybe they'd go shopping in Phoenix after they left the library. That would depend on what Mary Schmidt had to say.

***

Kerrie's plane arrived late and the airport was crowded. Sarah was in a self-explained tizzy and Dana wasn't feeling much better. When Kerrie rushed into Dana's arms, she sighed with relief. Everything was going to work out. Her daughter was striking in a blue suit with white accessories and would make a good first impression. Dana's own black dress and Sarah's designer pant suit completed their fashion statements. Gathering up Kerrie's luggage, they hurried off to the Escalade. It was a twenty minute drive to the library.

A crowd had already gathered by the time they arrived, Standing at the entrance they scanned the reception area for someone who resembled the murder victim. Moments later a pleasant looking woman approached them. After she had welcomed them, Kerrie asked to speak to Mary Schmidt.

"She was here earlier but had to leave. Mrs. Schmidt lost her daughter recently and isn't feeling well."

"I flew in from Denver to interview her for a magazine article," Kerrie said. "Is there a number where she can be reached?" Kerrie asked.

The plump, middle-aged woman seemed undecided.

"I'll be happy to feature the library as well."

The woman brightened. "Oh, how nice."

"I can send a dozen copies of the magazine for display."

"That would be lovely. Wait just a moment and I'll see what I can arrange." She turned and hurried off toward the reception desk.

Sarah whispered, "Did you really mean that, Kerrie?"

"It's a good story, although out of my circulation area. I might be able to link Murphy's murder with several others I've been investigating."

"The grieving mother angle?"

"Right, Mom. That and the similarity in the victims and their circumstances. Three victims were found in Colorado, New Mexico and Utah."

"All young women?"

"All in their twenties."

"Petite blondes?"

"Yes, how did you know?"

"The description fits Lori Murphy. We have a lot to talk about when we get back to the hotel."

Kerrie's brows lifted. "An Arizona murder would make it a Four Corners killing spree."

Dana noticed the welcoming woman weaving her way through the crowd toward them. Carrying a notepad and pen, her smile had been replaced by a frown.

"I was advised by the head librarian that I shouldn't give out Mrs. Schmidt's number, but if you'll give me yours, I'll pass it along."

Kerrie recited her cell number and they turned to leave.

"Aren't you going to stay for the celebration? You can interview the librarians and Friends of the Library."

"We'll come back later. I need to unpack at the hotel."

The woman seemed disappointed but handed Kerrie her card. Kerrie asked that she urge Mary Schmidt to get in touch. They then left the building.

Dana filled Kerrie in on all that had happened at lunch in the hotel restaurant. She then asked if the other murder victims had anything in common.

"None that I'm aware of. The bodies were all found in remote areas in all three states. The police are sitting on the information."

"So there's a good chance that Lori's murder is tied in with the others."

"I don't believe in coincidence, Mom, although one or more could have been a copy cat murder."

Sarah aimed her salad fork at Dana. "None of this makes sense. Unless—"

"Mark Stone killed the rest of the victims?"

"Right. And we're not even sure it was him. It could have been James Murphy."

Kerrie laughed. "Now there's a theory I can wrap my mind around."

"While we're waiting to hear from Lori's mother," Dana said, "we need to find out where the two men work. You can interrogate their employers."

Sarah didn't want to miss a meal in favor of information gathering. So Kerrie wrote down directions to the library and took the Escalade's spare key. She was not in the mood for interviews but would concentrate on information about the two suspects. Surely someone would know something about Mary Schmidt's son-in-law.

The crowd had tapered off at the library since her earlier visit. They had probably gone to a late lunch. She found a stern looking librarian seated behind a welcoming table and asked if she had time for an interview. That brought a smile to her face. Her name tag said Mary Lou Darnell.

After introducing herself and accepting a name tag of her own, Kerrie remarked how sad it was that Lori Murphy had died. The woman looked at her curiously as though she had strayed off subject. Kerrie realized her mistake and sat down to unpack her camera equipment.

The librarian insisted that she was not photogenic and asked that Kerrie only record her voice. Agreeing, Kerrie asked about the library's history, hoping that Mary Lou would eventually come back to Mary Schmidt. It didn't happen.

Others were beginning to return to the library, so Kerrie moved on. There had to be someone who was willing to gossip. While browsing a table of books, another librarian approached. There was someone she thought Kerrie would be interested in interviewing.

"Cornelia Connelly has been with us for over fifty years. She's someone you'll want to talk to."

Kerrie followed her to an area just off the main desk. A petite woman in her late sixties or early seventies sat waiting, hands folded in her lap. She smiled when she was introduced and extended a small, blue-veined hand. If anyone liked to dish, Kerrie was sure it was her. All it took was one question and they were off and running.

"I'm sure you've seen a lot of changes here since you began your job as a librarian," Kerrie said.

"Do you have a week or so to chat?"

"I'm afraid I don't but maybe you could touch on the highlights."

Cornelia grimaced and shook her head as if to clear it. "People were honest and returned their books on time when I first came here," she said. "Now, we're lucky if we get them back in one piece. And they dump overdue books in the return slot and don't want to pay their late fees."

"Is there anything else going on in the library that you don't approve of?"

"I've found some of those roll your own smokes hidden on book shelves."

"Marijuana?"

"I suppose that's what they were."

Some librarians lead sheltered lives. "Has anyone been caught doing it?"

The woman leaned forward and whispered, "I'd be fired if I told you."

"Someone in authority who has children"

The woman looked surprised. "How did you know?"

"A lucky guess. I would never reveal my sources, Miss Connelly. Your secret is safe with me."

"Well, I don't know."

"Could it be someone with the Friends of the Library?"

The woman opened her mouth in surprise. "You must be clairvoyant."

"Do you happen to know either Mark Stone or James Murphy?"

"They've both come in occasionally."

"With Lori Murphy?" Kerrie asked.

"Sometimes. Why?"

"I'll tell you if you promise not to repeat it—to anyone."

Cornelia pursed her lips and leaned her left ear towards Kerrie.

"Mark Stone is suspected of killing Lori Murphy."

She gasped. "I'm not surprised. He's the one who—" She stopped, apparently unsure if she should continue.

"Who hid marijuana in the library?"

The librarian nodded her head in the affirmative.

"Do you happen to know anything else about him?"

"Only that Mary Schmidt seems afraid of him."

"Do you know why?"

"I heard he was stalking her daughter."

Kerrie asked when Mark Stone had last frequented the library and was told that it had been several months. He had come in with a group of other men to borrow books.

She noticed several librarians grouped together frowning at her. "Let's talk about your time at the library," she said, taking her recorder from its case.

An hour later Cornelia Connelly had brought her up to date as recent as the 1980s. In order to escape, Kerrie said there were other librarians waiting to be interviewed. Miss Connelly reluctantly stopped her narrative and headed for the restroom.

One of the librarians from the group approached, taking Kerrie's hand. She was as plain as an unbuttered biscuit and in her mid-50s. She wanted to know whether Kerrie was focusing on the library or the unfortunate death of the Schmidts' daughter. Kerrie asked why. She knew that she had overheard her last interview.

"It seems strange that you would come all this way for a Friend's of the Library celebration. Don't you have them in Denver?"

"I'll tell you if you promise to keep it to yourself."

"Certainly."

Kerrie briefly told her about the murder investigation and watched her reaction. The librarian appeared nervous. When asked if she had information that might be relevant to the case, she hesitated and glanced in her companions' direction. They promptly turned their backs and separated.

"Is there somewhere we can talk privately?"

"I really don't know anything, except . . ."

Kerrie waited.

She moved closer to talk just above a whisper. "Except that some strange men came in several times at night to use the library."

"A group of them?"

"Four or five."

"Were they doing research or just checking out books?"

"Both."

"What kind of books?"

"Chemistry," the librarian said.

"How often did they come in?"

"Three times while I was here and once while my friend was on duty."

"Why did that frighten you?"

The woman sighed. "It was their eyes and the way they looked at me."

"You felt threatened?"

"Yes."

Kerrie asked for descriptions and wrote them down. One of the men sounded like Mark Stone and James Murphy. Another was described as looking like Mr. Clean. "The one in the TV commercials."

When the librarian finished, Kerrie asked a few general questions of the others and took a dozen photographs. She then left for the hotel. Later, after she summarized what the librarians had said, they sat discussing the information.

"Chemistry books?" her mother said. "That certainly ties in, doesn't it?"

Sarah grimaced. "Sounds like a conspiracy to me."

"If the small man with dark hair had been either Mark Stone or James Murphy, the librarian probably would have recognized him."

"Which is why he wasn't there. The men who *were* there must be part of a larger organization."

"Terrorist group," Kerrie said to herself.

"With plans to poison people with chemicals."

"We've got a lot more investigating to do." Dana pulled her profile printouts. Mark Stone's employer was listed as Zamco Chemicals in Phoenix. She circled the name and phone number and then handed the sheet to her daughter. Shuffling through the stack of remaining printouts, she found Lori's husband, who was listed as an environmental engineer.

Kerrie read the data on both men. "That's interesting. One of them works for a chemical company and the other's an environmentalist. Opposites and probably antagonists."

"But what does that have to do with Lori's murder? Or the others, for that matter."

"If Lori Murphy had discovered something the chemical company had illegally done and was going to report it—."

Dana's fingers drummed the hotel desk. "She could have been killed to keep her quiet."

"Let's assume that the chemical company has something to hide."

"Like what, dear?"

"Cutting corners. Disregarding regulations. Any number of infractions of the law. Violations that could bring local, state and national authorities down on them."

"You mean a fishing expedition?"

"Yes, I hope I can bluff my way into the supervisor's office."

Kerrie retrieved her cell phone from a side pocket in her purse to punch in the chemical company's number. Dana heard her ask for Zamco's supervisor. She then requested an interview concerning the chemical company.

"I'm sure you don't want lies and speculation about your company printed in a news magazine," Kerrie said when the supervisor refused her request for an interview. "The story'll be picked up by the AP and *the Times* on both coasts, and don't forget the broadcast networks."

There was a long pause before she said, "Two o'clock tomorrow works for me. Where shall we meet?"

Kerrie sighed when she clicked off. "That woman has hit the glass ceiling so hard she must have cracked her skull. You'd think I was accusing *her* of murder."

"Why would she think you suspected her of anything?"

"She's probably been questioned about her company's activities."

"I hope that's true, dear. That would mean we're on the right track and the company's under investigation."

"Or the supervisor may have a guilty conscience about something she or the company has done."

"The printout doesn't say what type of job Mark Stone has at Zamco. He might also be an engineer."

"That's something I plan to ask Ms. Dailey, Kerrie said. "I have a feeling the interview will be a real tooth puller."

"What approach are you going to use?"

"I haven't decided. We need more research, like recent chemical spills or whether Mark Stone has been involved in some environmentally unsound project."

They needed to locate Mark Stone's residence. James Murphy's house came to mind. Why wouldn't an engineer be living in a better neighborhood? Unless he was low man on the corporate totem pole.

"Shall we wait until after your interview to talk to James Murphy's supervisor?"

"I'd prefer to concentrate on one supervisor at a time. Tomorrow's interview may turn up questions I can ask the second boss."

While Dana took a meditation break, Kerrie scrolled through Phoenix newspaper articles. Dana had just dozed off when her daughter shouted, "Mom, we were right. Look at this."

Chapter 15

"A chemical spill happened in the Arizona Canal south of Scottsdale. A similar accident happened two months ago in another location."

"What kind of chemicals?"

"Sulfuric acid from a tanker truck which overturned and ruptured."

"Was Zamco involved?"

"It doesn't say and it may have nothing to do with the murder case."

"Sulfuric acid's dangerous, isn't it?"

"Oh, yeah. I looked it up on the Wikipedia. A terrorist named Ahmed Ressam used sulfuric acid to make bombs forty times more deadly than the average car bomb. He planned to detonate them at Los Angeles International Airport on New Year's Eve in nineteen ninety-nine."

"Why would the chemical company be hauling the acid?" Dana wondered aloud.

"It's used to make batteries and fertilizer."

"Like the fertilizer that blew up the federal building in Oklahoma City?"

"Apparently so. Although it's non-flammable, if spilled it can release hydrogen gas, which is highly combustible."

Dana frowned. "Two spills in the same area within a couple of months sounds suspicious."

"I was thinking the same thing."

"If Lori Murphy knew why the spills happened . . ."

"Whoever's responsible would want to keep her quiet."

"Mark Stone?" Dana picked up a pen to take notes.

"It points to him."

"How company-loyal would you have to be to kill the woman you love?"

"The guy's obviously a nutcase who doesn't care a whit about loyalty. Especially to someone who dumped him," Kerrie said.

"True, but there's got to be more to it than that."

"Crimes of passion happen all the time."

"But Lori's murder was premeditated. Who knows how long the killer chased her down the highway."

Dana tried meditating while Kerrie conducted additional research. Hoping to lull herself into a brief nap, she was plagued with questions about the murders. How could a chemical spill tie into a four-state murder spree? Were the murder victims all involved with chemical companies, or simply one employee, Mark Stone. And was the company Mark worked for responsible for the chemical spills?

They needed to locate James Murphy. If he wasn't home that night, they'd have to track him down. She wondered whether the address listed on the Internet was a previous one that had not been updated. Since they were in Phoenix, she wouldn't have to pay the online directory to locate the entire list of Murphys. Opening her eyes, she glanced at the desk where a phone directory was located, along with a bible someone had left behind. She didn't know which one to reach for first.

There was a knock at the door and she found Sarah waiting in the hall.

"You're just in time," Dana said. "You can help call Murphys to locate the right one."

Sarah was led to the desk and handed the phone book. Before she started calling, Dana brought her up to date on all that Kerrie had learned.

"Sounds like we're making progress."

"We've only scratched the surface, which is why we need James Murphy."

Sarah plucked her cell phone from her purse. "What about Mary Schmidt? Hasn't she called Kerrie yet?"

"Not yet but we'll find her if she doesn't get in touch. She has to leave home sometime."

"In an armored car with bodyguards," Sarah muttered.

Dana told her to call every Murphy listed in the book. "Someone has to know the widower."

Sarah complained that her phone would need recharging before she reached the end of the list.

"Then we'll stop and recharge. Calls from hotel phones are expensive."

Sarah laughed. "About time you stopped spending the rest of your inheritance."

"Whatever it takes to solve the case."

"Right. Our expensive murder solving hobby."

"No matter how much we try to avoid them," Dana said, "murders always seem to involve us."

"You do like to live dangerously, my dear friend." Sarah checked her watch. "Before I start calling, how about an early dinner and trip back to the Murphy house. It could save us a lot of phone calls."

"You're right. I'm sure Kerrie would welcome a break."

Her daughter promptly shut down the computer and reached for her purse. When they piled into the Escalade, Dana asked what they wanted first, dinner or a trip to the Murphy residence. Sarah said she was starving.

Nearly an hour and a half later, Dana double parked in front of the house and Kerrie left the Escalade. A light shone from a window so someone must be home. Dana circled the block and noticed Kerrie standing on the front porch talking to a middle-aged man. When she circled again her daughter was waiting.

"The current resident has lived here over six months. He doesn't know the former tenant."

"Back to the planning board and more phone calls from the hotel."

Sarah groaned.

Later that evening, Sarah reported, "Five no answers, two wrong numbers and twelve 'we-don't-know-hims'. I'm not even halfway through the list."

Dana sighed. "I've had no luck either. It's strange that the Murphys claim not to know each other. They must be protecting the widower. How could they *not* know about the murder? It's been in all the media."

"I'm hitting a blank wall too, Mom. It must be a coverup where the chemical spills are concerned. Guess I'll have to visit the county offices. Or the newspaper morgues."

"Maybe we should talk to Murphy's former neighbors."

"If he actually lived there, It may have been the wrong James Murphy."

Sarah left the desk to stretch. "What about Mark Stone?"

"I doubt he's still in the area."

"I wouldn't wanna snoop around *his* house, would you?"

Dana made a face. "Kerrie's interviewing his supervisor tomorrow."

Kerrie looked up from the laptop. "That reminds me, I need a list of questions for the reluctant supervisor."

Dana absently tapped a pen on her palm. "What was his specific job within the company? And was he involved in any way with environmentalists?"

"Was he a good employee?" Sarah added.

Kerrie's long fingers flew across the keyboard. "Did he investigate the chemical spills?"

"Good question, dear."

"I don't quite understand how two sulfuric acid spills could happen in the same area. Unless there was espionage involved."

"I'll check that out."

"Ask if Stone talked about Lori Murphy?" Sarah, the romantic.

Kerrie grinned. "It's a big company. I doubt a supervisor would know about her employees' love lives but I'll try to work the question in."

"Ask if Zamco is under investigation?"

"I doubt Ms. Dailey would admit that, Mom. I'll have to check with the prosecutor's office."

"By all means. Looks like tomorrow's a busy day."

***

Dana's cell phone rang not long after she got in bed. Walter was calling to apologize for not calling sooner.

"It's a real mess. Some guy killed his wife and son, then shot himself. No one seems to know why. He didn't leave a note."

"I'm sorry. I know how exhausted you must be after the ordeal here."

"I wouldn't mind if you were here."

"Walter Grayson, we agreed—"

"Sorry. We'll keep it on a friends only basis until I retire from this blasted job."

"How's the murder case progressing there?"

"We're doing a lot of research but there isn't anything concrete yet. Kerrie's here to help."

She heard him sigh. "I'm glad she's there with you, Dana. She's an intelligent young woman."

"Indeed she is."

"Call if you need me. Or just call to let me know how things are going."

"I will."

"And for heaven sake, stay out of the danger zone."

She agreed and said goodbye.

Dana didn't sleep well that night. There were too many questions circulating in her brain. She was wide awake long before the automated wake-up call rang. Sarah groaned in the adjoining bed and went back to sleep.

"Ham and eggs for breakfast, Sarah." That should wake her up.

"A side order of breakfast potatoes." Her words were slurred with sleep.

"Get dressed and we'll call to rouse Kerrie."

Sarah sat on the edge of the bed rubbing her eyes. "Why so early, Dana?"

"We have a lot to investigate. While Kerrie interviews Mark Stone's supervisor, you and I will visit the library."

Sarah yawned. "What're we researching?"

"For starters, Zamco, chemical spills, the Murphys, and Mark Stone."

"Can't we do that on the laptop?"

Dana reminded her that only the highlights of the day's news appear online. They needed to conduct more thorough research. Kerrie would drop them off at the library on her way to her interview at Zamco Chemical Company.

Sarah stumbled to the closet and selected a light green pantsuit. "Is this elegant enough?"

"More than enough. I was planning to wear a T-shirt and jeans."

"Not in Mary Schmidt's library."

"You're right. We need to be prepared for anything." Dana browsed the closet until she located a dark, short sleeved jumpsuit with a braided belt.

Half an hour later she tapped on Kerrie's door. She was ready and waiting. A runway model would not have looked better in a peach colored dress with matching jacket. Dana was impatient to get started. Opening the door, she waved the others into the hall. "Breakfast awaits."

***

Kerrie found Zamco, an eight-story block building on an industrial side street, after leaving her mother and Sarah at the library. Glad that she'd had the forethought to bring her recorder, she parked in the lot beside the building. Inhaling deeply, she gathered her gear and entered by the front door. A receptionist glanced up from her desk and asked if she had an appointment.

"Two o'clock with Sharon Dailey."

The receptionist punched in a number on her phone and announced Kerrie's arrival. While she waited, she looked at artwork on the stark white walls. Pictures of tankers in pristine settings monopolized most of the available space. She was about to check out a bank of framed certificates when her name was called.

A slender man with white hair and a face to match beckoned her to follow and they entered a nearby elevator. He said nothing as he punched in the number six on the side panel. When the elevator jerked upward she nearly lost her balance. Why didn't a big company like Zamco have better service? At least it was fast. Before she could catch her breath the door opened and she followed her escort down the hall. Told to wait in an outer office, Kerrie sat and looked over her list of questions. Twenty minutes later she was fuming. Dailey was deliberately ignoring her. Not the smartest thing to do to a journalist writing a story about her company. It was an obvious power play.

At last the office door opened and a woman dressed in a frumpy yellow outfit asked her to step inside. "Ms. Dailey will see you now," she said, opening the inner office door.

A small woman in her early fifties stood behind her desk and apologized for keeping Kerrie waiting. Her dark hair was short and she was dressed conservatively in a gray suit.

"Please be seated." She didn't offer her hand.

Kerrie sat and unpacked her recorder, notepad and pen.

Dailey shook her head. "No taping. What I tell you is off the record."

Kerrie sighed and put her equipment away. "I'd like to know about one of your employees, Mark Stone."

The supervisor hesitated. "What about him?"

"Is he still employed here?"

"He's taken a leave of absence."

"Since when?"

"You'll have to ask the personnel department."

"Is he an engineer or involved in chemical cleanups?"

"Not an engineer. He works in reclamation."

"Was he involved in the recent chemical spill cleanup on the Indian Reservation south of Scottsdale?"

"I couldn't tell you that."

"Why?"

"I'm not aware of who goes out on cleanups."

"Are you saying that there are so many of them that you can't keep track?"

"No!" The word reverberated off the office walls. "This is a very large company and I don't keep track of the comings and goings of all the employees."

Kerrie glanced at her notes. "Are you acquainted with James Murphy?"

"The name's familiar."

"He's an environmental engineer."

"Oh, that James Murphy." She said the name as though it left a bad taste in her mouth.

"You've had dealings with him?"

"On occasion."

"In what way?"

"That's privileged information."

So he's been on Zamco's case. "Did you know his wife, Lori?"

"I've heard about her unfortunate death and that her husband took it very hard."

"Do you have a phone number for him? I'd like to get in touch."

"I'm afraid you'll have to find him, yourself. He's not one of my favorite people."

"Has Murphy been here to investigate your sulfuric acid spills?" Dailey moved uncomfortably in her chair. "Just the first one."

Kerrie cocked an eyebrow and waited for the rest. The information wasn't forthcoming.

"Which environmental agency is he with?"

"I don't recall."

I'll just bet you don't. "Have all the spills happened on the Indian reservation?"

"All? There have only been two."

"And the causes?" Kerrie noticed the woman's hands grip the edge of her desk. She wanted the interview to end.

"Driver error," she said too quickly.

"Really? The same driver both times?"

"Of course not."

"So Zamco's under investigation?"

Dailey spoke as though Karrie were a child. "Whenever there's an accident involving chemicals, there's always an investigation."

"By whom?"

"State, local and federal authorities."

From the expression on her face, Kerrie almost felt sorry for the woman.

"It must have been an ordeal."

Dailey nodded and avoided her gaze. Her fingers inched over to her phone bank. A moment later the door opened and her secretary appeared.

"Ma'am?"

"Have the Collins reports arrived?"

"This morning by FedEx. I thought I told you—"

"I need to get to those right away."

Kerrie noticed a strange expression on the secretary's face.

"If you'll excuse me."

Kerrie rose and handed the supervisor a business card. "If you hear from Mark Stone, I'd appreciate a call. Or James Murphy, for that matter." She knew the card would be filed in the waste can the moment she left the room.

Kerrie turned back to face her at the door. "There's a murder investigation going on and I would hate to see you taken in as an accomplice."

Was that fear on Dailey's face or anger? Hard to tell. Kerrie left the office before the supervisor had time to throw something at her.

Chapter 16

Kerrie called her mother as soon as she buckled herself in.

"Where are you? I was just going to call."

"What's up, Mom?"

"Mary Schmidt's here."

"How do you know it's her?"

"We found her picture on a Scottsdale society page."

"Great. I'll get there as soon as possible."

"If she starts to leave, we'll waylay her."

Kerrie laughed. "Gently, Mom. Don't tackle her."

Traffic was heavy and her palms were sweating when she pulled into the library parking lot. Grabbing her purse, she hurried up the ramp to the back door. Disoriented, she scanned the area before making her way toward the large front windows. Temporarily blinded by incoming light, she noticed three women near the entrance backlighted by the floor to ceiling windows. She could only distinguish their silhouettes. One of them stood nearly a head taller than the rest, another plump, the remaining woman small. When her mother noticed her, she beckoned Kerrie to join them.

"Here's my daughter now." Dana then introduced Kerrie to Mary Schmidt. The petite blonde's depression weighed obviously on her shoulders. Her smile disappeared as she extended a manicured hand.

"Did my mother explain why I'd like to interview you?"

"Vaguely."

Kerrie glanced at Dana who had raised a brow.

"May we sit somewhere so that I can tell you why I've come?" Kerrie hoped the woman wouldn't question her wisdom of flying in without an appointment.

Mary Schmidt hesitated. Curiosity must have crowded out any doubts she may have had because she finally nodded consent. Without a word, she led Kerrie toward a lounge area at the east end of the library. Dana and Sarah took their cue and returned to a large table covered with newspapers and magazines.

Sarah plopped into a plastic chair. "Whew, did we time that right, or what?"

"We were lucky we recognized her before she left."

"I hope Kerrie can convince her to cooperate."

"She will when she realizes Kerrie might be able to help solve her daughter's murder."

"This is the most complicated murder case we've ever investigated, Dana."

"I'm aware of that. I hope Kerrie can learn something useful from the interview."

Dana was flipping through a news magazine when she discovered an article concerning chemical spills. One had taken place in Knoxville, Tennessee, in 2002. A hazardous materials team worked through the night to clean up thousands of gallons of chemicals that had spilled from an overturned railroad car.

"Listen to this, Sarah. The authorities evacuated eight thousand people after the sulfuric acid spill. It formed a heavy, billowing cloud of hazardous gas and people were evacuated within a five-mile radius, twenty miles from downtown Knoxville."

"Was anyone killed?"

"No, but fumes are an extreme irritant and direct contact with the chemical can cause blindness. Prolonged exposure can also cause extensive damage to the mouth, throat and stomach. If swallowed, the liquid form can cause death."

"I wonder if that happened on the reservation?"

"That we need to find out. There was another spill into the Santa Cruz River some forty miles south of Nogales. A train derailment caused two carloads of sulfuric acid to spill twenty thousand gallons, which flowed across the border. because the river runs north. All the fish died from Nogales to the international border."

"Nasty stuff."

"The Knoxville spill was a military shipment."

"Why would the military be shipping acid, Dana?"

"The article states that sulfuric acid is used in chemical munitions, car batteries, fertilizers or toilet bowl cleaners."

"Chemical munitions? What does that mean? Chemical warfare?"

"I doubt our military manufactures toilet bowl cleaners or fertilizers."

Sarah shivered. "That gives me cold chills."

***

Kerrie noticed the family resemblance when the Schmidt woman seated herself on a long couch facing her. Closing her light blue eyes she sighed, folding her hands across her lap.

"I know how difficult this is for you, Mrs. Schmidt, and I'll make it as brief as possible. I'm investigating a series of murders that may include your daughter Lori."

"I see."

"We need to locate Mark Stone and James Murphy."

"I haven't seen either of them since Lori died."

Surprised, Kerrie dropped her pen. "James didn't attend his wife's funeral?"

"No, he did not." There was anger in the woman's voice.

"Are the police looking for him?"

She shook her head, lowering her eyes. "I haven't talked to the police since they notified us of our daughter's death."

"I'm sorry. I hope my investigation helps to capture the murderer."

"Why are you doing this? Just for a magazine article?"

"Not only that. Mark Stone tried to kill my mother."

"Oh, that explains—"

"We're not even sure it was Mark Stone who killed your daughter. It could have been your son-in-law."

She gasped. "James wouldn't—"

"Are you sure? He could have been jealous."

Mary Schmidt merely nodded.

"The two men look enough alike to be brothers."

"First cousins, actually."

Kerrie caught her breath. "So rivalry existed between the two?"

Lori's mother shifted uneasily on the couch. "Ever since childhood. They never got along."

"Were they fighting over your daughter?"

"Lori was engaged to Mark but changed her mind. She said James was more affectionate and understanding."

"How long before the wedding did she break it off?"

"It was about two months. We had already purchased her wedding gown and invitations had been ordered."

"Where can we find her husband?"

"My son told me that James moved out of the house the day after Lori died. He told Stephen he couldn't live there any longer."

"Where did they live?"

Kerrie jotted down the address Mary Schmidt gave her. James Murphy worked for an independent environmental agency, the name she couldn't recall. Kerrie handed her a business card and asked that she get in touch when she remembered. She then asked what her daughter had done for a living.

"She worked for Zamco, a chemical company, as a lab technician."

"The same company Mark Stone worked for?"

"Yes. That made it difficult for her after the breakup."

"What does Mark's job entail?"

"He's in waste management."

"So he was responsible for chemical spill cleanups?"

"I believe so."

"Was your daughter afraid of Mark?"

"Not until he began stalking her."

"At work?"

"No, they were in different departments. He'd follow her home and try to gain entrance to her apartment."

Kerrie asked if the stalking continued after the wedding and was told that Stone followed her daughter whenever she left home alone.

He must have been watching her constantly.

"Do you know why was she driving Interstate 40 west of Flagstaff?"

"I wish I knew. My husband and I were out of town and didn't know she was leaving."

"So it could have been a spur of the moment decision on her part?"

"Probably. I remember now that she had mentioned a trip to Nevada several weeks earlier, but it wasn't definite."

"Did she usually keep you apprised of her activities?"

"Yes, we were very close."

"What about her friends? Did she have disagreements with any of them?"

"Not that I'm aware of."

"Clubs or organizations that she belonged to?"

Mary Schmidt paused before answering. "Lori belonged to an archeologist club that she occasionally went on field trips with. She was also a member of the Women's Health Club in Phoenix. As I recall, she did say something about a disagreement she had with the director."

"How long ago and do you know what it was about?"

"A month or so ago, and no, she didn't tell me what it concerned? Whatever it was she didn't want to talk about it. She just said she would find another gym."

"I'll check that out."

"She also had a disagreement with Martin Borrunski."

"What was it about?"

"I'm not sure. Lori usually didn't talk to me about her relationships."

"So Martin was a boyfriend?"

"That's the impression I had. He's a civil lawyer."

"Before or after her marriage?"

"Before. Lori was faithful to her husband."

Schmidt was growing edgy. Kerrie decided to end her questioning for the time being.

"May I call you if I have other questions?"

The woman pulled a card from her purse with a library logo in the right upper corner. She then struggled to her feet. Kerrie thanked her and followed her back to where her mother and Sarah were seated. They were still leafing through old newspapers, and smiled tentatively as Mary Schmidt walked by on her way to the entrance.

"What did she say?" Sarah whispered when the library door had closed.

Kerrie sat down and read from her notes.

"A great start." Sarah set the newspaper aside. "Where do we go from here?"

"I think we'd better follow up on the chemical spill," Dana said. "I'm reading about the stockpiling of chemicals by the military. Toxic chemicals stockpiled in Utah and various parts of the country. I also read about the dumping of tons of toxic chemicals into the Baltic Sea following World War II, off the east coast of Bornholm, a Danish Island. There's a reference to Bornholm Disease, a painful respiratory ailment called 'The Devil's Grip' by inhabitants of the island."

"Chemical warfare has been waged ever since the third century," Kerrie said. "I recall reading about the Sasanians using chemical weapons against the Roman Army."

"Even earlier than that, the Hindus in 400 BC forbade the use of poisoned and flaming arrows, but they allowed the poisoning of their enemies' food and water. And Chinese writings in 1000 BC contain recipes for the production of arsenic tainted tobacco."

Sarah asked what any of it had to do with the murder investigation. They were wasting time discussing ancient chemical warfare.

"I think Mom's wondering whether the canal chemical spill might be some sort of terrorist plot."

Dana shrugged. "Anything's possible. The spills could be directly linked to Lori's murder or simply a red herring."

"You can tell Dana's a mystery novel buff." Sarah got to her feet. "Red herring, indeed."

What's gotten into Sarah?

Kerrie suggested they first locate James Murphy. "I have his address but he hasn't lived there since his wife died."

"If he's not around, we can talk to the neighbors," Dana said.

Sarah was gathering up newspapers and magazines from the library table. "Let's get going. First an early dinner, then we'll interrogate the neighbors."

"Before we do that," Kerrie said, "I need to question the Phoenix woman's health club director. Mary Schmidt said her daughter had a fight with her." She checked her watch. "I think there's still time this afternoon."

***

Kerrie entered the women's health club by the rear door, hoping to pass for a member. Removing her bolero jacket, she grabbed a towel from a nearby rack to drape around her neck. Maybe they would think she had just arrived from work. When she located the director's office she knocked and entered before anyone could answer. Seated behind a massive mahogany desk was a young woman with short spiked hair and wearing a light gray sweat suit. She didn't appear happy to have a visitor.

"I don't recall having an appointment—"

Kerrie removed the towel from her neck and dropped into the nearest chair. "I'm investigating the death of Lori Murphy."

The woman looked incredulous. "You don't look like a cop."

"I'm with a news magazine reporting on the deaths of four young women."

"Four of them?"

"Someone close to one of the murder victims said that you had a serious disagreement with Lori Murphy."

Her name was Janet Jeffries, according to her desk name plate. And her expression said that she wasn't in the mood to cooperate.

"Lori and I were good friends."

"Did you attend her funeral?"

"No, but—"

"Then you must not have been very close."

"Close enough."

"What was the disagreement about?"

Jeffries made a face. "Nothing I care to talk about."

"That makes you a murder suspect." Kerrie watched the woman squirm in her seat. "The police don't know about your disagreement yet and they won't if you tell me what I want to know."

"Like what?"

"Lori's relationship with Mark Stone."

"They were engaged but she broke it off."

"Why?"

Jeffries hesitated. "He was into drugs."

"Selling them?"

"Probably."

Kerrie asked about Lori's relationship with her husband. Jeffries shrugged and was noncommittal. James was a nice guy, she said, but Lori was bored with him.

"Is that why she was seeing Mark Stone?"

"Mark was stalking her and she was afraid of him."

"Was she seeing anyone else?"

"I wouldn't know."

"Why did she drive to Las Vegas?"

Jeffries shook her head. "I have no idea. We weren't speaking by then."

"Why?"

"It's personal."

"Did Lori get along with everyone else?"

Jeffries' laugh was harsh. "Lori had a temper you wouldn't believe for someone her size."

"Anyone else mad enough to kill her?"

"I can think of several."

"Who?" Kerrie picked up her pen, ready to make a list.

"Friends that I don't care to implicate."

"Not even to clear yourself from suspicion?"

"Well—"

"They'll never know you gave me their names."

"Oh, all right." She pulled a personal phone book from her desk drawer.

"Talk to Maggie McGuire. I hear she and Lori had a real knock down-drag out."

"The reason?"

"You'll have to ask her."

"Anyone else?"

"Peggy Landers hated Lori but don't ask me why."

She then gave Kerrie the addresses and phone numbers.

Kerrie handed Jeffries her card and asked that she call if she remembered anyone else.

Chapter 17

They had a quick dinner before driving to Peggy Landers' place. She lived in a terrace apartment near the Phoenix-Scottsdale border. Kerrie debated whether she should call or just show up at her door. She decided that a surprise visit might work best, so they drove there, hoping Landers was at home.

Platinum blonde and of medium height, the Landers woman appeared at the door in a short filmy dress without a bra or apparent underwear. She must have been expecting her boyfriend and wasn't happy to find Kerrie standing on her porch. When told Kerrie was investigating the death of Lori Murphy, Landers sneered at her.

"Who cares," she said and tried to close her door.

Kerrie's shoe blocked the door and she tried another approach. "I hear that Lori was a real bitch. Am I right?"

The door opened wider and she was invited in. "You don't know the half of it, girl." She indicated a worn chair and Kerrie sat, notepad in hand. The apartment was small and inexpensively furnished so Landers must have not had a well-paying job.

"Why'd you come to me?" she asked

"I talked to some of Lori's friends."

"She didn't have any friends."

"Why's that?"

"Lori would charm new people and then stab them in the back."

"Is that what she did to you, Peggy?"

"She stole my boyfriend in high school."

"And you're still mad at her after how many years?"

"Nine."

"We were engaged in our senior year until Lori came along."

Kerrie scribbled on her notepad before she asked her former boyfriend's name.

"Mark Stone."

That took Kerrie by surprise. So Lori and Mark were sweethearts since high school. No wonder he went wacko when she married James Murphy. There was no wedding ring on Landers' hand so she probably hadn't connected with anyone else. No wonder she was bitter. Could she have murdered Lori?

Have you been to Las Vegas lately?" Kerrie asked.

"No, I can't stand the place."

"Why's that?"

She said nothing for several moments. There were tears in her eyes when she said, "Mark used to take part in the poker tournaments once a month and I went with him."

"While you were still in high school?"

"No, later."

Kerrie tapped the notepad with her pen. "So, Mark was seeing both you and Lori?"

"I begged him to break it off with Lori but he said she was blackmailing him."

"Did he tell you what she had on him?"

"No. He was afraid I'd blackmail him too."

"And you kept seeing him?"

When Landers nodded, Kerrie asked, "Have you visited Flagstaff lately?"

Landers wanted to know why she was being questioned, but Kerrie sidestepped the query. She then asked when she had last seen Lori Murphy.

"I avoided her like the plague."

"Do you know anyone who hated her enough to kill her?"

Landers laughed. "Besides me? About a hundred other people."

"Care to give me some names?"

"No. Whoever did it deserves a medal." Landers walked to the door and opened it. Kerrie left without a backward glance. So much for friendly banter.

Kerrie's next stop was across town at Maggie McGuire's neat bungalow. She hoped the McGuire woman would be more hospitable. She wasn't. Although she invited her into her modest home, her attitude was similar to that of Peggy Landers. Kerrie wondered if Landers had called McGuire when she left her apartment.

"So," she said, "you're investigating Lori Murphy's murder. Are you with the police?"

"I'm an investigative reporter from Denver."

"Denver? Well, our infamous friend was quite notorious, wasn't she?"

"How well did you know her?"

"Well enough. Actually, too well."

McGuire proceeded to tell the story of Lori Murphy's betrayal. It happened several years earlier when McGuire had been visiting her sick mother. Gone for three weeks, she had returned home to find Lori and her husband in bed. The discovery had culminated in the McGuire divorce. Lori then dumped the husband and moved on to destroy other marriages and relationships.

"Why would she do that? Do you know?"

"Spoiled, bored rich kid who didn't have anything else better to do, I guess."

"Do you hate her?"

"Just for a while. Until I realized that it was counter-productive. I've since met a great guy who asked me to marry him." She held her shiny new diamond ring for Kerrie to admire.

Kerrie congratulated her and noted the softening in her attitude. She asked if McGuire knew anyone who hated Lori enough to kill her.

"Mark Stone is the likely candidate. He's jealous and immature. He and Lori were a great match and I felt sorry for James when she married him. He's a nice guy who was taken advantage of at every turn."

"Did you know him well?"

"No, but friends told me how she treated him."

"Please don't take offense," Kerrie said. "Lori was from a rich family who probably didn't know about her *bad habits.* You and Peggy Landers don't seem to be from the same social background. I wonder why Lori didn't hang out with others in her own social strata."

McGuire laughed. "I wondered about that too. Lori felt she was better than the rest of us and it must have made her feel superior to associate with those of us from the middle class. She drove a BMW for a while that she traded in for a Mercedes convertible. That made her pretty popular with the rest of my friends. That is, until she started breaking up relationships and marriages."

"Do you have any idea who might have killed her?"

"How long are you planning to be in town? A month? That's how long it would take to talk to all the suspects."

"You're not exaggerating?"

"Not by much. It seemed that a new divorce was filed once a month among our group of friends."

"How did Lori have time—?"

"It was her main source of entertainment."

"But wasn't she seeing Mark Stone?"

"Oh, yeah, but he was on the road for long periods of time before he went to work for Zamco a couple of years ago. The bored, spoiled rich bitch had to have her fun."

"Wasn't she involved with a married lawyer?"

"I heard about that. I think his wife did too, so the affair didn't last very long."

Kerrie's eyes closed and she shook her head. *Talk about Peyton Place.* She needed to pay a visit to Lori Murphy's home.

Chapter 18

Next morning Dana drove to the address Mary Schmidt had given Kerrie at the library. The Murphy home was located in a quiet neighborhood, a two-story white colonial, which was a smaller version of Lori's parents' home. The grass needed mowing and the house appeared deserted.

Dana pulled the SUV into the driveway.

"Let's see if anyone's home." Kerrie opened her door and started up the walk. A few moments later she returned. "It looks like Lori's mother was right. No one's lived here for a while."

"I wonder if James Murphy's out searching for Mark Stone."

"He could be, Mom. Mary Schmidt said there was fierce rivalry between the two men. If Murphy thinks Stone killed his wife, he has good reason to go after him."

A next-door neighbor was watering her flowers so they sent Kerrie over to question her. Three women trooping onto her front lawn might have prompted her to escape what she thought were religious zealots. They watched as an animated conversation took place. The neighbor was tall and angular, nearly Kerrie's height, and she used her hands to illustrate her words. A quarter of an hour passed before Kerrie returned, smiling to herself.

"Let's go," she said when she reached the SUV. "I've got some information about James Murphy."

"What did she say, dear?"

"Murphy has not been home since his wife died. His neighbor thinks he has a girlfriend."

"Oh, my." Sarah leaned from the back seat. "Why does she think that?"

"She said she saw him with another woman in his car before the murder."

"Well, that complicates matters, unless it was his sister."

"Did she say where he works as an engineer?"

"The company is called the Safe Environmental Agency. It's located downtown. We'll have to look up the address."

"Does the neighbor know Mark Stone?"

"She remarked how alike the two men look."

"Does the neighbor know whether Lori and her husband got along?" Sarah asked.

"She heard them fighting on more than one occasion. She's obviously the type who snoops on her neighbors."

Kerrie filled them in on the rest, most of it gossip, as they drove back to the hotel for a phone directory. Half an hour later they were in the downtown district attempting to locate the address. They found the small, low gray building on a side street. A parking space was available half a block away and they left the Escalade. Kerrie entered the building alone while Dana and Sarah got their exercise by walking around the block.

"I feel left out," Sarah complained when they returned to the Cadillac.

"Why? Kerrie can ask the right questions without raising suspicion. She's much better at interviewing than we are."

"Even so—"

"When she leaves we're on our own."

"You know how I like to visit with people."

"We're much better at research. I'll buy another laptop so that we can both surf the web at once."

"I can't wait."

"You're too old for PMS. Why're you so cranky?"

"Chasing killers isn't as much fun as it used to be."

"So you'd quit in the middle of the investigation?"

Sarah said nothing as Dana unlocked the SUV. When they were both seated, Dana turned to face her. "We could fly home but Mark Stone might be there waiting for us."

Sarah groaned. "Two good reasons to stay here. You know how I hate to fly."

"I think we both need a good night's sleep."

"And a good man to snuggle up to. . . Speaking of good men, did you call Jeff Mailey to ask if he'll check on the mansion?"

Dana said that she would call and tell him where the door key was located. It was time to put him back on the payroll. When asked what was next on the agenda, she said, "We'll decide that when Kerrie gets here. We need to check on the chemical spill. I'm convinced it has something do with the murder."

Dana had just disconnected her call to Jeff Mailey when her daughter returned. Shaking her head, Kerrie said that James Murphy hadn't shown up for work since his wife's death. The people she questioned hadn't heard from him. Not even a phone call to say he needed time off.

Sarah's eyes widened. "Do you think Mark Stone killed him?"

Dana shook her head. "It's possible."

"Or he's on the run because he killed his wife?"

"The receptionist said they weren't getting along, which agreed with the neighbor I talked to." Kerrie picked up her notebook and read a quote she'd written earlier: "James came in a couple of weeks ago covered in scratches."

"Maybe his wife found out about the other woman." It seemed that Sarah had regained interest in the case.

Kerrie laughed. "At least she didn't attack him with a golf club."

"We don't know that either, dear."

"There're a lot of loose ends to tie up. And I can't stay much longer."

"I hope you don't mind a few more interviews before you leave," her mother said.

"With whom?"

"Good question. Let's go back to the hotel and regroup."

When they reached the hotel, they filed into Kerrie's room. Plopping down on the flowered bedspread, Kerrie retrieved her notepad, ready to make a list. They then sat staring in silence at each another. Dana finally asked if Kerrie had inquired about the chemical spill.

"I did, but they were pretty close mouthed about it. All I got were statistics. The tanker was carrying five thousand gallons of ninety-eight percent sulfuric acid, which entered the canal over an estimated ten minute period."

Dana frowned. "That would create a lot of toxic fumes, wouldn't it? It would make the driver and anyone else around there sick."

Kerrie retrieved her notes. "The plume of acid gradually spread out and initially contaminated one million gallons of canal water. But that slowly diluted as contaminated water flowed away from the site."

"But if someone downstream were fishing or kids were swimming and unaware of the spill—"

"They were in big trouble. The acidic balance on the pH scale was about one. Seven is neutral. The acceptable pH range for drinking water is six to eight point eight. So, the spill must have been devastating to marine life or anyone using the water."

"How long before the spill was discovered?"

"It's a rural area without much traffic, so it took almost half an hour before responders reached the scene. The driver died in his truck and several motorists who stopped were overcome by the fumes."

"We need to contact them."

"I tried to get their names but—"

"Can't we ask the chemical company?"

"Good luck with that, Sarah."

"Were their names in the accident report?"

"Tomorrow we'll check with the sheriff's department."

"Who responded to the accident, dear?"

"The firemen arrived first. When they decided what had been spilled, they spread soda ash all along the highway to neutralize the acid. Once the canal gates were closed, they added sodium carbonate or lime to the water."

"Who closed the gates?"

Kerrie flipped through her notes. "The first responders notified the project headquarters, located in Tempe. I was told that an operator at the canal project can push a button to close the gates."

"Then we need to talk to them as well."

"The acid was found as far downstream as the Sun City retirement village, which was briefly evacuated."

"I assume the reservation was evacuated too."

"Yes, but not before there were some sick people."

"Oh, my," Sarah said. "How could the driver have been so careless?"

"That's a mystery unto itself. I got the impression that he may have been shot before the accident."

"Shot? What makes you think—?"

"An environmental employee told me off the cuff that there was blood on the driver's seat, but he didn't know how it got there."

The puzzle pieces were beginning to come together, although a great many were still missing. If the driver had been shot, someone had planned the spill. But why? Did Lori Murphy know who was responsible and was that the reason she was killed? And were both Mark Stone and James Murphy involved?

Dana's cell phone rang. It was their former bodyguard Jeff Mailey. He reported that someone had been in the mansion while they were away. He couldn't tell whether anything had been taken but there was evidence that a bed had been slept in and food eaten in the kitchen. He found crumbs on the counter along with half a bowl of warm soup.

"You must have scared him off," Dana said. "Have you called the police?"

"I thought I'd better call you first, ma'am."

"Be careful," she warned. "He's armed and dangerous."

"I checked the house before I called. The alarm system has been disabled."

"Call the sheriff immediately and stay in touch." She then gave him her new cell number.

Had she been right in her suspicions that Mark Stone had gone to Wyoming to kill her? If it *was* Stone who had broken into the mansion, she hoped the Wyoming police would arrest him before he killed again. That still left the missing James Murphy, who might be dead. If only they knew who the mysterious other woman was. There must be a way to find out. Mary Schmidt might know. She had mentioned to Kerrie that she and her daughter had been close.

When told what Jeff Mailey had said, they gasped and asked what they should do.

"Jeff will take care of it. He's back on the payroll."

"But our things," Sarah wailed.

"Jeff didn't think anything had been stolen. The man's a killer, not a burglar. And anything taken can be replaced."

"Not everything."

Dana focused on her daughter, ignoring Sarah. "We need to visit the scene of the chemical spill."

"Right." Kerrie began making a list. "Newspaper office, sheriff's department, canal headquarters, James Murphy and his alleged girlfriend. I nearly forgot. The coroner's office."

"Coroner's office?"

"To check on the truck driver's cause of death. And to find out if the body contains any bullet holes."

"We need to find out if there are any John Does who might be James Murphy."

Kerrie cleared her throat and pointed her pen at her mother. "After you two left last night I watched the news on CNN. There was a feature about Phoenix, the kidnap capital, which made me wonder if that's what happened to James Murphy."

"Kidnap capital?" Sarah appeared frightened.

"An average five people disappear each week and there have been more than a few home invasions."

"Here? In the city?"

Kerrie nodded. "Most are drug debtors or illegal aliens who pay people called coyotes to smuggle them across the border. Some of the victims have been buried alive."

Dana shivered. "You don't think James Murphy reneged on some drug debts, do you?"

"An environmentalist who does drugs" Kerrie shrugged. "Stranger things have happened."

Dana knew she'd get little sleep that night. There were so many aspects to this case to consider. Did the chemical spill tie into the dealings of drug lords and James Murphy's disappearance? It didn't make sense. They needed to talk to Mary Schmidt again about her son-in-law. Was she aware of any indiscretions? Even more important was the question of whether the truck driver had been shot.

Chapter 19

Dana listened as Kerrie called Mary Schmidt the following morning. Glancing at her mother, she shook her head and began questioning the woman over the phone. She asked about James Murphy's habits and whether he and Lori had been getting along. The conversation lasted nearly ten minutes and Kerrie was frowning when she clicked off.

"She admitted that Lori and James had been fighting but was hesitant to tell me why."

"That's understandable."

"Lori accused her husband of cheating but he refused to confess. Mrs. Schmidt thinks that may be the reason her daughter left town. She asked me to keep the information confidential until her daughter's killer's arrested."

"Did you agree?"

"It was the only way I could get her to talk."

"What about Murphy's habits—other than cheating on his wife."

"She hinted at possible drug use. Both of them smoked weed, but she didn't think they used anything stronger."

"I don't know the price of marijuana, but would Murphy risk his life by not paying?"

"I'm sure the kidnappings only apply to people who buy in large quantities for resale, and don't pay the supplier."

"Let's hope the Murphys weren't into selling the stuff."

"She also said that Lori decided she'd made a mistake in marrying James. Lori told her mother that James would get phone calls and make excuses why he had to leave."

Dana sighed. "That may explain the reason for her trip out of town. She might have had a clandescent meeting with Mark Stone."

"And if her husband followed her, he could have killed her in a jealous rage."

"What's strange is that the Schmidt woman opened up on the phone. She could have told you all that in person."

"It's easier to unburden yourself when no one's staring at you, Mom."

"Like a confessional?"

"Exactly, but I hardly qualify as a priest."

Kerrie said the Schmidts were leaving on a business trip. They wouldn't return to Scottsdale for more than a week. The next thing on the list was the chemical spill. Kerrie called the canal supervisor to ask for an appointment. Within minutes, an eleven o'clock meeting was approved. She then called the coroner's office. He agreed see her at four o'clock that afternoon. Dana went back to her room to call the fire department while Kerrie finished her list of questions.

Sarah was still asleep. It was time to wake her, although Dana knew she would insist on breakfast the minute she was dressed. Dana looked up the number for the fire department and punched in the number. The woman who answered didn't know details of the chemical spill, so Dana held the line while she found someone who did. A few moments passed before a deep voice boomed in her ear. Momentarily stunned, she asked if his department had been the first to respond to the sulfuric acid spill.

"Why are you asking?"

Dana crossed her fingers to nullify the lie she was about to tell. "I'm a reporter for *City Magazine* and we're running an article about chemical spills."

"Never heard of *City Magazine.*"

"It's based in Denver."

He hesitated. "Well . . . I went on the call. We suited up in hazmat gear and got there within half an hour after it happened."

"Did an ambulance arrive to take the trucker to the hospital?"

"Not right away. There were a number of other people overcome by the fumes, including the patrolman who got there first."

"Were they motorists who stopped along the highway?"

"They were. The overturned truck blocked the bridge so they couldn't drive past."

"Was the driver still alive when you got there?"

"Not sure. EMTs attended to the victims while my crew cleaned up the spill."

"Where exactly did it happen?"

"On the bridge where the highway crosses the canal. The feds are still investigating."

Dana wrote down his name and hung up thinking it was too much of a coincidence that the truck overturned at that particular spot in the road. If the driver had been shot, the spill had to have been carefully planned by someone who wanted to contaminate the water.

Sarah yawned and pulled herself into a stretch. "What was that all about?"

"Get dressed and I'll tell you and Kerrie about the call over breakfast."

They joined Kerrie in the hotel restaurant where she read them the list of questions for her morning interview. Dana then told them of her call to the fire department. They agreed that the case was pointing to a conspiracy.

Sarah said, "Last night when I went for ice, I found a pamphlet about the reservation in the lobby." She pulled the brochure from her purse.

"The reservation is home to seven thousand members of the Pima and Maricopa tribes. It encompasses over fifty-two thousand acres and is located adjacent to the northeast section of the Phoenix metro area. It's best known for its two Indian gaming casinos on Highway one-oh-one."

"Gaming casinos?" Dana bit her lip. "I wonder . . ."

Sarah continued. "Besides the casinos, there's a golf course, shooting range, modern shopping center and a telecommunications company."

"Most reservations have gambling casinos, don't they?" Kerrie leaned to stare at the brochure.

"Probably. There's also a nineteen thousand acre natural game preserve."

"I wonder how close that preserve is to the chemical spill."

"We need to take a look."

Sarah unfolded the pamphlet to show the reservation terrain. "Twelve thousand acres are under cultivation."

"You'd have to be pretty twisted to spoil a place like that. Modern technology combined with native American culture." Kerrie closed her notebook and dropped it back in her purse.

Dana checked her watch. "I think we have time to drive out there before your first interview."

Kerrie picked up the check. "Let's do it."

Dana tried to take the breakfast bill from her, but Kerrie reminded her of her own share of Aunt Georgi's will. They had a little more than two hours before her appointment and they needed to get going.

While attempting to retrieve the car keys, Dana dropped her purse in the parking lot. The contents spilled next to the SUV. When she reached to scoop everything back into her purse, she noticed a gold colored key.

"Isn't that the one you found at the murder scene?" Sarah asked.

Dana groaned. "How could I have forgotten?"

Sarah spread her fingers and counted out each reason. "The murderer tried to kill you, you wrecked the RV, the flash flood—"

"Thanks for trying to make me feel better."

Kerrie was frowning. "What key, Mom? You didn't tell me about it."

"A post office box key I found near the body."

Kerrie reached for the key and turned it over in her hand. "There's no box number. How can you find the right post office?"

"I'm hoping postal authorities can help."

"What can you say to convince them?"

"I hate to lie but how about 'My elderly mother died and I found it among her possessions.'"

"But won't they ask her name?"

"Lori Murphy."

"I hope the post office is big enough that clerks don't know the patrons personally."

Dana sighed. "That could be a problem."

"Maybe we'd better start with the postal service before we drive to the spill scene."

They trooped back into the hotel where Kerrie pulled a phone book from the desk drawer. "Let's start at the post office nearest Lori Murphy's home."

Twenty minutes later they were on their way. Dana heaved a sigh of relief when they pulled into the lot. The post office was large, the lot filled with cars. Filing in, the others waited while Dana stood in line. Her hands trembled and she wondered whether she should have asked Kerrie to lie about the key. No, it was bad enough that she was prepared to perjure herself. When her turn came in line, a tall, balding, middle-aged man standing behind the counter had a questioning look on his face. Would he believe her?

She retrieved the key from her pocket and set it on the counter.

"Ma'am?"

"I found this key in my mother's possessions when she passed away last week. I thought I'd better check for bills so I can pay them."

"Admirable. Do you know the box number?"

Dana lowered her eyes. "No."

"Her name?"

"Lori Murphy."

His eyes narrowed and Dana felt her knees tremble.

"Name sounds familiar."

"Common name. There're a lot of Lori Murphy's in the Phoenix area." She hoped her voice didn't betray her fear.

"I reckon so. What's her address?"

"Address?"

Kerrie stepped forward holding her notepad. "Grandma had just moved to a new home before her heart attack." She ripped the address from the pad and handed it to him.

Nodding, the clerk turned and disappeared into the back of the building. Dana placed an arm around her daughter's shoulder and squeezed. Why had she forgotten about the address? Old age or dementia?

The clerk returned holding an index card. "Box 79205," he said, pointing in the direction of a bank of boxes. "Near the bottom row, as I recall."

Dana smiled her appreciation and took the card. It was all she could do to restrain herself. Easy, she told herself, Don't raise suspicion.

Kerrie took the key and stooped to place it in the lock. She then pulled the small door open and retrieved several envelopes. Smiling, she glanced at them before handing them to Dana. "Let's go," she hissed and led the way out of the building. Seated again in the Escalade, Dana sorted through the stack. Two envelopes were from credit card companies, one a power company bill, the other from an oil company.

"It's a felony to open them," Sarah warned.

"I know. We need the Schmidts to do that for us."

Kerrie whipped out her cell and punched in the number. A minute later she said, "Too late. They're gone."

Now what should they do? They couldn't legally open the mail. She wondered why Lori's parents hadn't tried to pay their daughter's bills. Maybe they were so distraught that they didn't think about clearing her debts. Not yet anyway. The bills would no doubt answer the questions about Lori's secret trip. They might even name her killer. She started the engine, curbing the urge to rip the envelopes open.

"If Walter were here, he'd insist we take them to the police."

"Yes, he would, Sarah. But would the police follow up on them? They're convinced that Mark Stone killed Lori. I doubt they'd consider anyone else."

Kerrie leaned forward from the back seat. "Maybe if I give them all the evidence I've collected from the other murder cases—"

"What if they place a gag order on the case?" Dana said. "What would happen to your investigative story?"

"It would be deader than Lori Murphy. That wouldn't set too well with my editor. And speaking of the magazine, I have to return to work in two days."

Dana hated the thought of her daughter leaving. Not just because of the case. It was good to have her near.

"Let's get you to your appointment. Then we'll view the spill area."

Chapter 20

They waited in the Escalade while Kerrie conducted her interview. She returned half an hour later. It was much worse than they suspected, she said. The surrounding towns had been briefly evacuated. Several people at the shooting range southwest of the highway had been overcome with fumes. Golfers at Eagle Mountain and Fountain Hills also reported respiratory problems when the wind had shifted in their directions.

Dana's frown matched her daughter's. "I wonder why we didn't read about it in the newspapers."

"Apparently it didn't make much of a splash in the local media. And we were concentrating on finding Mark Stone and Lori's parents," Sarah reminded her.

"True, but—"

Kerrie tapped her notepad. "Whoever planned this must have checked weather reports and scheduled it for a windy day to affect the greatest number of people."

Sarah snorted. "Sounds like a terrorist attack to me."

"A possibility," Dana said, "but how does it connect with the murder?"

"I don't know, Mom. Let's drive out Beeline Highway to where the chemical spill happened. Maybe we'll come up with some answers."

"Someone at the chemical company must have been in on the conspiracy. It had to have been an employee who knew the transportation schedule. It was probably Mark Stone or one of his cohorts. If it was Stone and Lori found out about it, he had reason to kill her."

Dana drove across the four lane bridge and parked along the highway. The terrain was fairly desolate although they could see the Usery Mountains in a haze to the east. The highway was deserted when they walked onto the bridge. The pavement still showed signs of the chemical cleanup. The traffic lanes were wide enough for an assassin to pull alongside the chemical truck to shoot the driver. There may have been two people involved although Dana reasoned that a shooter could have gotten off a shot if he had pulled to the inside edge of the road. But timing the shot so that the chemicals would spill on the bridge would take some mathematical calculations, including the speed the truck was traveling. The spill must have been well planned, but that was pure speculation.

Sarah tugged at Kerrie's sleeve. "It's nearly time for your appointment with the coroner."

Kerrie nodded. "We need to find out whether the driver was actually shot. He could have been cut by flying glass when the truck overturned."

"I have a strong feeling he was shot," Dana said. "It fits the pattern of Lori Murphy's death." She turned and started back to the SUV. The map Sarah had picked up in the hotel lobby had come in handy and they arrived at the coroner's office several minutes early.

"I'm glad you brought something along to read," Kerrie said, unbuckling her seat belt. "This may take a while."

Dana pulled a mystery paperback from her handbag. "I've been trying to find time to finish this Evanovich book since the murder."

Kerrie gasped. "My straight-laced mom is reading Janet Evanovich?"

Dana laughed. "There are a lot of things you don't know about your mom."

Kerrie rolled her eyes. "If I'm not back within an hour, call me on my cell."

"Why?"

"Some interviewees don't know when to stop talking. I'll probably get all the information I need within the first five minutes."

"Will do." Dana checked the dashboard clock, noting the time.

Sarah yawned. "I guess I'll take a nap. Hopefully my subconscious will come up with some answers."

"I hope so. I'm running out of questions."

Sarah was softly snoring when Dana laughed and woke her up.

"What's so funny?" She sounded grouchier than usual.

"I was just reading about Grandma Mazur prying open a casket in the funeral home."

"Why would anyone do that?"

"Why does anyone do anything, Sarah? I can't believe the things people do."

"Like shooting a young woman along the highway?"

"Yes. Was it road rage or a desperate attempt to save the killer's own life?"

Sarah sat upright in her seat. "If we knew that, we'd know who he is. Or she."

"It all seems part of a bigger conspiracy."

"You think the Four Corners murders are tied in."

Dana laid her book aside. "It would seem so, although the other three could have been committed to confuse the issue."

"We need to ask Kerrie the dates of the other murders. If they happened after Lori's death, it would seem to prove your theory."

"Good idea. You'll have to take a nap more often."

Sarah noticed Kerrie leaving the building.

"Uh-oh," Dana said. "She doesn't look happy."

Kerrie approached the Escalade shaking her head. They waited for her report, but she said nothing while she belted herself in. Sarah apparently couldn't tolerate the suspense a second longer.

"Well?"

"The driver was shot and died at the scene."

"And?"

"That's all they would tell me."

Sarah asked why.

"The feds are still investigating."

"FBI?"

"I assume so. They wouldn't say."

"Who's they, Kerrie?"

"I talked first to the deputy coroner. A woman in her late forties, early fifties. She said her boss had been called out on a murder."

"I wonder if it's connected to this case," Dana said.

"Turn on the radio. It might be on the news."

Dana flipped through the stations but could find nothing more than music and a few talk shows. It was five minutes before the noon hour when most stations carried the news. In the meantime, they'd find some food to quiet Sarah's growling stomach. Dana preferred a family restaurant but they didn't want to miss the broadcast. They were in line at Taco Bell when the newscaster reported that a body had been found in the McDowell Mountains.

Dana gasped. "You don't suppose it's Mark Stone or James Murphy? They're both missing."

Kerrie shook her head. "It's probably a kidnapped drug dealer who didn't pay his bill."

"You could be right. I'm grabbing at straws."

"Murders seem an everyday occurrence here, Mom. No big deal."

"Even so. It's worth looking into." Dana pulled forward to the menu board. "I wonder why we haven't heard from Jeff Mailey about the break-in at the mansion."

"Probably nothing to report."

"I'd better give him a call." Dana punched in the number and waited. Four rings later it went to voice mail. She left him a message and clicked off. Why didn't people leave their cell phones on? Didn't they charge them at night? Frustrated, she dropped hers back in her purse and reached for her wallet. They were next in line at the pay window.

Sarah tapped Dana's hand. "It's my turn to pay. I kinda feel like a kept woman."

"Suit yourself. I'm not really hungry. That body killed my appetite."

"Just some drug dealer, Dana. Don't let it bother you."

"Why do I have this feeling it's one of our suspects?"

"Maybe you're tired of the investigation and ready to go home."

Dana was adamant. "I can't quit the case until we solve the murder."

"Or the murderer solves us." Sarah handed Dana a twenty and settled back in her seat.

Maybe Sarah was right. They should probably return to Wyoming. Let the police solve Lori's murder. Whoever had broken into the mansion might have killed Lori as well as the man in the mountains. Wyoming was a great place to hide. Plenty of criminals had done so in the past. But was it safe to return home?

Handing an Indian woman with braided hair Sarah's twenty, Dana collected the change and pulled forward. Closing her eyes, she realized how exhausted she was. She questioned her own ability to continue. Sarah nudged her and she noticed a car length of space ahead of the Escalade. It was time to move on. When Sarah rifled through the bag containing their orders, she complained about the lack of napkins.

"Go inside and get some," Dana snapped. When she saw the expression on Sarah's face, she apologized.

"You need some serious time under a palm tree, my friend."

"I can't quit."

"Or maybe time in the hospital when you're completely run down."

"Sarah's right, Mom. You're taking this case much too seriously."

"Certainly not."

"Please go home and I'll keep you informed on a daily basis."

"From Denver?"

"Why not?"

"I'll take it under advisement. . . Let's drive back to the coroner's office so you can ask about the body."

Kerrie shrugged and bit into her burrito.

***

Dana's cell phone rang while they waited for Kerrie to return from the coroner's office. Jeff Mailey was returning her call. He sounded concerned.

"Don't know when you planned to come home," he said, "but I think you should stay put for a while longer."

"Why? What's happening?"

"I hope you don't mind that I snooped around the mansion."

"Of course not. That's why I hired you, Jeff."

"I didn't find anything out of the ordinary during my first sweep—other than the bowl of soup and slept-in bed."

"You found something else?"

"I looked in your bedroom closet and found an opened gun case on the floor."

"My Glock?"

"Yes, ma'am. You take the gun with you?"

"No. I should have. Is it missing?"

"Yeah, I couldn't find it anywhere. What I did find were a few shells that had rolled to the back of the closet."

"So whoever had broken in the house has the Glock." It wasn't a question. The chill down her backbone said it was true.

"I'm afraid so."

"Has the sheriff investigated?"

"He just left and I was about to call you."

"What did he say?" Dana asked.

"Not much. He said he'd send in the lab boys to take some prints."

"Does he know about the murder case here?"

"Some information came in over the wire. I filled him in on the rest."

"I'd appreciate it if you'd stay there, Jeff, until we get back."

"I was planning on it."

"Good. Keep your cell phone on and check in every day, even if you have nothing to report."

Dana disconnected and repeated to Sarah what he had said.

"I hope the killer doesn't commit a crime with your gun, Dana."

"I'm sure Jeff told the sheriff it's been stolen."

"You don't suppose he was planning to use it on us. Make it look like a murder-suicide?"

Dana hesitated. "It hadn't occurred to me, but it's a good possibility. Jeff thinks we should stay here."

"Let's not waste any more time. What's next on your agenda?"

Dana smiled. "It's good to have you back on the team. I was beginning to feel lonely."

Sarah reached across the console to pat her arm. "I never left. It's just frustration."

Kerrie returned to the SUV, unnoticed until she opened the door. Her expression said she hadn't learned much. The coroner was closeted in his office with his investigative team. No word on who the victim was or whether he had been murdered.

Jean Henry Mead

"There were other reporters present so I couldn't speak privately with anyone. The coroner or one of his staff will hold a press conference late this afternoon."

Dana started the engine. "Shall we come back or watch it on TV?"

"I can't toss out questions from the hotel room."

"True. What time is the press conference?"

"I left my number with the receptionist. She promised to call."

But would the receptionist call? Dana was losing faith in the promises people made. They should probably return by three that afternoon, just to be safe. In the meantime, a nap would help to recharge their batteries.

Dana pulled back onto the highway and glanced in her rearview mirror. Was that a dark red Dodge pickup truck behind them?

148

Chapter 21

"Don't turn around to look," Dana warned. "There's a red Dodge following."

Sarah gasped.

"Don't panic."

Sarah leaned to peer through the side mirror. "Looks like a dark haired man at the wheel."

"That's what I thought."

"What'll we do?"

"Stay in traffic," Kerrie said from the back seat. "That driver won't dare do anything with so many cars around."

Sarah pointed to a road sign. "Freeway's coming up."

Kerrie said, "It's too easy for him to shoot us and escape on the nearest off ramp. I'll call the police."

"Not yet," Dana said. "What if it's not the killer?"

"Make a quick U-turn at the nearest intersection. If he follows, he's our man."

Dana did as her daughter suggested. They then caught a yellow light and she turned in front of the approaching cars. Holding her breath, she glanced out her side window to determine whether they had been followed. Sarah reported that the truck had run a red light and nearly caused a wreck.

Dana told her daughter to call the police and to write down the pickup's license number. She watched in the rear view mirror as Kerrie turned in her seat to look. Pulling her notepad from her purse, she wrote the number down. Then, retrieving her cell, she called 911.

Dana weaved in traffic with an eye on the mirror. The pickup was nearly on their rear bumper when they heard a siren and noticed flashing lights behind them. The Dodge darted off onto a side street as the police cruiser pulled behind the Escalade, its siren screaming.

"Damn it," Kerrie said. "He's pulling *us* over."

The Escalade slowed and parked at the curb. Dana cut the engine and watched as the patrolman left his car and approached the driver's door. She rolled down her window and waited.

"Ma'am? You nearly caused an accident back there. I need to see your driver's license, registration and proof of insurance."

"We just called 911 about the killer following us. He escaped on a side street." She turned and pointed down the street.

The stocky cop raised an eyebrow. Dana had to admit it sounded like a lame excuse to avoid a ticket. But when Sarah and Kerrie chimed in, he nodded and took Dana's license and paperwork back to the patrol car. The moment he closed his door, Sarah complained that the killer had gotten away.

"Keep watching," Dana warned. "He might come back."

It seemed an eternity before the patrolman returned. "Your story checked out," he said, handing back the license and paperwork. "Under the circumstances I won't write you a ticket. But if it happens again—"

Before she could ask what she should have done, he said, "Follow me to the station so we can file a report."

Dana groaned. There was no way to prove the pickup driver was the killer. The police at the station would probably think she was having an anxiety attack. They'd also want to know why she and Sarah were still in Phoenix conducting their own investigation. That wasn't going to set well with the police.

"I forgot to give the officer the license number," Kerrie said.

"The killer's probably miles away so it doesn't really matter. We'll turn it in at the station."

They spent over an hour at the station while Dana filled out the report before submitting to questioning. As she had feared, the sergeant wanted to know why a killer was following them. After he checked with homicide and the Flagstaff police, the sergeant ran the license number. When he returned from his office, he refused to tell them who the pickup belonged to, but said an APB had been issued. They were then told they should be placed in protective custody.

They refused, citing Kerrie's need to return to Denver and their own trip back to Wyoming. Dana decided to call Walter the minute they reached the hotel. Maybe he could learn who the pickup truck belonged to, if not Mark Stone. There was also Jeff Mailey's friend at the police station in Wyoming, who had provided them information in the past.

They were free to go after they gave the officer their addresses and phone numbers.

Kerrie checked her watch. "There might still be enough time to catch the news conference, if we hurry."

"Maybe you should call the coroner's office," Dana said when they were buckled into the Escalade. "I knew that woman wouldn't call."

Kerrie's cell phone rang a moment later. Checking the caller I.D., she said, "Guess what mom? It's the coroner's office."

She said "Uh-huh" several times, and "thank you." She then hung up. "Twenty minutes. She had a long list of reporters to call. I guess I was last on the list."

Dana turned the key in the ignition. "I think we can make it."

Someone was testing the microphone at a small wooden podium when they pulled into the parking lot. A rotund woman stood nearby clearing her throat. Kerrie said she was the deputy coroner. When she stepped up to the mike, everyone was silent as cameras rolled and reporter's pens poised to take notes. Kerrie crowded in up front to join them.

The woman's voice wavered as she read from the report. She must be new, Dana thought as she edged closer to the small crowd of media.

"An unidentified white male, approximate age thirty, was found in the foothills early this morning by a group of hikers. Death was caused by a gunshot wound to the head. Time of death has not yet been determined but the body might have been buried for more than a week. The murder is under investigation by the sheriff's department."

When she finished her statement, reporters immediately began firing questions at her. A deputy stepped alongside and pointed to a young man wearing a colorful shirt.

"Any suspects?" the reporter asked.

"None that I'm aware of."

The deputy smiled when he pointed to Kerrie, who had her hand in the air.

Kerrie stated her name and that she was from Denver's *City Magazine*, which brought a curious look to his face.

"Was the victim buried or easily found? And were the hikers from the Phoenix area?"

"Partially buried but erosion uncovered the upper part of his body due to recent rains. The hikers were boy scouts from the city of Phoenix."

Everyone seemed to groan in concert. It had to have been traumatic.

Other reporters asked about the condition of the body, whether it had shown evidence of predators, and if the man was listed as John Doe. The coroner replied that they were checking the victim's DNA against missing person reports. Dana wondered whether that included Stone and Murphy.

Someone else asked whether there was evidence of drug use in the body. The secretary shook her head saying that the autopsy had not yet been conducted.

Back at the hotel, Dana called Walter. He had just gone off duty and sounded delighted to hear from her. He agreed to find out all he could, but insisted they return home post haste. Maybe he was right. The case was beginning to feel beyond their investigative skills. If only *she* were involved, Dana would see the case through to the end. It wasn't fair to involve her daughter and Sarah.

Kerrie would continue to investigate the Four Corners murders from Denver, while Walter kept them informed from California. When they saw Kerrie off at the airport, they should drive on home.

They were watching Fox news after dinner when Walter called. He insisted Dana leave Phoenix immediately. The license plates on the red Dodge had been stolen.

"It was obviously someone stalking you, Dana. He may be involved in the chemical spill, or the murders or both."

She told him about the body found in the mountains and regretted it when he said, "If I wasn't so wrapped up in this double homicide, I'd hop on the first plane to escort you home. Promise me you'll leave as soon as Kerrie's plane takes off." He paused. "I have a better idea. I want you all to leave on the same plane and catch a commuter flight to Wyoming."

Dana sighed. "Good idea, Walter. Why didn't I think of that?"

She wondered whether the Phoenix police would want them to stay to identify the killer. She would call them in the morning. In the meantime she could do more laptop research. When she reached for the computer, she noticed Lori's bills on the desk. Dare she risk opening them?

No, she needed to give them to the police. She then remembered steaming envelopes open as a teen, but they had no tea kettle. Opening the closet door she noticed a steam iron in the closet on a shelf above an ironing board. It was still illegal but she could say that she dropped the envelopes when it rained. When Kerrie left for Denver and Sarah was distracted, she'd steam the envelopes open so they wouldn't be accomplices to a federal crime.

Telling Sarah she would come right back, she left for Kerrie's room. Seated at the desk, she asked about the Four Corners murders. Opening the laptop, she began typing notes. All four women were young, petite blondes but they seemed to have nothing else in common. The first victim, a cocktail waitress in Farmington, New Mexico, was twenty-three and living on her own. She had been shot and killed on her way home from work after two a.m.

The second blonde was a twenty-seven year old nurse in Durango, Colorado, who had been found shot to death in her car on a lonely highway, much like Lori Murphy. The third victim was twenty-six and had also been shot in her car while driving home after dark from her job as a sales manager. Other than their appearances, there didn't seem to be anything else to link them together, although Kerrie was determined to learn if they had anything in common.

"Did the first three murders happen before Lori Murphy was killed?"

"They did." Kerrie recited the dates of each death, which happened within the same week.

"Not much to go on, is there?"

Kerrie eyed her mother, frowning. "I thought you and Sarah were going home with me. You're not thinking of staying, are you?"

"I haven't decided."

"That man who followed us may be an accomplice to the murders. Or the killer himself."

"Or was it a coincidence the pickup driver made that U-turn behind us."

"You don't believe that, Mom. Neither of us believes in coincidence."

"Stranger things have happened, dear."

"Solving this case is not worth the risk."

"It's not safe at home. And the killer hasn't had time to leave the mansion and drive back here yet."

Kerrie's expression was one of worry. "Are you sure? What if there are two of them taking turns driving?"

"It's possible, but how would they know we're driving an Escalade?"

"Someone who works in the police department would know. Or the rental car agency. Someone at the hotel."

A lump rose in Dana's throat. "I hadn't thought of that."

Kerrie reached to hug her. "Please don't risk your life or Sarah's. It's not worth it."

"Yes, you're right. We'll try to get tickets on your flight for tomorrow."

Kerrie sighed. "I'll turn my investigative notes over to the police as soon as my article's published."

"When will that be?"

"With luck, a week."

"A week? A lot can happen by then."

"I know, Mom, but I've got so much sweat equity in this case that—"

"Sarah and I will fly home and let the police muddle through."

Kerrie laughed. "Good thinking mom. I'm so relieved you'll both be out of harm's way."

"Let's hope so. We may find the killer at home."

"I'm glad Jeff Mailey's there to protect you."

"Jeff's a good bodyguard but he allowed himself to be captured by the drug lords in South Dakota. Remember?"

"I'm sure it won't happen again." Kerrie reached to open the desk drawer and handed her mother a phone book. "Call the airlines before they're booked solid."

Dana dutifully called and was told that two seats were available on a later flight. Glancing at Kerrie, she agreed to book them. There was a six-hour wait when Kerrie's plane left the terminal. They would have time to do what? She would think of something to help with the investigation. When told of the schedule, Kerrie said she would take a cab to the airport, but Dana insisted on seeing her off. It was an 8:20 flight so they'd have to get an early start. She kissed her daughter goodnight and returned to her room. Sarah had gone to sleep watching television.

Dana opened the closet door and retrieved the steam iron and board. Quietly setting them up as far away from Sarah as possible, she filled the iron with water from the sink. She then picked up the envelopes containing Lori Murphy's bills. When the iron finally steamed, she ran it over the back of the first envelope. The paper crinkled and she knew it would never look the same. Peeling it open, she pulled the bill from the envelope. The MasterCard statement listed fuel in Flagstaff on June 17, three days before Lori's death. The next fuel stop had been in Kingman, Arizona, the third in Las Vegas. Three days later she had filled up in Vegas and again in Kingman, the last charge on the statement. What had the murder victim done for three days in Vegas? And who had she met there? Mark Stone, James Murphy or someone else?

Dana placed the statement back in the envelope and tried to iron the envelope free of wrinkles. In the process the flap tore and the iron left a burn mark. Now what was she going to do? A brief vision of herself behind bars flashed through her mind. Nauseated, she sank onto the colorful flowers of the hotel bedspread. Maybe she could plead with Lori's mother and ask for forgiveness. But how forgiving could a grieving mother be? She looked again at the other bills and reached for the Visa statement. It would undoubtedly tell where Lori had spent the night in Vegas. Dana had already committed a federal crime by opening the first bill. She might as well open the rest.

The Visa bill listed several purchases from a Target store in Phoenix, and fast food in Flagstaff and Kingman. The next item was a room at the Crystal Palace and food in Kingman the following day. Too bad the purchases didn't list the times.

No food purchases in Las Vegas either meant Lori didn't eat or someone else paid for her meals. Unless she had won money that she used to buy her food or had taken some with her.

The last Visa charge was an Avis car rental in Las Vegas. Why would Lori rent a car when she had driven her own there and more than halfway back?

Sarah groaned and turned over in her bed, the TV still blaring. Dana slipped the unopened power bill into her purse. The credit card bills followed. She would use money orders to pay them all. Then no one would be the wiser. Sarah was getting so forgetful that she would hopefully forget about Lori's bills.

Instead of flying to Wyoming, they could drive back through Vegas and stay at the Crystal Palace. Dana might be able to find a clerk or busboy who remembered Lori Murphy and the man she was with. Another couple came to mind. James Murphy and his alleged mistress. If the man found murdered *was* Murphy, had the woman killed him? Or, if she were married, was a jealous husband involved? And what about the strange men who invaded the library reading and borrowing the chemical books? They must be involved in both the chemical spills and the murders. Did Lori and James Murphy know them?

So many loose ends were giving her a headache.

This was not the time to call it quits.

Chapter 22

Dana was awake long before the alarm sounded. She hadn't slept much during the night. Too many questions plagued her. The first order of business was to see Kerrie off on her plane. She wouldn't say a word about driving home until Kerrie had reached Denver. Dana was aware of what her daughter's reaction would be, and she wasn't looking forward to telling her. Or, Walter, for that matter. The only problem was Sarah. She couldn't talk her into flying home on her own. Sarah was the original white-knuckled flyer.

She woke her friend, telling her they didn't have much time. They would have breakfast at the airport. Their bags were packed and standing near the door. Dana wondered when would be the best time to tell Sarah they were driving home. Definitely after Kerrie left. Sarah loved to play the slots in Vegas so she didn't anticipate a problem but Dana's hand trembled when she applied her lipstick.

"Better call Kerrie to make sure she's up and ready," Sarah called from the bathroom.

A moment later she heard a knock at their door. Kerrie was not only ready, she was impatient. "It's time to go, ladies," she said as she picked up two suitcases.

When Dana sputtered, she said, "My luggage is already downstairs in the Escalade." She handed her mother the spare key.

Sarah appeared in the doorway, a foamy toothbrush in her hand. "What's the hurry?"

"Check-in time's longer in big cities."

"They'd better not use a taser on me." Sarah waved her toothbrush like a Samurai sword.

Kerrie laughed. "Just don't give security any trouble. . . By the way, I didn't have time to check on one of Lori's boyfriends. A lawyer named Marty Borrunski. According to her mother, he and Lori had a serious spat."

***

They found an airport café that had not yet filled with travelers. After a quick breakfast, they hugged and said goodbye. Kerrie then strode down the tarmac like a soldier off to war. Watching her, Dana's chest filled with pride. Relieved that Kerrie was flying out of the danger zone, she knew she had placed herself and Sarah in jeopardy. Sarah could play a dotty old lady quite well, so there was a good chance they'd get away with asking questions, without raising suspicion. They could rehearse during the drive to Vegas.

Sarah eyed her curiously. "You've got something up that sleeve of yours. I can see it in your eyes."

Dana raised her sleeve to stare at her arm. "Ah, what's this? A free trip to Las Vegas and all the slot machines you can play?"

Sarah's eyes widened. "Are you saying that I don't have to tranquillize to fly home?"

"Right. We're going to drive."

"Did you tell Kerrie?"

"I plan to when she arrives in Denver."

"You realize you're in trouble."

Dana took Sarah's arm and led her back to the parking garage.

"So that's why you insisted on coming back later for the luggage? I never realized what a devious person you are, Dana Logan."

"Before we leave, we need to have a talk with Martin Borrunski."

They stopped for coffee at a nearby café. The clerk loaned them a phone book which they used to find Martin Borrunski, an attorney with a Phoenix firm. Dana wrote down questions in a notebook before she called.

Mr. Borrunski was with a client, the receptionist said. She would have him return their call. An hour and two cups of coffee later, Dana's cell phone rang. The lawyer would see them at one o'clock. Checking her watch, she wondered what they should do for the next three hours. She started the engine and pulled into traffic. A black Chevy pickup pulled in behind them.

"I've been thinking," Sarah said, distracting her.

"About what?"

"That body found yesterday in the mountains."

Dana glanced in the rearview mirror.

"With both Stone and Murphy missing, it could be either one of them."

"I think so too."

"Maybe we should call the coroner's office to see if he's been identified."

"Good idea. Why don't you try?"

Sarah retrieved a phone book from the pouch behind the driver's seat. A couple of minutes later she punched in the number. After a long wait, Dana listened to her ask for the coroner, who wasn't there because she then asked for the deputy. The black pickup was now two car lengths back, keeping pace with them.

When Sarah hung up, she said, "You'll never guess who the victim is?"

"Who?"

"James Murphy."

Dana sighed. "I had a strong feeling it was him."

"Mark Stone must have killed them both. But why?"

"I wish I knew. It must have been Mark Stone who was camping out in the mansion."

"Better call Jeff and alert him to the fact. He might even have some news for *us*."

"I think he would have called." Dana glanced in her rearview mirror but the black Chevy was gone. *Thank God!* She wiped each hand on her jeans. *Maybe this isn't such a great idea.* "Dial the number for me, will you, Sarah."

Sarah handed her the phone and Jeff Mailey answered after two rings. She then filled him in on all that happened since their last conversation. He said he had nothing further to report, but wasted no time admonishing her for her plan to drive to Las Vegas.

"We'll be fine. I'll call each night to check in. And don't forget to tell Sheriff Barnes we think it was Mark Stone who broke into the mansion."

"Will do, ma'am. Be careful."

Dana clicked off, a little agitated that everyone thought she was incapable of taking care of herself. She was only sixty, for heaven sake. Not a helpless elderly matron.

"Bawl you out, did he?" Sarah laughed.

"He doesn't know what a one-armed bandit freak you are."

"Slot machines haven't had levers in eons, Dana. You're showing your age."

I'm beginning to feel it.

Kerrie had not had time to visit a newspaper morgue, so Dana decided they should spend a few hours at the *Arizona Republic News*. They might discover a clue concerning James Murphy's death. Sarah wasn't in the mood to sift through more newspapers but agreed to go along. Dana knew her mindset was already in Vegas playing the slots.

Sarah spotted the first article about Murphy's death. She read the first paragraph to Dana: *Environmentalist James Murphy's body was discovered Friday in the McDowell foothills an estimated week after his death. The coroner's office reported that he was killed with a small caliber, foreign-made bullet of undetermined origin to the back of his head. The case is under investigation by the sheriff's department.*

"A foreign made bullet?" Dana said. "A terrorist must have killed him. But why James Murphy?"

"He could have uncovered a terrorist plot. Maybe Mark Stone didn't kill him, after all."

They searched for more than two hours without finding anything else to enlighten them about the case, so they left the newspaper office.

It was time for lunch. A family restaurant came into view and Dana drove into the parking lot. She grabbed the city map from the dash and told Sarah to locate the law firm while they waited for their meals. An hour later they parked in front of Martin Borrunski's office, an imposing three-story brick building with an ornate two-pillar façade. Were they out of their element?

The receptionist lifted a penciled brow while she looked them over before telling them to have a seat. Ten minutes later she ushered them into Martin Borrunski's office. Plush hardly described the furnishings with its soft leather furniture and oriental carpet. The desk in itself was a work of art. A small man sat behind the desk, his fingers tented, a bored look on his face. He didn't bother to stand when they entered.

"What can I do for you?" He had that same scornful expression as his receptionist.

Dana asked about Lori Murphy and he asked what business it was of their's. When Dana told him about the murder, he said he was well aware that she had died. He didn't seem emotionally involved.

"So she was merely a client?"

"Yes."

"Rumor has it that she was more than that."

"I'm a happily married man." The lawyer turned several framed photographs of his family around for them to see.

"We've heard that you had a serious disagreement with your client."

"I never discuss my relationships with clients."

Dana asked if he knew of anyone else who might have been angry enough to kill Lori Murphy.

Leaning back in his chair, he gazed at the ceiling. "There were several, I understand."

"Who?" Dana took a notepad from her purse and poised to write the names.

He laughed. "I really shouldn't tell you this, but Lori swung both ways."

"Names please."

"I don't remember her name, but the director of some women's health club was more than a friend."

Is he telling the truth or just trying to divert attention away from himself. "Anyone else?"

"I wasn't her father confessor."

"Was she into drugs?"

"Isn't everyone?"

"No," Sarah said, glaring at him.

"What about her husband?" Dana said quickly to cover Sarah's lapse. "Was James into drugs and cheating on his wife?"

"He smoked a little pot now and then but the guy was straight. I think that's why Lori was bored with him."

"So Lori was cheating on her husband."

He shrugged.

It was time to ask the question she'd been leading up to. Did he know Mark Stone? He didn't answer immediately but resumed his gaze at the ceiling. Dana thought he wasn't going to answer when he finally said, "Now there is a logical suspect."

"Why?"

"The guy's a nutcase. He's not only dealt drugs, I've heard that he's involved in some paramilitary group."

"To guard the country?"

"Hardly. To take it down's more like it."

"Do you think he's capable of murder?"

The lawyer said, "In my opinion Mark Stone's capable of anything."

Checking his watch, he said, "Two more minutes and you're on the clock. My time's valuable."

"All we need is another name—someone who might have more information about the murders."

He made a face, obviously trying to decide whether to tell them. He finally said, "Talk to Len Keller. Ask him about Mark and Lori."

"Where can we find him?"

He reached into a desk drawer and withdrew a phone directory. When he found the address he read it to Dana, who wrote it down.

She then asked, "Anything we should know about Len Keller?"

He smiled. "Oh, you'll find out soon enough. I'd go over there without calling."

They rose from their chairs, Dana towering over him, and shook hands. They then thanked him and left.

"That guy gives me the creeps," Sarah said, once they were on their way.

"Why?"

"He's so—"

"Len Keller is probably even worse. Let's reserve our judgment until we learn more about Mark Stone."

Sarah routed them on the map through the downtown district to an outlying industrial area south of Phoenix. The address was a warehouse that had already seen its salad days. A cracked and weedy sidewalk led to an office door with a diagonally cracked glass insert that probably hadn't been cleaned since it had been installed. Sarah shuddered and hung back until Dana took her arm. There was no way she was going in there alone.

The building's interior was as shabby as its exterior and they looked about for an office door. Dana wondered whether sending them there had been a joke. She couldn't imagine Martin Borrunski associating with the likes of anyone who worked there.

A deep voice startled her and Sarah yelped with fright.

"What can I do for you ladies?" The man was huge and dressed in grimy overalls. His thinning hair was combed in a swirl over his high forehead.

"Are you Len Keller?"

"Who wants to know?"

"Dana Logan," she said, pointing to her chest, "and my friend, Sarah Cafferty."

"Come on in my office."

Was he or wasn't he Len Keller? Dana resisted the urge to run from the hell hole filled with trash. He opened a door at the end of the warehouse and swiped at dust on a couple of metal chairs. When he seated himself behind his littered desk, they remained standing.

"Martin Borrunski suggested that we come to talk to you," Dana said.

"Old Marty. I'll be damned. Haven't seen him since the war."

Dana didn't want Keller to elaborate on the war, whichever one it was. From the looks of him, it must have been Vietnam. She asked about Mark Stone and would question him later about Lori Murphy.

His eyes seemed to glaze over when she mentioned the name. Stone may have given Keller an alias. She described him.

"Oh, him," he said. "Yeah, he's been around."

"Did you sell him anything?"

"A couple of guns. Some ammo."

"A private sale?"

"I'm no gun runner. Why do you ask?"

"Someone killed Lori Murphy and her husband."

"I heard about that. Too bad." He seemed sincere.

Dana asked if he knew Lori and he said she'd been in a few times with Stone. Six months ago, maybe seven. That must have been just prior to her wedding. But if Keller hadn't seen Martin Borrunski since the war, how did he know about Keller's guns? Or that Mark and Lori had been to see him? Lori must have told him. If that were true, they had been closer than he would admit.

She then asked about Stone's paramilitary affiliations.

He laughed. "Mark's planning to take back the country."

"How do you mean?"

"He hates politicians and wants to get rid of them."

"You mean he's an anarchist?"

"If not, he's the next thing to it."

"Oh, my," Sarah said. "Bullets instead of ballots."

"That's about it."

"Is he capable of murder?" Dana asked.

"No doubt in my mind. He even makes *me* nervous."

"What about Lori. Was she also an anarchist?"

"I doubt it. I think Stone just provided her with a few thrills."

Both women sighed. "I hope you're right," Dana said. "It would break her parents' hearts."

She wondered aloud whether Stone had been there recently and was told not for at least a month. During his last visit Stone had bragged about a group he'd trained, "a bunch of armed misfits ready and willing to do battle." Keller thought he might be making the entire thing up. Dana and Sarah glanced at each other, hoping he was right. But from all they'd learned about Stone, he was probably telling the truth. Mark Stone was a psychopath.

"One last question before we go," Dana said. "Did Stone mention anyone else who might have been supplying him with weapons? Make that two questions. Did he try to sell you drugs?"

"Yes on both counts. He tried to trade drugs for weapons but I didn't go for it. I've been clean and sober for twelve years now."

"Good for you. And the other supplier?"

"I wouldn't tell the cops this because I don't know if it's true. Stone claimed that a little old lady on Second Street traded him weapons for drugs."

Dana gasped, knowing Sarah was equally shocked. "Do you know her name?"

Keller thought for a moment. "Sadie, Shirley, Sabrina or something like that. She lives in a small apartment in the rear of the Sound of Music Pawn Shop, which she owns."

They thanked him and left.

Once seated in the Escalade, they glanced at one another in disbelief. Next stop the pawn shop. They expected it to be as shabby as Keller's warehouse but the shop resembled a gingerbread house with holiday lights lining the windows. Jewelry and all manner of miniature radios and iPods were featured on display. When they entered the shop, a musical rendition of the Sugar Plum Fairy played for a full minute. While they were browsing the display cases, a tiny, white haired woman dressed in a native Swiss costume appeared from the back room. Smiling, she greeted them as though they were old friends.

"Lovely shop you have here," Sarah said. "I'll bet you have lots of customers."

"Not this time of year. Christmas is my best season, like everyone else."

"Do you sell many guns?" Dana asked.

The smile vanished and a guarded look took its place. "You two looking for guns?"

Dana explained that they were traveling and that she had left her Glock at home. "I would feel safer with a gun for protection."

The proprietress said that she understood, but that she usually didn't take guns in exchange for loans.

"That's strange," Dana said. "Mark Stone said he trades for them here all the time."

The woman was visibly shaken. "He told you that?"

"He also said that we could trade you some weed for a gun."

"He lied!"

Sarah laughed. "Mark must have been joking. I can't imagine somebody trading anything for weeds." She was into her dotty old lady mode.

The woman looked at Sarah as though she were an imbecile.

"How well do you know Mark Stone?" Dana asked.

"Who said I know him?"

"He did."

"Well," she said, running a tongue over her dentures, "he does come in once in a while."

"Has Lori Murphy come in with him?"

"What are you? Undercover agents?"

"Friends of Lori Murphy. We're trying to track down her killer."

"I heard they killed her husband too."

"They?"

"The killers. Who else?"

Dana leaned across the counter, her voice just above a whisper. "Do you know who the killers are?"

"How would I know that?"

"Mark Stone must have told you."

She backed away from the counter as though readying for an escape. "Well, it could have been that crazy bunch he hangs around with."

"Who are they and why would they kill the Murphys?"

"They call themselves the Saviors, and they're likely to threaten anyone who gets in their way. I have no idea why they would kill the Murphy couple."

"Do you know where they're headquartered?"

"I don't want to know and I want nothing more to do with Mark Stone." Her expression was one of fear. Turning her back, she began sorting receipts from the cash register.

End of interview. They'd get nothing more from her.

Walking back to the Escalade, they noticed a dark red Dodge parked on the opposite side of the street. How many of them had been produced? It could be the same one that had been stalking them.

"This was a really fine idea."

"Don't panic. There're a lot of dark red Dodges."

"Why do they all have to follow *us*?"

"You're exaggerating, Sarah."

"We should have switched cars before we left Phoenix."

"I was thinking the same thing."

"And bought some wigs and sunglasses."

"Ninety-five degrees is too hot for wigs."

They decided to take the interstate back to the airport to exchange vehicles. Northbound traffic was light when they noticed the Dodge behind them pick up speed and drive into the passing lane. Dana pulled into the passing lane and stepped down hard on the accelerator. She wouldn't allow him to pull alongside and get a shot off shot at them.

Sarah looked as though she were going to swallow her tongue.

"Lean forward with your head on your knees. Hurry!" *No sense us both getting shot.*

The Escalade was fast but the Dodge was faster. When their bumpers made contact, Dana lurched over the steering wheel, the seatbelt cutting into her waist. She knew she had a whiplash and hoped Sarah wasn't hurt.

"Are we dead yet?" Sarah yelled, clutching the edges of her seat.

"We might be soon. Call 911."

A quick glance in the passenger side mirror told her another pickup a few lengths back was in the outside lane. They were approaching an off ramp. If she could cut in front of the other truck, she might be able to take the ramp at the last second before the Dodge could follow.

The Dodge was taking another run at the Escalade and she cut the wheel sharply to the right, taking the off ramp just short of the barrels. Afraid to look back, she heard Sarah shriek. "That Dodge was hit broadside by another truck."

Dana's heart leaped into her throat. The last thing she wanted was someone else hurt. "How bad, Sarah?"

"He won't be following us again for a while."

Dana hesitated, taking her foot from the accelerator. Should they stop?

"Keep going." Sarah sounded like a drill sergeant.

The Escalade eased onto the secondary road at the bottom of the ramp and raced up the opposite side to the highway. Glancing in the mirror she saw that the Dodge had been hit broadside and rolled. Traffic had been light and no other vehicles seemed involved. Hopefully no one else had been hurt. Flashing red lights came into view and Dana again hesitated. Should they go back and talk to the patrolman? She pulled to the side of the road.

"We need to go back," Sarah said. "It's the law." No traffic was coming through so both lanes must be blocked. Dana pulled across the median and waited for a lull in southbound traffic, which was literally crawling by. Lots of lookie loos gawking at the accident. Steam poured from the pickup's engine as it lay on its side. Didn't their assailant look in his mirror before following them? As they crept past the Dodge, she noticed a man gesturing with his hands as he talked to a highway patrolman. He then pointed in the direction they had taken down the ramp.

Dana switched on the turn signal and pulled into the median strip next the patrol car. Getting out, she walked over to where the two men stood.

"That's the SUV," the pickup driver said, "and she's the one that guy in the Dodge was ramming. Then they both pulled right in front of me."

Dana held her hands in a peaceful manner. "The driver of that rolled Dodge was trying to kill us. The only way we could escape was to take the off ramp, officer." She looked at the overturned truck and gulped back her fear before apologizing to the man for involving him in the accident.

"I was about to get involved anyway," he said, touching her shoulder. "That was a smart move on your part."

"Thank you. Is he dead?"

"No, ma'am. He crawled out of the truck and took off running down the ramp. I ducked because he had a gun in his hand."

Dana's knees threatened to buckle.

The patrolman said, "Better get back to your car. You look a little unsteady on your feet. Maybe I should call an ambulance."

Dana rubbed her aching neck and turned to Sarah who was standing behind her. Sarah shook her head so Dana thanked him and resigned herself to filling out yet another report. Where had the driver gone and would he try to shoot them from his hiding place? Dana thought she was going to lose her breakfast.

Sarah slammed the passenger door. "We'd better drive back to the airport and trade in the Escalade."

"Good idea. I don't think I can drive much farther today, anyway."

"We need to leave for Vegas," Sarah said, leveling her hands to demonstrate how steady they were. "I'll drive. I'm just madder'n hell."

Sarah drove to the airport where they traded for a Jeep Cherokee. Dana then made arrangements for an employee to transfer their luggage from the Escalade to the Jeep, in case anyone was following. She wondered whether they should fly home instead. Sarah was adamant. No killer was going to keep her from slot machine heaven.

"We may have been followed, Sarah."

"Time for a disguise."

"I guess we should take evasive action in case we're being followed."

"Let's hit an airport boutique and change clothes. Get some big hats and flowered shirts."

"Great idea, but how will I disguise my height?"

Sarah looked about and spotted an airport wheelchair. "Problem solved. Follow me."

Halfway down the corridor was an airport boutique. Dana bought a light blue T-shirt, beige walking shorts and matching baseball cap. Sarah's purchase was a subdued Hawaiian muumuu which she accessorized with a wide straw hat. They left the shop separately with their purchases well hidden in shopping bags and slipped into the nearest restroom. Sarah emerged first and collected the wheelchair. Wheeling it into the ladies room, she told Dana to have a seat. She then piled bags on her lap and pushed her down the corridor toward the rent-a-car lot.

The dark green Cherokee was parked at the end of the first aisle. Dana hoped their bags had been transferred. If not, they couldn't afford to wait. They'd buy more clothes later. Sarah pushed the wheelchair to the Jeep's passenger side and pretended to help Dana into her seat. Pushing the wheelchair aside, Sarah took the driver's seat.

"Lean your seat back as far as it'll go," Sarah whispered. "We're out of here."

"Drive normally and don't call attention to yourself," Dana whispered as she leaned nearly into the back seat. "Take that hat off as soon as we're on the street."

"Gotcha." Sarah was bareheaded by the time they left the lot, and complained about the sloppy braking system. "I think they gave us a lemon."

"We'll trade it for a different car in Flagstaff."

"If we make it that far."

"If the brakes are that bad, we had better find another rental agency."

Sarah glanced in the mirror before changing lanes. "I'll get used to them. It's mostly uphill to Flagstaff."

"Are you sure?"

"As sure as I'm natural blonde."

Dana laughed. "Keep an eye on the rearview mirror."

"I already am. No one seems interested in us. Yet."

Dana sat up in her seat and twisted the bill of her cap to the back of her head. "I think we need to check our blood pressure."

"Mine's fine. There's nothing to worry about."

"What in heaven's name's gotten into to you, Sarah?"

"I'm tired of being scared. Whatever will be, will be."

"Give me some of whatever you've been drinking."

"Take a nap, Dana. You worry too much."

Dana repeatedly checked the side mirror until her neck was in pain. *The whip lash.* She needed to get it checked, but where? Las Vegas? "We should have flown home."

"And miss a chance to catch a Wayne Newton show?"

Chapter 23

They had an early dinner in Flagstaff, then drove the length of the long main street and back again to make sure they weren't followed. Clouds loomed dark and heavy over San Francisco Peak, which cast a gloomy mood over the Jeep's occupants. Dana kept a constant eye on her side mirror. Before they reached the interstate, they located a rental agency where they traded the Jeep for a tan suburban.

Sarah sighed. "Too bad they didn't have a camouflaged model for mountain driving."

"I think we created enough attention with our tourist duds, don't you?"

"Good thing we changed at the gas station. My muumuu was like traveling in a bed sheet."

"I love it when you talk dirty."

Dana had taken back the wheel when they filled up in Flagstaff. They would switch cars and drivers again in Kingman. As they approached the small town of Williams and a sign announcing the gateway to the Grand Canyon, Dana noticed that Sarah had fallen asleep. Reaching to nudge her, she scolded her for not keeping watch on the other vehicles.

Sarah yawned. "Nothing to worry about. If he was going to attack, he'd have done it by now. We've long passed the place where he shot Lori."

"He's probably waiting for us to let our guards down. That's when he'll strike. Or they. I'm not so sure this isn't a group conspiracy."

"But how would they know we're headed for Vegas?"

"If we've been followed all along, they'll know that we talked to Lori's mother. They could have followed us to the Murphy home and the post office to get her mail. It doesn't take a genius to figure out where we're going."

Sarah sat upright in her seat to glance in the side mirror. "So you think we haven't lost them?"

"I don't think we can count on it."

Sarah managed to stay awake until they had reached the town of Kingman, where they found a motel just off the main highway. Their outside room was on the second floor and carrying the luggage up a flight of metal stairs was exhausting. Dana generously tipped the night clerk and asked that he keep a close eye on any unregistered guest who climbed the outside stairs.

The carpet was well worn and needed cleaning, but their queen-sized bedspreads appeared to have been recently laundered. The distinct smell of cleaning solvent made Sarah cross.

"We'll survive the night," Dana said before her friend could complain. "If he tries to break in, the smell should drive him away."

Sarah plopped down on the bed nearest the bathroom. "When are you going to let me in on your plan? And what's the real reason we're going to Vegas?"

"Can you keep a secret, Thelma?"

Sarah laughed that deep throated laugh of hers. "You know me better than that, Louise."

"That's what worries me."

Dana reclined on the other bed, plumped the pillows and laid out her plan. Sarah nodded agreeably until she nodded off. She was softly snoring when Dana covered her with the bedspread. Talking about her plan helped to solidify it. With any luck it might work. They would rehearse all the way to sin city.

The rental agency in Kingman had an assortment of small cars and a pickup truck with a camper shell, which Dana reluctantly agreed to take. The four-wheeled drive Ford was big and black, reminding her of a villain's truck she had once seen in an action movie. At least it was a match for anything the stalkers could attack them with, unless they hijacked a tank from a local armory.

"This'll do just fine," Sarah said. "Reminds me of the truck my brothers taught me to drive, while growing up in Nebraska. Without the stick shift, of course."

"A model T?" Dana teased.

Sarah grimaced but said nothing as they stowed their luggage in the camper shell. She then climbed in on the driver's side. It was only half past eight but the temperature was rising rapidly. A black truck in this time zone wasn't a great idea. No wonder someone had dumped it in Kingman. Dana noticed small sections of peeling paint on the edges of the doors and wondered whether they were making a mistake by trading away the suburban. Sarah was gunning the engine, anxious to be on their way. She was like a kid with a new toy.

The landscape between Kingman and Vegas was boring at best and sweltering at its worst. Most of the terrain was flat and occasionally punctuated with cactus and clumps of scrubby undergrowth. Dana fought the urge to doze off and worried that Sarah might fall asleep at the wheel. To stay awake, they talked about past experiences and the murder cases they'd solved. Tired of talking, they found an oldies music station and sang to the songs of the sixties.

Halfway to Vegas the air conditioning stopped working. Opening the windows was like sitting in a furnace. Dana's shoulder length hair whipped across her face, blinding her.

Thank heavens Sarah's curly blonde hair was short and didn't impair her vision. The thermometer registered 108, with no service station in sight. Why had they traded for the black pickup truck from hell?

Sarah grumbled, "Now what, Louise?"

"Slow down before we melt and blow away."

"The faster we go, the quicker we'll get to Vegas. Or at least a service station."

Dana retrieved a map from the glove box. Holding her hair back with one hand, she traced their route with the other. "There's nothing out here for miles."

"Another fine mess you've gotten us into."

"Quit changing characters on me, Thelma. Oliver Hardy, you're not. This isn't even funny."

Sarah stepped on the brakes and pulled off the highway.

"What're you doing?"

"There's a tree with some shade."

Sarah maneuvered the big truck as close to the trunk as possible. The truck cab darkened and cooled considerably. A few moments later Sarah announced that it was only 91 degrees.

"Only?"

Sarah glanced into the rearview mirror. "Red pickup truck coming up fast. I think we'd better leave, don't you?"

Dana yelped with pain when she turned to survey the road. She definitely had a whip lash. "Time to get back into the furnace. Let's go."

A long white patch of alkali ran beside the highway. They could either back up or take a chance on getting stuck in the chalk-like earth. Sarah's foot jammed the gas pedal as Dana gripped her neck with both hands. Dust swirled into the cab, making them both cough.

"Watch where you're going." Dana reached for the grab handle as the truck roared back on the highway. The red pickup had to have been traveling over a hundred miles an hour when it passed them in the outer lane.

"Crazy fool," Sarah muttered to herself. "We could have stayed under the tree."

"For how long, Thelma? Until dark?"

Sarah briefly turned to glare at her. "I'm tired of playing Thelma and Louise. Now I know why they drove over the cliff."

"They were in a convertible with the top down."

"Even worse in this blasted heat."

Dana cringed. They'd look like dried prunes by the time they reached civilization. All that expensive face cream applied for nothing.

Sarah slowed to fifty-five and wiped the sweat from her forehead. "This is hell on earth. How could anyone live in this heat?"

"Plenty of people do so don't complain. At least we're alive and the truck's still running. It could be worse."

"Not by much." Sarah placed a finger to her lips and leaned over the steering wheel. "Hear that?"

"Hear what?"

"That noise."

"What noise?"

"The engine. It's thumping."

"It's your imagination. I don't hear—"

A wisp of steam sailed past. Sarah looked down at the engine temperature gauge and gasped. "Two hundred-fifty degrees and rising." The truck was losing speed and Sarah managed to pull to the side of the road.

"What are you doing, Sarah? There's no shade tree for miles."

"The pickup overheated and the engine shut down."

"Ohmygosh. In this heat?"

"And I haven't made out my will."

"Fine time to think about that now." Dana lifted her cell from her purse. No bars meant no signal. There probably wasn't a tower within fifty miles. It was too hot to stay in the truck so they climbed out and walked to the side of the road. It wasn't long before their clothing stuck to their bodies. Peering down the road they could see nothing moving in any direction. Heat radiated from the pavement, like steam from the truck's radiator. Although they both wore sunglasses, it was impossible to see more than half a mile.

Sarah was right. Hell wasn't somewhere underground. It was right here on the Arizona-Nevada border.

Chapter 24

The pickup was stifling but standing in the heat was even worse. Dana decided they needed to raise the hood to signal other motorists they were in trouble. No telling how long the emergency flashers would last before the battery ran down. Steam still poured from the radiator and the hood was too hot to lift, so they rummaged through their luggage for something to use as hot pads. Sarah had several pairs of heavy socks which she pulled over her hands.

"Why'd you bring those along?" Dana asked.

"It wasn't that warm when we left Wyoming."

"Let's get that hood up." Dana reached inside the truck for the hood release and wrapped a denim scarf around her hand.

A car raced by while they were attempting to lift the hood. They grumbled obscenities beneath their breaths.

"We're sitting ducks if the killer stops, Dana."

"Stop thinking and lift."

Several moments passed before the hood raised and they jumped back to escape a blast of steam. They needed water for the radiator but all they had were two small bottles of Dasani. And those might keep them alive. At least for the rest of the day.

Another car passed without slowing down.

"If we were young, good-looking chicks someone would stop to help."

"Too anxious to lose their money in Vegas, Sarah."

"Wouldn't it be great if our friend Ruby stopped by in Old Bertha."

"Talk about wishful thinking."

Sarah stepped around the pickup to peer back down the road. "Speak of the devil—"

Dana joined her as a large truck slowed to pull in behind the Ford. It wasn't Ruby but a middle-aged man about Ruby's size. Grinning, he climbed down and introduced himself as Chuckwagon Charlie. He obviously liked to eat. Lifting his baseball cap, he scratched his balding head.

"Too hot for you ladies to be standin' out here in the sun. Why don't I give you a lift into Vegas?"

Sarah grinned. "Is your truck air conditioned?"

"Sure 'nuff is."

"Let's go."

The driver could be a serial killer but Sarah didn't care. Better to die in an air conditioned cab than roast to death in the scorching sun.

The truck driver helped them load their luggage into the sleeper and Dana climbed in among the suitcases. Sarah was more than happy to ride up front with Charlie. She could hear them chattering while she pushed luggage aside and reclined on the remaining space. It wasn't long before she fell asleep. When she awoke they were parked in a truck stop. She hoped it was Vegas. Sarah and Charlie were nowhere in sight. Panicking, she made her way into the cab and pushed the passenger door open. Sarah was standing next to Charlie at a diesel pump, still chattering like a chipmunk. Sarah looked up and waved at her through the window.

Dana climbed down.

"Don't just stand there, Thelma. We need to rent another car and book a hotel room."

"Charlie wants to buy us dinner. I'm starving. Aren't you?"

"First a shower. Then we'll buy *him* dinner."

"Motel's right across the street," Charlie said.

Dana looked where he had pointed. A dingy building with a faded roof was all that stood in that direction. She shuddered but agreed. They could take a shower and leave. Sarah made a face but helped Dana unload their luggage from the sleeper.

"Half an hour in that place should do it. Then we'll buy *Charlie* dinner and rent a car. We're not spending the night with the bed bugs."

Twenty-five minutes later they trudged back across the street towing their suitcases. Within an hour they were all stuffed with enough steak, potatoes and gravy to last them for a week. Charlie winked at Sarah when they left the cafe.

"He asked for my phone number," Sarah said, giggling like a school girl.

"You didn't give it to him, did you? He's wearing a wedding ring."

"He's getting a divorce."

"How old are you, Sarah?"

She ducked her head and said nothing.

"It won't be long before you get a call from an angry wife who found your number in her husband's wallet."

"I didn't think of that."

Dana gripped her shoulders and told her not to move. "Don't turn around. There's a familiar dark-haired man in the parking lot who looks like Mark Stone."

Sarah's expression was fearful. "He must have followed us. Why didn't he just kill us in the desert?"

"Maybe he thought we'd die of heat prostration. And our deaths couldn't be traced to him."

"But I thought he was in Wyoming at the mansion."

"Let's go back inside and call Jeff Mailey. Maybe he knows Stone's whereabouts." She wanted to hear him say that Mark Stone had been captured.

A busboy was clearing their table when they returned to their booth. Dana told him they had decided on dessert, so he waved a waitress over.

"What if he comes in and spots us, Dana?"

"Hold a menu in front of your face."

Dana reached into her purse to retrieve her baseball cap. Pulling it low over her forehead, she lifted her cell phone and punched in Jeff Dailey's number.

"No sign of him," Jeff said when she asked. "He must have left town before I moved into the mansion. Sheriff Barnes's got an APB out on Stone but no one has seen him. He disappeared like a ghost."

"Then it must be him in the truck stop parking lot."

She told him where they were and filled him in on their day's adventure. He didn't mention that they were crazy, but she could hear it in his voice. Reassuring him they'd be fine, she clicked off and told Sarah to follow her to the ladies' room.

Sarah sputtered. "But my cherry pie—"

"I'll buy you a case of them *if* we ever get home."

Once in the restroom, they changed clothes. Sarah wore her muumuu and Dana tucked her hair under her cap. Buttoning on an oversized shirt, she pushed it into her jeans. Moving from the stall to the mirror, she scrubbed off her makeup, hoping she could pass for a man in the distance. Thank heavens she was small breasted. She had never appreciated it until now.

Sarah's hat had been discarded so she wrapped a scarf around her hair and knotted it in back. A transom window was partially open at the rear of the large restroom and they pushed out the screen and squeezed the suitcases through the opening, dropping them to the pavement on the other side. Sarah would leave first and casually circle around to the back of the building. If the parking lot was clear she would inform Dana through the restroom window.

Dana waited for what seemed an eternity before she heard Sarah whisper outside the window. "He's still out there, pacing around the parking lot waiting for us to come out. Good thing he doesn't know what *I* look like."

The window had been just big enough to push the suitcases through, but was it large enough for her? Dana looked at a nearby trash can. Turning it upside down and spilling its contents, she prayed no one would enter the restroom before she could escape. She sat on the edge of the metal container and swung her legs up past the metal frame. Turning as though a pole vaulter, she pushed her body through the window to her thighs. She then realized she was stuck.

Sarah urged her to unbutton her jeans and push them down past her hips. "Then suck in your belly."

Dana inched her way back into the restroom to unbutton her jeans. Sarah then pulled them down to her knees. Edging back through the window she found it still a tight fit but she was out as far as her chest when someone opened the restroom door.

"What'n hell are you doing?" a large woman asked.

"Escaping from my former husband. Please don't tell anyone."

The dark-haired woman placed a hand on her ample hip. "Sure, honey, I got one of them myself. Here, let me help you."

"He's out in the parking lot. Would you distract him for a few minutes so I can get away? I'd be glad to pay you."

"Keep your money. What's he look like?"

Dana described Mark Stone down to his tennis shoes, then remembered he was young enough to be her son. She hesitated before adding, "I married a younger man."

"So did I, honey. I guess that makes us cougars."

Dana forced a laugh and, with Sarah's help, dropped to the pavement. "Thank you," she said through the opening, but the woman was already gone. Would she keep her promise to distract Mark Stone, if that's who he was? They didn't stay long enough to find out. Angling away from the restroom they towed their suitcases toward a bus stop out of sight of the restaurant. Dana thought ditching the suitcases was a good idea but Sarah insisted that they could throw them at Stone, if he came after them.

Sarah noticed a bus. "Doesn't matter where it's going."

"I agree. We can hide out in one of the casinos after we book a hotel."

They climbed aboard and made their way to the back of the bus. Once seated, Dana peered out the window as Stone came running toward the bus. Had he sent the woman into the restroom to look for her?

The driver had already closed the door and placed his foot on the accelerator. When he noticed Stone, he lifted his foot and the bus hesitated.

"He's trying to kill us," Sarah screamed. "Go, go, go."

The driver stomped on the accelerator and the bus jerked away from the curb. The few passengers aboard all turned in their seats to stare at the odd couple seated in the back of the bus.

"If he noticed the bus's destination, he'll be waiting for us, Dana."

"We'll get off at the next stop before he has a chance to follow. We can leave the suitcases. Maybe the driver will save them for us."

Sarah nodded and they pushed their luggage beneath the seat before making their way forward. Dana nearly lost her balance when the bus hit a pot hole and swayed. The sober-faced driver acted as though he would cooperate. The luggage would be stored at the terminal for a week. He wished them luck.

As soon as the bus stopped two blocks down, they hurried down a side street and entered a restaurant by the back door. Dana led the way through the kitchen to the restroom. Panting,

Sarah grabbed for a paper towel to mop her brow. "We can't stay in here forever. I'm getting tired of this restroom tour."

Dana looked about for a window but the small restroom was enclosed. "I'm afraid we're out of luck."

"Why not call a cab and have him meet us at the back door."

"Good idea. Unless Mark Stone's waiting for us."

"I'll grab a frying pan when we go back through the kitchen."

Dana retrieved her phone to call information for a cab company. The dispatcher said there would be a half hour wait so they dabbed their faces with wet paper towels and leaned against the tiled walls. Restaurant customers came and went, giving them wide berth. Dana realized how strange they looked and removed her cap to fan herself. The air conditioner must be set at 80, but it felt like 110 degrees.

Sarah checked her watch after a young woman with three young daughters closed the restroom door. "It's time."

"How do we know the cab's out there?"

"I'll go see. Mark Stone doesn't know what I look like unless he noticed my picture at the mansion."

Sarah reached for Dana's cap. A bit large, she pulled it down over her ears and headed to the kitchen. Moments later she returned, breathless.

"The cab's waiting and there's no sign of Mark Stone."

Dana took a deep breath and took possession of her cap.

Chapter 25

Sarah left the kitchen while Dana handed the cook a fifty dollar bill in exchange for a cast iron skillet. Several others in the kitchen were holding knives as though to protect themselves against the intruders. The outside door pushed inward and Sarah stuck her head inside.

"Hurry. I hear a police siren in the distance. There's no sign of Mark Stone or his red pickup."

One of the kitchen helpers must have called the police and she couldn't blame them. She and Sarah must look like escaped mental patients. Once they were seated in the cab, Dana whispered, "Maybe we should wait for the police."

"The way we're dressed, they'll think we're—"

"I know." Leaning forward, she told the driver to take them to the Crystal Palace.

"What about our luggage?"

"We'll have to get it later."

Dana turned to glance in the rear window, causing sharp pains to stab at her neck. When she winced Sarah told her she needed to see a doctor. Not until they reached home. There was no time for self-indulgence. They needed to discover why Lori Murphy had spent three days in Vegas before she died.

And who had been with her? It had to have been Stone. Why else would he follow them to Vegas? And how in the world did he find them? His companions must have been watching them since they left Phoenix.

"We'll rent a car and have it delivered to the hotel. Then we can pick up our luggage at the bus terminal." Dana opened her purse to retrieve her wallet. Counting the few remaining bills, she said she was running low on money. Thank goodness for credit cards.

The taxi driver must have taken the scenic route because it was nearly half an hour before they reached the hotel. Dana had five dollars left when they exited the cab and Sarah's stash amounted to two ones and a twenty.

"I won't be playing many slot machines."

"We'll worry about that later. We'll book a room before we call that company that delivers cars."

"First a restroom to make ourselves presentable."

Half an hour later Dana pushed a card into the lock at room 342. It was small room with two queen beds but neat and clean and they were both exhausted. The temptation to take a short nap was irresistible and they awoke sometime later to the sound of sirens.

"Fire trucks," Sarah said, still groggy from her nap. Making her way to the window, she reported they'd driven by.

Dana sighed as she reached for a phone book. "Time to call for a car."

Another Suburban was delivered within the hour and they followed a dispatcher's directions to the bus terminal, repeatedly checking for red pickups.

"Looks like we've lost him, Dana."

"Don't be too sure. He always manages to find us."

Once they retrieved their suitcases and returned to the hotel, they showered and changed, and decided it was time for dinner. Should they eat in their room or chance being spotted at one of the hotel restaurants?

Sarah insisted on a small casino café. Dana knew she'd gobble down her food so that she could spend more time at the slot machines. While she lost the rest of her money, Dana would show the manager Lori Murphy's photo. If that didn't work, she'd try the busboys and cleaning maids. Someone had to recognize her.

The night manager was in a meeting so Dana roamed the halls searching for a maid. She finally gave up and decided to try again the following morning.

The casino was wall-to-wall people and Sarah was no-where to be found. Dana searched each row of machines, paying special attention to Sarah's favorite, video poker. Maybe she had run of out money and gone back to their room. No. Sarah would have found an ATM machine and continued gambling.

Where was she? Dana's stomach felt as though she had contracted the flu. Was it the BLT sandwich or fear that Mark Stone had kidnapped Sarah? Not in a crowded room. He would have waited until they had gone to bed.

Dana retraced her steps, starting with a row of machines nearest the far wall and working her way through the maze. Flashing lights, cigarette smoke and general noise were nearly more than she could bear. A huge lump formed in her throat, triggering tears.

Where was Sarah? Dana hurried to the nearest restroom where she called Sarah's name. When no one answered she tried another. Still no Sarah. At the third, a strange voice answered. The woman's name was Sarah but she looked nothing like her friend.

Dana dabbed at her eyes and decided to call her cell phone. The call went directly through to Sarah's voice mail and she left a message to meet at their room. Immediately. She then took an elevator to the third floor. Sarah wasn't in their room and she waited fifteen minutes before her cell phone rang. The man's voice was one she'd never heard.

"Your friend is lonely," he said. "If you want to see her again, follow my instructions carefully."

Dana caught her breath and reached for a hotel notepad and pen.

"Take Highway 15 to 160 and the sixth exit. Follow the road until you reach a steel building off the gravel road. Four of my men will escort you there. Don't tell anyone or your friend will experience an early end to her miserable life."

"Miserable?"

"You heard me. Leave now! If you're not here in twenty minutes, all you'll find is Sarah's remains."

They knew her name. But how did they know who she was? There had to be a number of people involved in the conspiracy. And what did the conspiracy involve?

Dana grabbed her purse and cell phone. She had to call someone in case she and Sarah were murdered. At least they could find their bodies. Hurrying to the elevator, she decided to call Jeff Mailey. She would leave a message for Walter. There was no way they could reach her in time to save Sarah but at least they would know what happened.

"Don't go," he warned. "I'll call the Las Vegas police."

"Sarah will die either way. I have to go."

"There's nothing you can do," he said. "And they'll kill you both."

"I got Sarah into this mess and it's up to me to get her out." She gave him directions to the steel building and warned him not to contact anyone. She clicked off as the elevator opened into the hotel lobby. Punching in Walter's cell number, she raced out into the parking lot to locate their rental car.

Walter ordered her not to go. "This is insane, Dana. I warned you not to get involved. I'll catch the next plane out of Sacramento. Stay put until I get there."

"What about your murder case?"

"Suspect's in custody. I was just gonna call you when my phone rang."

"Suspect? I thought it was a murder-suicide."

"The guy who killed the family tried to make it appear that way."

Dana checked her watch. "They'll kill Sarah if I'm not there in twenty minutes. "Make that eighteen." She reached into the side pocket of her travel purse to retrieve her keys.

"Don't go," he pleaded.

Pulling the phone away from her ear she disconnected the call. Only seventeen minutes remained. Checking the slip of paper she'd torn from the hotel pad, she pulled from the parking lot onto the busy highway. Hands trembling, she nearly ran a stop sign. A large truck's horn caused her to jog halfway into another lane. Was someone following her? Heart pounding in her throat, she threaded her way through traffic until she reached the onramp to 160.

Two dark red pickup trucks drove side by side several car lengths back. They must have an entire fleet of them. Whoever was driving didn't seem to care that she knew they were following. They were obviously herding her to the site. Would they allow her to see Sarah? She knew she should have left the case to the police but felt compelled to go.

Her cell phone rang and she debated whether to answer. After the third ring she decided it might be Sarah's captors. The I.D. said it was Walter and she dropped the phone back into her purse. Somewhere in the back of her mind she realized how cruel she was treating him, knowing that he loved her. But she didn't love him. Or did she? She didn't want to love him. Her lips trembled and she allowed herself to cry. What a mess she'd gotten them all into.

Chapter 26

A moment later her cell phone rang again. She thought it was Walter but had to make sure. The screen said unknown caller. It must be the kidnappers. Add murderers to the list, she thought, gritting her teeth.

The same man's voice said, "You disobeyed orders and talked on your phone."

"I just answered incoming calls. I thought it might be you."

"We'll check your phone when you get here."

Dana mentally crossed her fingers. "I didn't tell anyone about this."

"I don't believe you."

She heard Sarah in the background. "Don't come," she screamed. She then heard a sound like a slap and Sarah groaned.

"Don't hurt her. She doesn't know anything. And neither do I."

"That right?"

"All we know is that a young woman was shot and killed and a man's body was found in the mountains."

"What were you doing out on Beeline Highway?"

"We're tourists on our way home."

His laugh was brutal. "Tell me another one."

Dana paused. "My daughter's writing a story about the Four Corners murders. That's why—"

"Oh, you mean Kerrie Compton, who works for *City Magazine* in Denver?

Dana's heart sank into her knees. "How do you know?"

"We know everything, Miz Logan. You drove yourself into a cesspool."

Dana was unable to speak.

"The off ramp's coming up. Make sure you don't miss it."

The call disconnected. Hands trembling, she rested the phone on the steering wheel and deleted her previous calls. In the process, she nearly missed the ramp. A horn blared from behind her and she knew it was one of her pursuers. Crimping the wheel sharply, the Suburban narrowly missed the outside shoulder, swaying dangerously close to the edge. Heart pounding, she stepped on the brakes, slowing to a crawl.

Her cell phone rang again. Hands trembling, she pulled to the side of the road when she reached the end of the off ramp. The same man's voice growled, "Do that again and your friend is a dead woman."

From the corner of her eye Dana noticed someone attempting to open the passenger door.

"Unlock the door and let him in." It wasn't a request. It was a demand.

She could stomp on the gas and leave but what would happen to Sarah? Reluctantly pressing the unlock button, she watched as a huge man with a tanned shaved head jerked the door open. Dressed in a T-shirt and jeans, he resembled Mr. Clean with aviator glasses. He even smelled like soap.

"Don't even do anything stupid," he said, adjusting the shoulder strap and buckling himself in. A pickup pulled in ahead of the Suburban and backed up close enough to block an attempted escape. Dana wondered whether they had remote cameras trained on her, like patrol cars. How else could the man on the phone know exactly what she was doing?

Had they noticed her erase the cell calls? Hitting her hand on the steering wheel, she silently berated herself for trying to rescue Sarah on her own. Jeff and Walter must have called the police, but how could they help her?

Mr. Clean lifted his hand, signaling his partner to lead the way. Dana followed. "Why are you doing this?" she asked.

The big man simply laughed.

"I know you're going to kill us, so why not satisfy my curiosity?"

He turned to stare at her, a smirk altering his homely face. "The whole damn country will know soon enough."

Dana caught her breath. "You're planning a terrorist attack?"

"Something like that."

"With sulfuric acid?"

He laughed again. "Figured it out, did ya?"

"Why shouldn't I know *why* if I'm going to die, along with thousands or even millions of other innocent people?"

He remained silent.

There had to be a way to get through to him. "Don't you have a wife and kids? Think of all the innocent children that will die?"

"Who would marry somebody like me?"

"I have a friend who would love someone like you." She cringed inwardly, knowing Sarah just might be attracted to him."

"Oh, yeah. Where is she?"

"You and your boss captured her."

"Oh, *her*," he said, apparently disappointed. "She's old enough to be my mother."

"Plenty of lonely women would love a big, strong man like you."

"Yeah. Sure."

"Come to Wyoming and I'll introduce you—"

"That where you're from?"

"That's where Mark Stone broke into my house." She held her breath, hoping he would confirm that Stone was involved.

"I heard about that."

"Is he your boss?"

He laughed. "That wuss."

"He nearly got me killed in my motorhome."

"He's a real tough guy with the ladies."

"Then who's smart enough—tough enough—to head up this nationwide terrorist attack?"

"If I told you, I'd have to—"

"Kill me? Where have I heard that line before?"

The big guy was smiling and seeming to enjoy himself. Was there time to find out more? "Why would anyone want to kill his fellow countrymen?"

"I'm just on the payroll, I don't make the decisions."

"What about your mom? Won't she be killed too?"

"She died when I was a kid."

"Sorry to hear that. How did it happen?"

"Some druggies broke in the apartment."

Dana glanced at him again. He was younger than she had originally thought. Mid to late forties. He might even be younger. His biceps bulged conspicuously under his white T-shirt. There was no way she could overpower him.

"What about your dad?"

"Never knew him."

"Your grandparents?"

"Them too." There was an edge to his voice and Dana realized she'd hit a nerve.

She glanced at the terrain. Civilization had been left behind. The land was flat with small scrubby hills in the distance. It seemed as though no one else had ever been there, with the exception of the road crew responsible for this narrow stretch of pot-holed heaven.

"I hate talking to someone whose name I don't know."

His lower lip protruded. "I guess it doesn't matter if you know my name is George."

Dana forced a smile. "My uncle's name was George. He was a young seaman during World War II. Stationed on a ship torpedoed and sunk in the Pacific."

"Too bad," he said as though he meant it.

Did she dare ask? Dana hesitated. "What will happen to our country after the terrorist attack?"

"Martial law after they take out the power grids."

"You mean first the acid attacks, then no electricity or communications?"

"Among other things."

"Suicide bombings?"

He folded his arms across his chest and sighed. "I've said too much already."

"What difference does it make, if you're going to kill us."

"Can't be helped." He turned his head to gaze through the side window.

The pickup ahead engaged its right blinker and began to slow. When they turned into a gravel lane, George told her to keep her speed to ten miles an hour. She soon learned why. The narrow path was like driving over a washboard.

"Not far now," he said, pointing to a large steel building setting alone in a rocky field about a quarter mile from the gravel road. "Pull through that open bay door."

Her heart rate felt as though it were well over a hundred, her breathing labored. It was dark inside the bay, except for the Suburban's headlights. A shadowy figure tapped on her side window, motioning for her to release the lock. When the door opened, a strong smell of fuel filled her senses.

Before she could react, a hand grabbed her arm and pulled her from the driver's seat. She nearly lost her balance and swore beneath her breath.

"Go easy on 'er," George said. "She's a nice lady."

"Who cares?" the smaller man growled. "Get her inside with the other one."

George gently took her arm and towed her out the back door and into a side entrance in the L-shaped building. A step down led to a large room with an exposed concrete floor. Tied to a metal chair in the far corner was Sarah, who cried, "Oh, no," when she saw Dana. At least they hadn't gagged her. Dressed in her navy blue polyester pantsuit, her newsboy cap appeared to have been jammed on her head.

George retrieved several pieces of oily rope and another chair, which he arranged several feet from Sarah. Ordering her to sit, he told her not to move while he tied her up."

Dana had taken part in a self-defense training class but George's size intimidated her. He could easily break both her arms. She glanced about the empty room with its small row of high windows. The only door was the one they had just entered. She leaned toward Sarah to offer an apology when George began to tie her wrists. Dana winced when he pulled the rope too tight.

He loosened the rope a bit, saying, "I can't let you get away. The boss'll have my neck."

She smiled. "I wouldn't want to get you in trouble, George."

Ignoring her sarcasm, he tied her to the chair and stood back as though to admire his work. "I'm sorry," he said and left.

Sarah looked incredulous. "What was that all about?"

"Just trying to make a friend we may need later," Dana whispered back.

Sarah pointed with her chin to a revolving camera high on the east wall. So they were being watched and listened to. They had to be careful what they said.

"George is a terrorist or mercenary," Dana whispered. "He's not just a member of a home grown volunteer group of anarchists."

"That means they're organized and funded by some foreign group."

"Frightening, isn't it?"

"And we had to stumble into the middle of it."

"I'm afraid everyone will be in the middle of it soon."

Sarah's face crumpled and tears rolled down her cheeks.

"How did they kidnap you?"

"Some guy tapped me on the shoulder while I was at the video poker machine. He said you'd been hit by a car in the parking lot. And you wanted me to ride in the ambulance with you."

"Good heavens."

"Once we got to the parking lot, they shoved me into a van and took off like a scalded cat."

"They didn't hurt you, did they?"

"A couple of slaps." She turned her head so that Dana could see the bruises.

Dana groaned.

"They're going to kill us," Sarah whimpered.

"They're keeping us alive for a reason. They must think we know something."

"That means they'll torture us. What could we possibly know?"

"What worries me most is they know about Kerrie and her research on the Four Corners murders."

"How could they know that?"

"We've obviously been watched."

"Then Kerrie's in danger."

Dana hung her head. "I didn't have time to warn her."

Chapter 27

"Dana! Do you hear the sirens?"

"No. It must be wishful thinking."

"Listen carefully."

Dana strained to hear but Sarah's hearing was no doubt better. A moment later she said, "I think I hear them now. They sound a long way off. Maybe from the highway."

Dana's heart quickened. She had forgotten she'd given directions to Jeff Mailey. He must have called the police. But would they find them there?

The door creaked open and a squat man entered the building. He was holding a roll of duct tape. Dana groaned, realizing what he had in mind. He wasted no time wrapping the wide gray tape over her mouth and Sarah's. He then returned with tarps, which he draped over them. She heard Sarah moan, knowing she was claustrophobic.

The sirens grew louder and Dana wondered why the police didn't arrive quietly instead of announcing their raid. Concentrating on what was happening outside the building, she heard screeching tires and doors slamming. She then heard men's voices but couldn't comprehend what they were saying. It seemed an eternity before the door to their building opened and a man said, "Just some old diesel engines under the tarps. They've been there forever."

The door then slammed shut. She should have moved or tipped her chair sideways enough to fall before the officers left, but it happened so fast that she didn't have time to think. Sarah was groaning, obviously trying to express her disappointment. Tears ran heavily down Dana's cheeks.

Would the greasy man return to untarp and untape them or were they destined to remain that way until they died? After a while, she heard car doors slamming and engines starting. The police must be leaving. A few minutes later she heard the door to the building creak open and footsteps growing louder. The tarp was jerked from her and a nasty voice said, "You're in trouble, lady."

Dana shook her head until he ripped the tape from her mouth. It felt as though her skin had gone with it.

"Why am I in trouble?"

"You called the cops."

"No, I didn't. My friend called from home and I told him where I was going. Would you have done the same?"

He shrugged. "The boss ain't gonna be happy when I tell him."

"Then don't. How will he know if no one tells him."

"You're one sassy broad. You and your friend are still in trouble."

"Sarah didn't do anything wrong. Let her go. I'll stay and take your boss's punishment. There was no harm done. You convinced the cops it was a crank call. You should pat yourself on the back."

He seemed undecided.

"Please unwrap Sarah. I know she's hyperventilating."

He jerked the tarp, taking Sarah's cap with it. But he seemed a little more gentle with the tape. Gathering up the tarps he left.

Sarah whimpered.

"What's wrong?"

"Something crawled across my foot."

Probably a rat. "Kick as hard as you can if it happens again."

Sarah sighed. "Why do I always get captured? It hasn't been that long since that drug gang took me prisoner in the Laramie Mountains. It's like déjà vu."

"How well I remember, but at least you're not alone this time."

"I don't wanna solve any more crimes, Dana. I've had enough."

"I've come to the same conclusion."

It wasn't long before Sarah dozed off, her chin dropping to her chest. Dana continued to scan the building, looking for a possible way to escape. After what seemed hours, the florescent lights went out, leaving them in near darkness. Flickerings of starlight could be seen through the small windows near the top of the metal wall. It must be at least ten o'clock. Dana tried to twist her wrist to see her lighted watch dial but it was covered by the grimy rope.

Sarah gasped when she awoke. Complaining that she was hungry, she said, "This must be the beginning of our torture. No food or potty breaks. I'm glad I'm wearing a diaper."

"You are?"

"I put one on so that I wouldn't lose my video poker machine."

Dana wished she was wearing one, remembering the astronaut who drove cross country to kill her rival.

A few moments later they heard a clicking noise and the sound of an opening door. A flashlight illuminated a small area of the floor, which made its way toward them. When it reached Dana's chair it stopped and a voice whispered, "I brought some food and water."

"Bless you, George."

"I'm not George. He sent me."

Of course it wasn't George. This man smelled more like diesel fuel than floor cleaner.

Their visitor dropped bags of potato chips in their laps.

"Untie our hands so we can eat," Dana said.

"I'm not allowed to do that but I can feed you," the man said. He placed the flashlight beneath his arm and tore open a bag.

"My friend's afraid of germs," Sarah whispered. "Did you wash your hands?"

No. But if you're not hungry, *I'll* eat them."

"Not hungry," they said in unison.

They watched the flashlight as it made its way back to the door.

Dana sighed. "This is insane."

"At least they're in no hurry to kill us."

They heard an engine start outside the building. Was it their benefactor or someone else? The door again creaked open and a small overhead light above the door switched on. A short man wearing a dark hood made his way toward them. When he arrived, he said in a low voice, "George wants you to come with us."

"Where *is* George?" Dana asked.

"In the van. He doesn't want the camera to see him."

Before Dana could ask why *he* didn't mind the camera, the man reached to untie everything but her hands. He then untied Sarah. Tugging them to their feet, he marched them to the door where a dark van waited.

"Looks like the same van that brought me here," Sarah whispered.

The van's rear door was opened and they were pushed inside. Blankets had been placed on the floor and they were forced to lie on their backs.

Was that George in the driver's seat? Dana winced in pain when she craned her neck to look. The man behind the wheel was also wearing a hood. His smaller companion opened the passenger door and got inside. The van then crept along the side of the building, without its headlights. What in the world was going on?

"Lie still and be quiet," the shorter man said.

Faint light filled the interior of the van. What did George have planned for them? It had to be better than killed by unknown terrorists. Then again, it could be worse. Moving next to Sarah, she whispered in her ear, "Pray for all you're worth."

Sarah nodded and closed her eyes. They rode for what seemed an hour before the van stopped and the passenger door closed. When the back door opened, the shorter man reached for Sarah. He pulled her into a sitting position and out of the van. He then reached for Dana. She saw her chance and took it. Jerking knees to her chest, she kicked at the man's chin with all her strength. He didn't make a sound as he fell backward onto the road.

Dana scooted to the opening and pushed herself over the edge, her feet making contact with the man's body. Sarah, who was standing nearby, placed a foot on the man's throat while Dana regained her balance.

"Run."

Dana's long legs soon outdistanced Sarah's short, plump ones. Running into the field away from the passenger side of the van, Dana tripped and fell, knocking the air from her lungs. When Sarah caught up she tried to untie Dana's hands, although her own were still securely bound. They heard the driver's door open and George yell to his partner. Thank heavens the moon was only a sliver.

Dana was still trying to catch her breath, the pain in her chest easing. "No time to try to untie ourselves. We've got to get further away." She lifted her head to peer at the van. Taillights illuminated the big man who was kneeling beside the injured one. He then turned his head to stare in their direction. Shaking his fist, he yelled, "I tried to help you stupid women."

Taking his gun from a shoulder holster, he fired into the darkness. Sarah flattened herself beside Dana and they watched George help his partner into the van, which swung in a wide arc and stopped to shine its headlights in their direction. Moments later the van was floorboarded back toward their headquarters. Dana almost felt sorry for George, wondering what kind of punishment he had in store. He had obviously been ordered to kill them.

"Where are we, Dana?"

Dana worked the rope until she could see the lighted dial on her wrist. "About an hour out of Vegas. I have no idea which direction they drove. We'd better call 911."

"They took my purse. My phone's in it."

Dana patted her jeans pocket. Her slim line phone was still there, but was cell service available in the boondocks?

"Untie me, Sarah, if you have to use your teeth."

Sarah worked for quite a while before the ropes were loose enough for Dana to pull free. She then untied Sarah's wrists. Easing her phone from her jeans pocket, she flipped the cover open, noting that the battery was still charged. There were three missed calls from Walter. Two from Jeff. Another from Kerrie. Thank heavens she had shut off her cell before she'd been captured. Punching in the emergency number, she waited. When a dispatcher answered, she said they had just escaped their kidnappers and gave her their approximate location.

She decided not to say anything about the terrorist camp. Not yet. They would think it was a crank call. If the cell battery died, they'd probably die along with it before help arrived. She told the dispatcher she was shutting off her phone. She'd turn it on again for five minutes on the hour to conserve the battery. Turning off the ringer, she made sure it was on vibrate.

It was a quarter past midnight. They needed to take turns standing guard in case George's cohorts returned to search for them. She decided to take the first watch while Sarah slept. At one o'clock she turned on her phone and waited for a call from the police. She turned it off when nothing happened. She'd better call Kerrie.

The call went directly to voice mail and she left Kerrie a message, telling her not to call. She also told her daughter to place herself in protective custody. Dana didn't tell her about the predicament they were in. Kerrie had enough to worry about.

Sometime later, Dana had nearly dozed off when she heard a vehicle slowly driving their way, a searchlight scanning both sides of the road. Was it the police or the terrorists? Dana flattened herself next to Sarah and squinted to determine whether there were mounted lights on top. The vehicle stopped opposite them and doors opened.

Two men got out, one of them pointing into the darkness in their direction. The passenger who walked in front of the headlights was wearing a dark hood. It had to be George and his partner again. But why the hoods out here in the middle of nowhere? Unless it was someone else who didn't want to be recognized. That must mean they were only planning to recapture them, not kill them.

Dana placed a hand over Sarah's mouth and whispered in her ear. She awoke with a start. The two men carried flashlights and would soon discover them if they didn't leave their current position.

Dana led the way on hands and knees, crawling parallel to the two lane road and out of the men's current path. Rocks bit into her palms and knees and she clenched her teeth to keep from making a sound. She wondered how Sarah was faring behind her. When they were out of the men's direct path, she stood and helped Sarah to her feet. They then moved as fast as Sarah's wedgies would allow. Thankfully they were wearing dark colors.

Eyes at last adjusted to the darkness, Dana spotted a nearby boulder and they stopped momentarily to rest. The flashlight beams had almost vanished as both men searched in the opposite direction.

"I wonder why they didn't come after us in the van," Sarah whispered.

"Lots of rocks out here could flatten the tires."

"Or maybe your friend George is trying to help us get away."

"Why would he do that?"

"Shush, they coming back this way."

"Let's go."

Dana noticed a faint light in the distance and headed in that direction. Was it a house, another terrorist van or a car traveling on a parallel road? At least it would keep them from walking in circles. She heard Sarah puffing behind her and hoped she could keep up. She didn't exercise, as Dana did, and was out of shape.

Sarah sneezed. They were in a clump of tall weeds and Sarah's hay fever was going to give them away. Dana stopped walking long enough to locate the flashlights. Had they heard?

Chapter 28

They had to act fast.

"Sarah," she whispered. "We've got to circle around them and beat them back to the road. If the keys are in the van, we can steal it and drive for help."

Dana felt the ground for a palm-sized rock. Standing, she threw it away from the road and in the general direction the men were located. She watched as the flashlights swung toward the sound. She then gripped Sarah's hand and crept straight for the back of the van, whose taillights served as a beacon. Swinging wide so they wouldn't be visible in the red glare, they crossed the road well behind the van and into the field on the opposite side of the road. When they were even with the van, they crouched low and crept up on the driver's side. Dana prayed the driver had left in a hurry, without taking the keys, and that no one else was waiting inside.

"Get in as fast as you can and slide across the seat," Dana whispered as she reached for the handle. The door opened without a squeak and Sarah climbed inside, but not without a groan. Dana reached to push her along the bench seat, then got behind the wheel. Fumbling for the keys, she found them in the ignition, grateful to the driver who had left them behind.

"They're going to shoot at us so keep your head on your knees." Dana knew she sounded like a drill sergeant.

"What about you?"

Dana pushed the seat back as far as it would go. "The window upright will protect me," she said, although she didn't believe it.

Memorizing the road ahead, she turned off the headlights and floorboarded the van. Seconds later they heard gunshots and the thud of breaking glass. She lifted her foot from the accelerator and allowed the van to slow, hoping the men would shoot across the road ahead of them until they were out of ammunition.

"You all right, Sarah?"

"Leg cramps are killing me."

"We'll stop when we're out of shooting range."

The sound of gunfire ceased and she picked up speed, biting her lip until it bled. She imagined the men running toward the road and watched for flashlights behind the van. None yet but it wouldn't take them long—unless they stumbled and fell. Hopefully, they were out of ammunition. If that were true, they would have to stop to reload. She jammed her foot on the accelerator, praying they wouldn't drive into the ditch on the right side of the road. A few moments later, she reached for the headlights. They had to be out of range.

Dana gasped when a bullet smashed her side mirror. Shutting off the lights, she yelled at Sarah to keep her head down. She then deliberately drove off the left side of the road. Bumping along in the rocky soil she was risking a flat tire but only long enough to get them out of shooting range. A few minutes more should do it.

It was then she saw the light. Driving toward them at a distance was another car—if that's what it was. More terrorists or the police at last? She wouldn't stop until she got a good look at them. If they were backup for the men on foot, speed was her only defense. She doubted the van had been built for a race track but would put it to the test.

Reaching into her pocket for her phone, she handed it to Sarah.

"Call 911 and tell them what's happening."

As though to punctuate her sentence, a bullet struck the van. They must have rifles with infrared sites. *Please don't let them hit the gas tank.* She might as well drive on the road. Dana picked up speed, gripping the steering wheel until her fingers grew numb. The oncoming headlights were blinding her. Switching the van's lights from bright to dim, she signaled the other vehicle to do the same.

"No one's answering or we just lost cell service again," Sarah reported from her crouched position.

"Did it ring?"

"Only once."

Dana shielded her eyes from the approaching headlights, which had refused to dim. At least there were no more gunshots. The shooters were probably afraid of hitting their fellow terrorists.

Sarah sat bolt upright. "They're blinking their lights. They want us to stop."

"No way." Gritting her teeth, Dana clung to the wheel as she stepped down on the accelerator.

"What if *they* shoot?"

"We'll have to take that chance. Get down."

Dana aimed straight at the blinding lights, hoping the other car would stop or go into the ditch. Not much chance of either happening.

"There's signal," Sarah shrieked. "The phone's ringing."

Dana lifted her foot from the gas pedal and allowed the van to slow to ten miles an hour. The approaching vehicle seemed to have done the same. "Ask if a patrol car's out here."

"They're in the area. That must be them ahead of us."

"Why don't they dim their lights?"

"They might think we're the terrorists."

"Tell them—"

"I did. The dispatcher's notifying them."

Dana punched in the emergency flashers and waited for the other car. When it pulled alongside, the car's overhead lights were visible. Relieved, she sank back into her seat. When two sheriff's deputies approached the van with guns drawn, she rolled down the window and raised her hands. Sarah did the same.

"The kidnappers are back there," she said, nodding in the direction they had come. "We got away and managed to steal their van."

"You're not going to arrest us for that, are you?" Sarah asked from the passenger seat.

The young officer nearest the van smiled. "No, ma'am, if you can prove who you are."

"They took our purses," Dana said, "but they missed my cell phone." She took it from Sarah and handed it to him.

"I'm Dana Logan and this is my friend, Sarah Cafferty. We were kidnapped by suspected terrorists."

"Terrorists?" He opened the door and ushered them into the backseat of the patrol car. His partner then drove the van into the ditch for safe keeping. Calling for backup, the driver gave their approximate location and they waited for others to arrive. Meanwhile, the women told them of their harrowing experiences, from the time they found the first murder victim until the present. Both officers laughed when told of Ruby McCurdy and the chase in the produce truck. Their laughter ended when the patrol car accident was mentioned.

"Do you know if they survived the wreck?" Sarah asked.

"We heard that two patrolmen didn't make it," the driver said. "Four or five truckers are in the hospital with serious injuries."

Both women hung their heads, Dana wondering whether it was *their* fault the accident had happened. There was little they could have done differently. Sarah would have to live with the memory, as well as Ruby.

Three groups of backup officers arrived within the hour. Fanning out over the area, they searched for the terrorists, some of them wearing SWAT labels across their backs. Faint light was streaking the horizon when Dana checked her watch. It was past five o'clock. Sarah had already fallen asleep in the back seat of the patrol car when it made a U-turn to take them to the station to fill out yet another report.

They hadn't received word of the terrorists' whereabouts but Dana was sure that a helicopter would soon be flying the area. She couldn't help but wonder whether George had been lying about the planned terrorist attacks. She didn't think so. Everything that had happened pointed to a plan to take down the country's infrastructure and kill millions of people.

Exhausted, she leaned her head against the seat and fell asleep. Visions of power outages and running feet filled her dreams and she awoke in the parking lot of the sheriff's substation. More paperwork awaited and she doubted she could stay awake long enough to fill them out. Maybe they could borrow a cell with two empty bunks for a nap. Bright lights caused her to squint and she hung onto Sarah as they followed the sergeant into a corner office. They were much too tired to make sense.

The first question asked was, "Can you describe the place where they held you captive?"

Sarah couldn't wait to tell the sergeant about the aborted police raid on the terrorist hideout and of her kidnapping from the casino lot. Dana filled in the rest. When asked why they had gotten involved, they looked at one another and sighed.

***

Dana's phone rang a few minutes past noon, wrenching her from a nightmare. Strange men had been pursuing her and Sarah with attack rifles.

"I just heard your voice mail," a familiar voice said. "I forgot to put my phone on the charger last night."

Dana sat upright in bed. "Kerrie, are you all right?"

"I'm fine. Why do you sound so worried?"

"Long story. We escaped a group of terrorists. They may be after you too. You need to stay away from the office and your apartment?"

"Terrorists? Why me?"

"It's all tied in with the Four Corners murders and the sulfuric acid spills." Dana briefly filled her in on what had happened since she had flown out of Phoenix. "I know it sounds like science fiction but you're in danger."

"I was just going to call you about the murdered women when I noticed your message."

"What about them, dear?"

"Hold on, Mom. Someone's here."

"Wait! You don't know who—"

"He's holding a badge."

Chapter 29

A tall, handsome, sandy-haired man in an expensive, gray suit stood before her desk. He held his badge at seated eye level long enough for her to read "FBI" before he returned it to his breast pocket.

"Kerrie Compton?"

"Yes."

Mid to late thirties, he gave her a smile that made her spine tingle.

"Do you know why I'm here?"

"Not sure, but I just talked to my mother."

"Then you know we're investigating possible terrorist activities?"

"I've been doing some investigating of my own."

"That's why I'm here." He pushed a vase of silk flowers aside and sat on the corner of her desk.

Surprised, she slid her chair back toward the wall. "Let me get you a—"

"No need. I won't be here long. Is there somewhere we can talk privately."

Kerrie glanced about the office and shook her head. "How about the coffee shop down the street. It should be empty by now. There's a booth in the back."

He smiled again and offered his arm. As they prepared to leave, her boss raised a questioning brow.

"Coffee break," Kerrie said, turning her back before she could object.

Once they were on the street, she gazed up at the agent and sighed. He had to be at least six-five. And no wedding ring. Once seated in the back booth with cups of steaming coffee, the agent introduced himself as Roger Brandt.

"From?"

"The Denver office."

She smiled. "A local officer."

He nodded. "I'd like to ask a few questions, if you don't mind."

"Not at all."

"During your research, did you discover a connection between the four young murder victims?"

"As a matter of fact, I did. This morning I read a news article about a convention held in Vegas. I was about to tell Mom when you walked in."

"All four women attended?" he asked.

"Right."

"What kind of convention?"

"Archeology. They were all amateur rock hounds. The article said that they referred to themselves as the Goldie Diggers. All young blondes."

He frowned. "So the fact that the murder victims were from four different states has no bearing on the case?"

"Apparently not. The article said they met at a previous convention and formed a group friendship. I guess the fact that they looked so much alike had attracted them to each other."

"I wonder how that ties in with the terrorists."

"I didn't know about the terrorist angle until I called my mother."

"And?"

"The Goldie Diggers went on a group dig where they found a large, recently buried box."

His eyebrows raised in surprise. "What was in it?"

"Electronic diagrams of some sort."

"Power grids?"

"I'm not sure. They took their find to a Vegas museum."

"Which one?"

"I don't remember. I'll have to look that up."

"Is the article at your office, Miss Compton?"

"My desk drawer."

He stood and offered his hand. "Shall we go?"

"Hold on. I handed you a valuable piece of information. Now it's your turn."

The agent hesitated before resuming his seat.

"Mom briefly filled me in on what's going on. She said my life's in danger. Don't you think that I deserve to know why."

"I'm sorry. I can't tell you."

"Sure you can," she said in a conspiratorial tone. "Why am I now a target?"

"Strictly off the cuff?"

"Of course."

"Your mother should have been told not to talk about the case."

"Not even with me?"

"Not under the circumstances."

"What circumstances? We're talking about my life."

"It's a matter of national security."

"What about *my* security?" Kerrie wailed.

"It's being taken care of."

"How?"

"We'll discuss that later."

He said they could talk more privately in his car. When she balked, he sighed and tried to reassure her that she was perfectly safe in his company.

"What I have to tell you is confidential and should not be overheard by the workers in this shop."

She accompanied him down the block to his late model non-descript sedan. Once seated she pressed him for details, knowing he was hesitant to discuss anything of importance with a journalist. Kerrie assured him she protected her sources and would keep everything he told her confidential. She insisted that she had a right to know about the terrorists' activities.

"I'm telling you this against my better judgment," he said, staring through the windshield. "If the information gets out it could cause a public panic."

She waited, sitting perfectly still.

"The bureau has been following members of the terrorist group for some time. Mark Stone raised red flags last year when he flew to Afghanistan during his two-week vacation to attend a special training camp."

"Terrorist camp?"

"Yes."

"What about James Murphy and his wife Lori?"

"Murphy was recruited to investigate Stone's activities. He was working with a female agent."

Kerrie gasped. "So he wasn't having an affair?"

"Not to my knowledge."

"But the two men were antagonists. How could James find out what Mark was doing?"

"They had mutual friends whom Mark Stone had tried to recruit to his cause."

"But why was Lori Murphy murdered?" Kerrie asked.

"We're not sure. Stone may have tried to recruit her or she might have found out and threatened to expose him and his group."

"Maybe she followed Stone when he buried the box. Or she could have ridden out with him because he thought she was joining the terrorist gang. That would explain how the Goldie Diggers knew where to dig."

Roger's grin ignited his eyes. "You solve puzzles well, Ms. Compton."

"Kerrie," she said, matching his smile.

"I hope you realize that you're among those with targets on their backs."

She groaned. "So you're saying that everyone involved in the case is in danger."

The agent nodded.

"What can we do to protect ourselves?"

"I've assigned an undercover agent to shadow you."

"Follow me around?"

"You probably won't notice him and he won't approach you to tell you who he is. If anyone does, run for your life."

Kerrie smiled. "I have a karate brown belt."

"Don't underestimate them. They've probably earned the equivalent of our black belts and won't be traveling alone."

"Are they planning terrorist activities to take down the country?"

He nodded in the affirmative.

"There must be other ways to protect ourselves, like the Israelis? Didn't they hide in their homes in plastic lined rooms sealed with duct tape, wearing gas masks when scud missiles were hurled their way?"

"So I've heard."

"There must be something we can do."

He tapped the steering wheel with his fingertips. "It's always a good idea to have emergency rations on hand and backup lighting and heat sources."

"You mean like for hurricanes and floods?"

"Right."

"But what if the electronic grid system goes down?"

"It'll bring the nation to its knees. That's all I'm going to say."

Kerrie made a face. "Here I am sitting on the story of the century and I can't even write about it."

"Sorry."

"I like you Roger Brandt but I feel like kicking you."

He smiled but it didn't reach his eyes.

"I've said much more than I should. I'm trusting you not to repeat it."

"Not even to my mother?"

"I'm sure she already knows. Tell *her* not to talk about it. We don't want to cause a panic."

"This really sucks."

The agent opened the driver's door. "I'm trusting you, Kerrie, not to repeat what I've told you to anyone. Let's go back to your office and take a look at the news article."

Although Kerrie was six feet tall, she had to trot to keep up with him. The walk back to the office took half the time as the stroll they'd made to the coffee shop. He resumed his seat on the edge of her desk while she hurried through the article. "Here it is." She read the name and handed him the news magazine.

"Mind if I borrow this?"

She hesitated. "It's research for my Four Corners story."

"I'll see that you get it back. How about tonight?" He fished a card from his wallet and handed it to her. "Call if you dig up anything else."

They both laughed at his unintended pun as she handed him a business card of her own. Before he turned to leave, he warned her to not to open her door to anyone she didn't know.

Kerrie nodded. Tonight? Was he suggesting a date? She didn't think that law enforcement officers were allowed to socialize with their—what? Witnesses, suspects, contacts? What did he consider her? Maybe he only planned to use her as bait for the terrorists. Fingering the card he'd given her, she slid it into her jean's pocket. It was time to call her mother again.

***

Dana was relieved to learn that Kerrie was to have her own bodyguard, although a distant one. She feared the terrorists planned to kill her, not just kidnap her. Had the police arrested them yet? Tiptoeing to the hotel room TV, she switched on the set with the volume on low. After twenty minutes of news, she decided the public hadn't been informed. And probably never would.

Sarah moaned in her sleep. She must be having a nightmare of her own. Dana tented her fingers, saying a silent prayer for her daughter's safety as well as Sarah's and her own. Sleuthing was a dangerous hobby but one to which she was addicted. Kerrie's account of the Goldie Diggers explained Lori Murphy's trip to Las Vegas. But if the terrorists had somehow acquired the plans for the nation's power grids, why would they bury them? Maybe they thought the police were on to them, or they left them for another group of terrorists to implement.

She was tempted to wake Sarah to tell her the news but decided to let her sleep. Dana reclined on her own bed and closed her eyes. Sleep evaded her. Thank heavens the FBI was guarding Kerrie. She wondered whether she and Sarah had their own shadow guards.

Next morning Dana awoke at dawn. What did Kerrie say was the name of the museum? The Archeological Historical Museum? Dana rose from the bed to open the desk drawer. When she found the phone number she wrote it down and decided to call when the museum opened at nine o'clock.

Quietly booting her laptop, she scrolled through news articles concerning the archeological society's convention. Halfway down the page she found pictures of the Goldie Diggers and searched each face to determine which one had been Lori Murphy. Two of the petite blondes dressed in khaki shorts and hiking boots were crouched beside a dig area while the other two looked on.

They all wore smiles and it appeared that Lori still had friends among the group. Probably because the others lived at a distance and she wasn't acquainted with the men in their lives. Or maybe she had decided to keep them as friends by not betraying them. That was a mystery in itself.

Following breakfast they returned to their hotel room and Dana placed a call to the archeological museum. Dana introduced herself as a concerned citizen and after a few moments of chit chat, asked about the box that had been delivered by a group of amateur archeologists. The curator hesitated before she told her about the break-in and stolen artifacts.

So the thieves took enough of the displays to disguise the robbery's purpose. She asked the curator if the electronic diagrams had also been stolen."

"I'm afraid so. They were taken before we were able to determine what they were."

"The police haven't come up with any answers?"

"Not as far as I know. Why are you asking?"

Crossing her fingers, Dana confessed to being a private investigator. She wasn't lying entirely.

"I wish someone would let us know what's going on. The phone's been ringing off the hook. And we've even had two visits from the FBI."

Dana gripped the receiver tighter. "Sounds serious."

"Indeed."

"The women who brought you the box of diagrams?"

"Yes?"

"Were they nervous? Or seem frightened?"

The curator hesitated. "I would say excited is a better word. They women insisted that we catalog the discovery immediately."

"That's strange."

"I thought so too."

"Were you able to—"

"No, the break-in occurred that night."

"Do you have any idea why someone would steal the diagrams?"

"Not unless they're of national importance."

That's what worries me. "Thank you for your time. I hope you're able to recover the stolen artifacts soon."

Dana clicked off before the woman could ask about her investigative credentials. After a moment's reflection, she picked up the phone again and punched in the number for the sheriff's department. She would feel a lot safer if she knew the culprits had been arrested. She was handed off four times before the deputy answered who had taken her last report.

"No such luck," he said.

"But how could they have gotten away?"

"If the organization is as large as we suspect, they were picked up before we had a chance to locate them."

"Then that means—?"

"That you and Miz Cafferty are still in danger. A deputy will pick you up."

"For what reason?"

"Protective custody, ma'am."

"But isn't the FBI watching us?"

"Not to my knowledge. They don't keep us informed."

"Great!" She imagined herself and Sarah behind padded bars.

Chapter 30

Walter called. He had arrived at the airport and would be there as soon as he could rent a car. She was almost glad to hear from him although she knew she was in for a lecture. He'd repeatedly told her not to get involved in the murder case.

Sarah had fallen asleep and Dana turned off her phone, hoping that Walter wouldn't find them until they'd had some sleep. Forty-five minutes later he was knocking at their door.

How did he do that? Dana wondered as she slipped into her robe. The sheriff had grown a lot more resourceful than he'd been as a dog trainer. He also seemed more attractive and distinguished. Dana's heart skipped a beat when she opened the door and saw Walter in his slightly rumpled uniform. But she couldn't let *him* know that. Rubbing her eyes and yawning, she motioned him inside.

He apologized for waking her and took a chair beside her bed.

"Can't we talk later?" she asked, resisting the urge to recline.

"I haven't much time. The perp I arrested is appearing for arraignment tomorrow afternoon. It wasn't a murder-suicide as we first thought. All three family members were killed during a home robbery."

Dana groaned and shook her head. "So you told me. Why are you here?"

"Dana!"

She remembered that look from an exasperated seventh grade teacher.

"You two manage to get yourselves into some of the damndest situations."

"But we manage to get ourselves out."

"With a little help from your friends."

She closed her eyes and nearly nodded off.

"Now what's this about being kidnapped by terrorists?"

"We don't know for sure but they certainly fill all the requirements."

"What's that mean?"

She told him briefly what had happened.

"That's the sloppiest bunch of terrorists I ever heard of."

Dana sighed. "No one said they were geniuses."

"I've heard some of 'em are."

"They've been sneaking across the border with the Mexican nationals and spreading all over the country."

He nodded in the affirmative.

"But the ones who kidnapped us seem the home grown variety. Hopefully they're not connected with the foreign groups," Dana said.

"You mean like Timothy McVey?"

"I'm afraid so."

"What makes people turn on their own countrymen?"

"Money. Thrills. Religious fanatics." Before she could speculate further, her phone rang. A worried Jeff Mailey, their Wyoming bodyguard, was on the line. She could hear relief in his voice. He told her that the local sheriff had called with word that Mark Stone had been arrested in Nevada, and that he had been trying to reach her for hours.

"Thank God. I was afraid —"

"We're fine, Jeff. Sheriff Grayson is here. He just flew in from Modesto." She apologized for not calling him to let him know they had survived their kidnapping.

"I guess you can fill me in on the rest when you get here, ma'am. Have any idea when that'll be?"

"Hopefully soon. Please stay at the mansion until we get there. There are terrorists on the loose."

"Terrorists? You and Miz Cafferty manage to get into some of the darndest—"

"I know. The sheriff has been telling me that."

"I'll camp out here until you're back."

"Be careful, Jeff. The terrorists might just decide to hide out there."

Before he hung up, he promised to alert the local sheriff and keep a watchful eye on the mansion.

Despite her exhaustion, Dana smiled at the thought of Jeff Mailey camped out in a tent on the living room floor.

"What's that smile about?" His jealous expression was back.

"Mark Stone has been arrested. That's one less bad guy to worry about."

"You think he's responsible for all the murders?"

"Yes, Walter, I do."

He grinned. "Say that again."

"You're incorrigible."

"No, just in love."

"Get yourself a room. We'll see you later this morning." Dana pulled down the bedspread and crawled between the sheets.

The sheriff sighed. "I'll see myself out."

Dana was asleep before the door had closed behind him.

Chapter 31

Kerrie felt like a school girl preparing for her first date. How strange, she thought. She'd dated a number of men since college and had been engaged to a fellow journalist she discovered had been unfaithful. She hadn't trusted any man since. Maybe Roger would prove himself trustworthy. She changed clothes several times before deciding on a royal blue suit with a gold silk blouse and matching pumps. With *her* luck he'd want to go bowling.

Checking her reflection in the mirror, she was satisfied he would be impressed. While she was changing earrings someone knocked at her door.

"Who's there?" she called.

"Roger Brandt at your service, madam."

She recognized his voice and unlatched the security chain. She was pleasantly surprised when she opened the door. He was even more handsome in a navy blue suit and gray shirt with paisley tie. His shoes were so well shined that she could see his reflection in them.

He also smelled of British Sterling.

Handing her the magazine he'd borrowed, he waited at the door while she tucked it into a desk drawer. She then invited him in for a small flute of champagne.

He smiled as he accepted the glass and seated himself on the sofa. "What's the occasion?"

"We just heard that Mark Stone was arrested."

He took a small sip. "Yes, that happened this afternoon."

"That should put a crimp in the local terrorist group."

"Eight known members of the group are still at large."

Kerrie sat beside him. "But they're under surveillance, aren't they?"

"We have a general idea where they are."

Kerrie raised her flute to his and the glasses clinked like a small bell tolling. "Here's to the demise of the Saviors. May they spend the rest of their lives behind bars."

Roger raised the flute to his lips to drain the rest of the bubbly. Checking his watch, he said, "If you're ready, we should be on our way. Our carriage awaits."

"Carriage? How romantic."

"I certainly hope so." He rose to his feet and offered his hand.

Kerrie rinsed the flutes in the sink and reached for her purse. After locking up, she took his arm and asked their destination.

His grin was mischievous. "Like Italian food?"

"Love it."

"I made a reservation at the Trattorio del Lupo. We may be a little overdressed but afterward—"

"Yes?"

"I have tickets for the Nevada Ballet Theatre. They're performing Puccini's La Boheme."

"Are you serious?"

When he nodded, she said, "I'd love to attend."

He smiled and pushed the elevator's down button.

Kerrie turned to look back when they left the elevator. A short, dark-haired man dressed in a loose fitting black suit exited the elevator to the right of the one they just left. His eyes were trained on her. So that was her bodyguard. Roger took her hand and led her into the parking lot where a limousine was waiting.

"I feel like Cinderella," she gushed, then realized how immature she sounded. "But all my dates pick me up in limos."

Roger's eyes lighted. "So you're impressed?"

"You might say that."

From the corner of her eye, she noticed the black-suited man move to her left and extend his arm. Was that a gun in his hand? Before she could scream a shot reverberated like a cannon. Roger groaned, clutched his chest and fell to the pavement. Kerrie's arms were wrenched behind her back. When she screamed, a calloused hand grasped her mouth and squeezed so hard that it hurt.

"Keep quiet or you'll join your friend in the hereafter." The man's voice was raspy and cold.

Kerrie was shoved into the limousine where her attacker joined her, pushing a gun into her throat. *They killed Roger.* Tears fell as she contemplated her own fate.

***

Walter had time for an early breakfast with them before he left for the airport. He looked exhausted and Dana asked him to stop flying from California unless or until he was needed. He reluctantly agreed. She then allowed him to hug and kiss her goodbye.

When he left, Sarah glared at her until she asked why.

"Fine way to treat a gentleman and officer of the law."

"You know I'm not ready—"

"Poor Walter. You treat our dog better than him."

Dana groaned. "Poor Bert's been in the kennel for over a month. He won't know us when we go home."

"If Micki didn't have all those cats we could have taken him with us."

The kennel bill would be astronomical but at least their San Joaquin Valley friend was getting well. Despite all the problems they'd encountered during their return trip home, Dana was glad they'd rushed to California to see her. If only Sarah hadn't balked at flying.

A deputy arrived at the hotel within the hour. Dana woke a confused Sarah and helped her into the bathroom to splash her face with water.

"They're not going to put us in a cell, are they, Dana?"

"I hope not, but anything's better than terrorist bait."

"I hope they have good mattresses. I could sleep for a month."

The deputy knocked at the bathroom door. "Let's go, ladies. My shift ends soon."

Dana grumbled to herself as she opened the door.

The deputy turned to leave. "I'll wait outside."

She noticed the deputy's sour expression and decided not to aggravate him further. They gathered up their clothes and stuffed them into suitcases, then applied some makeup and combed their hair. At last ready, Dana left the card key on the dresser and opened the door to their room.

The hotel hall was dimly lighted and the deputy was nowhere in sight.

"Probably went for coffee," Sarah said.

"We did keep him waiting."

Sarah gasped. "Dana, those men—"

"What men?"

"The ones coming down the hall with guns."

Dana backed against the door. They were trapped without a card key. She glanced down at her computer case and over at Sarah. "When they get close enough, hit the shorter one in the crotch with your train case and run for the elevator."

Sarah whimpered like a frightened puppy.

"It's our only chance."

"What if they shoot?"

"They won't."

The larger man resembled George and she wondered whether they were brothers. His smaller companion snarled before he reached them. "Down on your knees and don't look up."

"Now," Dana yelled as she drove her computer case into the larger man's groin. Sarah shrieked like a Ninja as she did the same with his surly companion. Both men groaned and doubled over.

Dana grabbed Sarah's hand and raced for the elevator. Punching the down button she peered down the hall. The smaller man was already standing upright and pointing his gun at them.

"The stairs." She grabbed Sarah's arm and jerked her around the corner and along the L-shaped hall. Sarah's breathing was so labored that Dana feared she'd have a stroke.

"Down two floors, then turn to your left," she said as Sarah followed her down the stairs. "There's a janitor's closet on each floor next to the stairs. We'll hide in there."

When they reached the second floor, she heard the door above them close. If either she or Sarah fell it was all over. Wrenching the door open, she reached for Sarah's arm and they made a quick left. The door to the janitor's closet was unlocked and they closed it behind them. Sarah sounded as though she were hyperventilating. Dana's own breath came in short, painful gasps. What if the men had heard them? She prayed they'd continue descending the stairs. Just in case, she groped for the broom she had seen before they closed the door. She handed Sarah a mop. There were no other weapons available. Breathing shallowly, they waited for what seemed an eternity, nearly gagging on the smell of cleaning fluids.

***

"Knock off the blubbering," the large man said, pressing the gun into Kerrie's cheek. She had no doubt he'd pull the trigger. Gulping back tears, she shuddered at the thought of the FBI agent dying on the parking lot pavement. She then heard a wail of what she hoped was an ambulance coming in their direction.

The limo briefly pulled off the side of the road and she watched a fire truck race by, followed by an ambulance. She prayed the paramedics would save Roger's life.

"Where are you taking me?"

Her answer was another jab from the gun barrel. Her only chance at survival was to take the gun away from him. Leaning forward and pretending to choke with tears, she ducked sideways and grabbed for the barrel. Pushing it away from her, she heard the gun go off. The blast felt as though it had burst her ear drum as the limo driver slumped over the wheel. Realizing they were going to crash, Kerrie took advantage of the gunman's surprise by chopping down hard on the large man's wrist, dislodging the gun from his grip. She then drove her elbow into his throat.

The limo crossed over the passing lane and crashed into a concrete highway abutment.

***

Dana stood ready to jab her mop handle at the throat of anyone who opened the door.

"Where did you learn all these mean tricks?" Sarah whispered.

"When Kerrie told me she was into karate I decided to take a self-defense class of my own. That was several years before I met you."

"Thank the Lord and pass the ammunition."

"Ssshhh, I hear someone coming." Dana pointed the broom handle in an upward position, ready to thrust if the closet door opened. Holding her breath, she heard footsteps stop and the door handle turn. When it opened the hallway lights nearly blinded her as she jabbed with her weapon. A scarecrow of a man with a shock of gray hair howled in pain and backed away from the door.

"J-Janitor," he said. "What are you doing in there?"

Dana shushed him and motioned for him to come closer. She then told him about the armed men, with whispered interruptions from Sarah.

"That explains all the cops in the lobby."

"Did you notice two men with guns running down the stairs a few minutes ago?" Dana described them.

"Yeah, one of them fools about knocked me down."

Dana wondered if the police in the lobby were FBI or uniformed officers, and whether they had captured the terrorists. She asked if the janitor would find out all he could while they remained in the closet. He hesitantly agreed.

"Make sure they're police before you tell them where we are," Sarah said.

The janitor nodded and left.

The stench of cleaning fluids was making breathing difficult. They couldn't possibly stay there much longer.

Chapter 32

Kerrie regained consciousness to the sound of waning sirens. Her head hurt as it never had before. Someone was groaning beside her and the memory of what had happened gradually returned. Attempting to move, she found that she was blocked between her own seat and the one behind the driver. Shoving with her shoulder, she was able to move the front seat a few inches but not enough to extricate herself. A man's leg was twisted at the ankle, the foot hanging at an angle inches from her face when she managed to turn her head. Neither Kerrie nor her abductor had been wearing seatbelts.

The limousine seemed to have landed on its side and she couldn't regain her balance. If the sirens she'd heard were from emergency vehicles, why hadn't someone opened the limo door? Fighting the urge to drift off again, she heard a man's voice but didn't know where it was it coming from.

She yelled for help. "These men have kidnapped me. The driver's dead or critically wounded."

"Don't move," the voice warned. "We'll cut you out of there. The limo's badly damaged."

Kerrie envisioned the "jaws of life" she'd seen during her first month as a news reporter. She twisted to look over her shoulder at the broken window behind her. A sharp pain in her back caused her to whimper, "Where are you?"

"Right here beside the limo. Don't move. You don't want to make your injuries worse."

Closing her eyes, Kerrie gave in to the warm, swirling sensation which overcame her. Visions of Roger holding his FBI badge swam in a distorted image. She then heard the gunshot and watched him fall to the pavement.

"No!"

A hand grasped her shoulder. "We've got you now. You'll be all right."

Kerrie drifted off again and awoke in a hospital bed. The odor of disinfectant made her wince. Disoriented, she tried to raise her arm to hold her throbbing head, but realized she was strapped down. She struggled to free herself until a soft woman's voice told her to lie still.

"What happened?"

"You were in a serious accident."

"What happened to the others?"

The nurse paused. "I'm afraid they didn't survive."

"Thank goodness," Kerrie said beneath her breath.

The nurse looked stunned.

"Long story," she said. "I was kidnapped by terrorists."

The nurse raised a brow and patted her arm. "You've had a serious bump on the head. What happened will come back to you."

Kerrie's vision slightly blurred and she tried to focus on the petite, white-haired person standing next to her bed. She knew the nurse didn't believe her. Remembering Roger Brandt, she asked if he had survived.

"I can check for you, if you like."

"Thank you." *Please let him be alive.* She managed to tent her fingers at hip level, cursing beneath her breath that they had restrained her. They must think *she* was one of the terrorists.

Kerrie groaned. Of course they thought she was one of the bad guys. Birds of a feather.

***

Sarah gasped when someone tapped the door. Terrorists wouldn't knock. They'd simply jerk the door open. She turned the knob and peered through a narrow crack.

The janitor stood there grinning. "You'll be happy to know that your friends just got busted."

"Friends?" Sarah's tone was hostile.

Dana asked how and where it happened.

"The fools came running into the lobby with guns in their hands. The cops jumped 'em before they knew what was happening."

Both women sighed and left the closet.

Dana wondered how many more of them were still at large. Her cell phone rang as they were waiting for the elevator. A woman who identified herself as a supervisor at a Denver hospital, said that Kerrie had been involved in an accident but was recovering nicely.

"What happened?

"She was riding in a limousine."

"In Denver?"

"Yes, and I'm afraid her companions didn't survive the crash."

"Companions?"

"I'm sorry. I can't tell you more."

"But my daughter said that she had a date tonight. Was he also involved in the accident?"

"As I said before—"

"Never mind. I'll catch the first plane to Denver." Dana clicked off before the woman could say another word.

When she explained to Sarah what had happened, they hurried to the lobby where they were immediately stopped and interrogated. Dana at last convinced them they had to leave for Denver. One of the officers offered to take them to the airport.

241

While waiting for their flight, they watched a television broadcast about the accident. Photos of the men killed were flashed across the screen.

"Sarah, that looks like George and . . . Mark Stone?"

"How can that be? Jeff said Stone was arrested here in Nevada."

"Maybe the terrorists bailed him out in time to kidnap Kerrie."

The news anchor said an FBI agent had been shot and badly wounded outside Kerrie's apartment shortly before the accident. He insinuated that Kerrie had been under arrest when rescued by her cohorts, following the shooting of Roger Brandt.

"Kerrie is under arrest at the Denver hospital," Dana said. "We've got to see her before she's taken to jail."

"Call the hospital and ask for her."

Dana sat on the nearest bench and dialed information. When the hospital receptionist answered, she said that Kerrie wasn't permitted calls.

"What do you mean I can't talk to my own daughter?" Dana's voice rose and others were staring.

Sarah insisted that she call Walter. He would straighten things out.

"But he just flew back to Modesto. He can't afford to keep flying."

"He'd spend his last dollar on you, Dana."

Dana picked up her cell and called. When he answered Walter sounded as though he had just awakened. Dana apologized and told him of Kerrie's arrest. He agreed at once to call the Denver police department. While she waited for his return call, she sank into a blue funk that deepened when Sarah told her their flight to Denver had been delayed. The airport was crowded with people leaving and going to the casinos. She was surprised that Sarah wasn't searching for a video poker machine.

As they waited in line to board the plane, Dana's cell phone rang. The caller I.D. said it was Walter. He didn't sound happy when he said, "She's been transferred to a more secure section of the hospital with a concussion and contusions. She'll be okay but they're waiting to talk to Roger Brandt before they release her."

"Kerrie's date? Is he all right?"

"Roger Brandt survived his surgery but hasn't regained consciousness."

"Will they let me visit Kerrie?"

"I arranged a meeting with a Lieutenant McGregor for you. He'll see that you get in to see her, if only for a few minutes."

"We're boarding the plane right now. I'll call after I visit Kerrie."

"I love you, Dana."

She hesitated. "I think I love you too, Walter."

He sighed and clicked off.

Was it love or gratitude? She wasn't sure but she didn't know what she would do without him.

***

They fell asleep during the flight and awoke with a start when the captain's voice announced their approach to Denver International Airport. A lack of luggage made them suspect and they hurried off the plane to catch a cab to the hospital. Visiting hours were over and they were told that Kerrie had been moved.

Dana swore beneath her breath. She didn't dare cause a scene. Hospital guards would turn them over to the local police. She had to contact Lieutenant McGregor. He must know by now that Kerrie wasn't a terrorist. The FBI agent would testify to that, *if* he regained consciousness. What was his name? Roger somebody.

Sarah remembered that it was Brandt and they hurried to admissions. A woman of latin descent informed them that because they were not related, no information about Roger Brandt's condition would be forthcoming.

They walked back down the hall and took a seat in the nearest waiting room. Dana called the number Walter had given her for Lieutenant McGregor. She hoped it was his cell phone. When he answered he said he was in the middle of a late dinner and that he would call her back. Dana fumed as she flipped the cover of her phone and replaced it in her purse.

"What's wrong, Dana?"

"No one seems to care that an innocent young woman is being held against her will. An injured one at that, who needs her mother."

"She's a grown woman."

Dana's temper flared. "She needs me, Sarah."

Sarah grimaced, mumbling something about her own daughter.

Dana's cell phone rang and she scrambled to open her handbag to retrieve it. Lieutenant McGregor apologized for the delay and said that he had arranged a brief visit with her daughter.

"How brief?"

"Five minutes."

"But I flew all the way from Las Vegas to see her."

"Best I can do."

Dana bit down hard on her lip to keep from screaming. "You can't suspect my daughter of terrorism."

"Not my call to make. She was with the FBI agent when he was shot. She might have been under arrest when it happened."

"She had a *date* with Roger Brandt. I hardly think he would have arrested her."

"That's conjecture, I'm afraid."

"What if Brandt dies before—"

"We'll investigate further."

"Lieutenant, my daughter's a staff writer for Denver's *City Magazine*. You can call her editor."

"Someone from my office will call in the morning. In the meantime I suggest that you visit your daughter before she's transferred."

"To where?"

"City facilities."

This can't be happening. She clicked off and repeated the conversation to Sarah. "This is my fault that Kerrie's involved."

"Kerrie was already investigating the murders before we discovered Lori's body. The terrorists already knew about her, Dana."

"Only because we got involved."

"What's the old adage about hind sight?"

Dana checked her watch. It was nearly ten o'clock. "Let's go see Kerrie before we decide what to do next."

Chapter 33

Kerrie was sleeping soundly when they entered the room. No one was visible at the nurse's station so Sarah followed Dana into the small, one-bed room. Dana hated to wake her daughter but time was of the essence. She knew a nurse would soon arrive to order them out.

Kerrie awoke as though she'd been drugged. An IV was attached to her right arm, the large bandage covering her hair resembled a white helmet. She was strapped to the bed in several places, which made her mother angry.

"Look what they've done to her, Sarah. She's not a criminal."

Squeezing Kerrie's hand, she leaned to kiss her forehead below the heavy bandage.

Kerrie's eyes flickered open but a moment passed before she responded. "Mom? Sarah? Am I dreaming or are you really here?"

"Sarah and I just flew in from Vegas."

"Vegas?" She didn't seem to comprehend.

"How are you feeling?" Sarah asked, patting her arm.

"Like a catcher hit in the head with a baseball bat."

Dana clucked sympathetically.

"Have you heard about Roger?" Kerrie asked.

"Just that he survived his surgery."

"He's the one, Mom. My prince charming."

"How can you know that from a first date?"

"It wasn't even a first date but I know."

Dana and Sarah exchanged questioning glances. Kerrie's head injury must have been worse than they feared.

A middle-aged, overweight nurse bustled in. Stopping short, her mouth dropped open. "No one's supposed to be in here," she snapped, attempting to shoo Kerrie's visitors away.

They had permission from Lieutenant McGregor, Dana explained, but she was told they hadn't been approved by the head nurse. "And she won't be on duty until tomorrow morning."

"Merciful heavens," Sarah said. "We hopped on the first plane from Vegas and I'm scared to death of flying."

"Las Vegas?" The nurse appeared horrified. "No wonder this young woman's incarcerated. She has gamblers for role models."

Kerrie laughed and immediately groaned. "It hurts, Mom."

Dana drew herself up to her full height and scowled at the short, heavy nurse. "Don't even think about making us leave. My daughter is in pain and needs me."

Backing out the door, the nurse rushed down the hall.

"She's going to call security, Dana."

"After all that we've been through, hospital security doesn't scare me." She gently hugged Kerrie and hurriedly briefed her on everything that had happened since they left Phoenix. Kerrie then told them about her kidnapping and the FBI agent who had charmed her. She begged them to find out how he was.

"Ma'am?" The security guard's voice was a near tenor. "Visiting hours are over. You'll have to come back in the morning."

When Dana started to protest, Kerrie said, "It's okay, Mom. Just knowing you're here makes me feel better."

Sarah gripped Kerrie's arm. "As Governor Arnold once said, "I'll be back. . . bright and early in the morning." Her Austrian accent left something to be desired.

Kerrie smiled and waved goodbye from the strap on her wrist.

***

They booked a room at the Brown Hotel. Wiping a tear form the corner of her eye, Dana first called Walter. Maybe he could learn how well the young agent was recovering. Kerrie needed some good news. When she told him the hospital had her daughter strapped down, he was angry.

"Those idiots. I'll fly to Denver tonight to straighten them out, if I have to."

"What about your job?"

"To hell with the job. I'm retiring in a couple of months, anyway."

"Don't risk your retirement. If we can't straighten this out tomorrow, you can make some calls from your office."

"Whatever you say, Dana. You know I'll do what I can."

"You're my hero, Walter, but don't risk your future—"

"Our future."

"We'll talk about it later." She hung up before he could say another word.

Sarah was already asleep in her queen-sized bed, so Dana undressed and climbed into her own. It was close to midnight and she knew she'd get little sleep, thinking of Kerrie. Her pillow was damp when she nodded off.

Sarah woke her at six the following morning, hungry and ready to leave. Moaning from lack of sleep, Dana got dressed with half-closed eyes and decided to forgo her makeup. When she thought of Kerrie, she grabbed her cosmetics bag and followed Sarah from their hotel room. Breakfast was eaten in the hotel dining room where Sarah called a cab to take them to the hospital.

"We're a little early for visiting hours. Think we can sneak in like we did last night?"

"If we're caught, I know they'll make *you* leave. You're not a relative."

"Sure I am. I'm Aunt Sarah Cafferty."

"You're not tall enough to be a member of our family."

"From Kerrie's dad's side then."

Dana smiled for the first time in days. "He was six feet six."

"But they don't know that. You could have married a midget."

"Okay, Auntie Sarah. You can be my sister-in-law from Nebraska."

They skirted the admissions desk and headed for the nearest elevator. Few people were moving about. Those that were wore hospital uniforms and didn't seem to notice them. Not until a nurse accompanied them in the elevator as far as the fifth floor. They sighed with relief when she left.

When the elevator opened on the top floor, Dana craned her neck to look down the hall in both directions. When no one appeared, they crept to Kerrie's room. They found her asleep and still in restraints. Dana resisted the urge to swear like a drunken sailor.

Checking her watch she wondered whether Lieutenant McGregor was in his office. Posted hospital rules mandated no cell phone use, so Dana locked herself in the restroom to call. When McGregor answered, he seemed evasive. He said he hadn't had time to contact the Arizona police. Dana responded with quiet fury.

"You may not be aware that my daughter is an award-winning photojournalist. You're not going to smell like roses when she writes her story about police incompetence and the Four Corners murders."

"You threatened me with her job earlier," he said.

"There's also the matter of the terrorist conspiracy to take down the country's power grids and annihilate millions of people."

"What?" He sounded shocked.

"The FBI hasn't filled you in?"

"Where did you get the information?"

"My friend and I were kidnapped by terrorists in Las Vegas." She thought she heard him snicker.

"I'll get back to you, Miz Logan."

"Release my daughter or I'll go to the *Denver Post* and tell them everything."

Dana heard a click as the phone call was disconnected. A moment later she not only heard but felt an explosion that rocked the building.

Sarah jerked the restroom door open, her eyes wide. "Did you hear—?"

"It felt like an earthquake."

They both rushed to the windows.

Sarah reported smoke rising from the nearby L-shaped hospital wing. "Oh, my Lord. Someone is trying to blow up the hospital."

Clouds of smoke and debris saturated the air and were moving in their direction. Chunks of concrete rained down on the parking lot, striking cars, and several people were face down on the pavement. The fog-like cloud soon made the windows in the room opaque and they couldn't see a thing.

Dana rushed to Kerrie's side and worked to free her of her restraints.

"What's happening, Mom?" Kerrie's worried expression mirrored her own fear.

"We're getting you out of here."

They could hear people screaming and the sounds of sirens in the distance.

"Sarah, find a wheelchair for Kerrie. We've got to leave before the entire building collapses."

Dana carefully removed the tape securing the IV to Kerrie's arm. She then slowly pulled the needle. Grabbing a tissue from the bedside table, she pressed down on the puncture wound to prevent it from bleeding. Kerrie winced but didn't make a sound. Moments later Sarah arrived with a wheelchair and they helped Kerrie into it.

Sarah wore a pained expression. "Smoke's filtering into the hall and it's getting hard to breath. We'd better hurry if we want to use the elevator."

"We're not supposed to use the elevator if there's a fire," Kerrie said.

"We have to use it. We can't take the wheelchair down the stairs. Good thing this is a detention floor. There doesn't seem to be anyone in the other rooms."

Grabbing a blanket to cover Kerrie, Dana pushed the wheelchair down the hall. Anyone else on the sixth floor must have taken the stairs. Dana repeatedly pushed the down button but the elevator seemed stalled on a lower floor.

"What'll we do, Dana?"

"Two more minutes and we'll have to carry her down the stairs."

"I can walk, Mom. Just help me out of this chair."

"No, Kerrie, You might have injuries you're not aware of."

"It's better than becoming a crispy critter."

"If you're sure."

Kerrie raised both arms for help and they pulled her from the chair.

"You're barefoot." Sarah turned to run back to the room to retrieve Kerrie's slippers. In the meantime, the elevator door opened and Dana helped Kerrie back into the chair and pushed it inside. She then reached to hold the door open. A smoky mist soon filled the interior and they both began to cough.

"Sarahhh," Dana yelled. "Forget the slippers." She noticed a green garbed hospital employee running in her direction. When she stepped into the elevator, she pushed the down button and ordered Dana to release the door.

"My friend's on her way."

"Close the door!"

"No!" Dana's size and anger must have intimidated the petite woman. After a moment's hesitation, she left when Dana told her to take the stairs.

The smoke grew denser and they were coughing when Sarah appeared with the slippers. Dana pushed the lobby button and the elevator jerked downward. It was like peering through San

Joaquin Valley fog when she glanced at her companions. Dizzy, she told Sarah to join her on the elevator floor. It seemed an eternity before the door opened into the lobby. Firemen were already there helping people into the parking lot. Some were on gurneys, others in wheelchairs. A few were walking wounded. The lobby was crowded and they had to wait their turn.

Between coughing spasms, Kerrie asked about Roger Brandt. "We've got to find him, Mom." She seemed on the verge of hysteria.

A young male nurse directed them to the northern section of the parking lot where medics were holding triage. Once there, they saw a huge gaping hole in the side of the building with smoke billowing from it. How many people had been killed or badly injured? And why bomb the hospital? To kill Kerrie and the FBI agent? That was too farfetched to believe.

Smoke billowed from the building as medics rushed from the lobby pushing patients in wheelchairs and on gurneys. Some were bleeding and hadn't received medical attention. Others staggered from the lobby and collapsed onto the parking lot pavement from smoke inhalation. There were not enough doctors and nurses to tend to everyone. Dana thought she saw a wounded doctor through the fog of smoke and debris.

Thank God they were able to get Kerrie out of the hospital in time. She glanced down at her daughter who looked so pathetic in the wheelchair with the huge bandage covering her head as well as scratches and bruises on her pretty face. Everyone was still coughing and covered with debris that had rained down on them.

It wasn't long before more emergency vehicles arrived, among them ambulances from other hospitals. The parking lot was already crowded with the injured as well as the dying. The screaming of sirens filled the air along with that of human voices. It was a nightmare first class.

Dana wanted to rush to help the injured but was afraid to leave Kerrie. Sarah sat on the pavement holding her head and coughing. She needed attention as well. Dana felt like screaming but knew she had to remain calm. There was nothing she could do besides comfort her daughter and best friend.

A male voice repeatedly called Kerrie's name and they turned in his direction. A handsome young man lying on a gurney was facing them, a portable IV attached to his arm. Kerrie immediately tried to move her wheelchair toward him. It had to be Roger Brandt.

Dana helped Sarah to her feet and tried to maneuver Kerrie's wheelchair through the rubble. Sarah helped to clear a path by picking up pieces of concrete blown from the building until a narrow path led to Roger's gurney. They left the two young people alone for some time as they talked together amid the confusion. Watching them from twenty yards away, Dana noticed them holding hands. They had to be the only people among the injured who were smiling.

Dana's spirits rose although there didn't appear to be a solution to their problems. Only two of the terrorists had been killed, and two others captured by the police in Las Vegas. She prayed that the rest of the gang had been rounded up by Roger's fellow FBI agents. Regardless, the country was still in danger.

She could only speculate about how many people had been killed or injured in the blast. The terrorists were inhuman. She reached to wipe tears from her gritty face and wondered what she could do to help. She noticed an older man lying on the pavement and rushed over to him. His head was covered in blood and he didn't seem to be breathing.

"No," she screamed. "This can't be happening."

***

Roger gave Kerrie his best smile although he flinched before it faded. He was obviously in a great deal of pain. She reached for his hand and kissed it, telling him how happy she was that he had survived.

"Just thinking about you kept me going," he said.

"You're echoing my own thoughts."

"Do you believe in love at first sight?"

She smiled. "I do now."

He groaned and closed his eyes.

Kerrie sat watching him for several moments before fear prompted her to squeeze his hand. She sighed with relief when he opened his eyes. They were oblivious to the chaos going on around them until an orderly rushed over to move Roger's gurney farther away from the building. Kerrie then realized that smoke still billowed from the hospital and a steady stream of patients and their visitors continued to leave the lobby and move to the outer borders of the parking lot where ambulances were waiting.

She turned back to Roger. "Wasn't the FBI watching the terrorists?" The pained expression on his face told her that this was not the time to discuss the bureau's failure to apprehend the Saviors.

***

Five men dressed in green scrubs and carrying large black medical bags crept down a hospital corridor on the main floor. They wore white gauze masks, which served not only to disguise them but to help them breath in the smoke filled corridor. Three of them checked to make sure no one else was in the wide hallway before they halted at the gift shop, locking the door behind them.

The frightened shopkeeper hadn't stopped long enough to lock up following the explosion. It had probably been an employee who wasn't concerned with possible looting. If the door had been locked, they were prepared to force it open. A fourth man stepped into an alcove and crouched near the shop to watch while his companions completed their work.

Each emptied the contents of their medical bags on the floor and set about putting the ingredients together while the fifth man patrolled that section of the hospital. If any of them had been stopped and searched before they entered the gift shop, the contents of their medical bags might have raised suspicion but would not have caused undue alarm under the circumstances. With so many people injured and dying, a few hospital orderlies were the least suspicious suspects in the area. Or so they hoped.

When the detonator had been set, they only had fifteen minutes to escape the resultant blast. The man who had been lurking in the alcove rapped on the glass door and motioned for them to hurry. Holding his left arm across his chest, he pointed to his watch. It was time to set the next charge.

***

Dana noticed a tall, dark-haired man approach Roger's gurney. After a brief exchange, Kerrie nodded and moved her wheelchair away. When Dana hurried in her direction, Kerrie signaled her to stop. She wasn't ready to leave the FBI agent just yet.

A second explosion directly under Kerrie's former room nearly lifted Dana from the pavement. She heard Sarah scream as everyone who could, ducked and ran for cover. Clouds of debris filled the air, reminiscent of the 911 explosions. Dana ran to push Kerrie to safety. In her haste, she missed a chunk of concrete on the pavement that had exploded from the hospital building. Catching her foot on the edge, she tripped and fell headlong to the pavement. The screams of the injured faded as she slipped from consciousness.

Kerrie had her back turned and crouched in fear at the second explosion. She was far enough away that she wasn't struck with falling debris but the dust storm coated her with grit and concrete dust. She could taste the powder and smell the lime residue.

She didn't see her mother fall. From her vantage point, she watched the fire department rush into action with hoses trained on the resultant blazes. She wouldn't tell her mother her suspicions that the bombs had been set to kill her and Roger.

Why would anyone go to so much trouble? Craning her neck to determine where the agent had pushed Roger's gurney, she was relieved when she noticed him raise his hand to wave at her from the northern edge of the parking lot. The lot was so littered with debris that she couldn't maneuver her wheel chair in his direction.

Dust and debris still rained down as she managed to pivot 180 degrees, looking for another route to Roger's gurney. When dust began to clear she noticed Sarah leaning over someone injured on the pavement. Whoever it was had auburn hair like her mother. No, it couldn't be. Kerrie pushed the wheelchair forward as far as it would go, then tried to lift herself to her feet.

"Mom," she screamed.

Sarah must have heard for she raised her head to stare at her. Holding her hand to caution Kerrie to not move, she carefully rolled Dana onto her back. Unaware of how badly her mother was injured, Kerrie cried out in frustration. How could any of this be happening?

Someone in green scrubs rushed toward Kerrie wearing a white gauze mask. When he reached her, she told him to push her to her mother's side. Instead, he wheeled her in another direction. Kerrie continued to scream but no one noticed. There were too many injured people crying out and not enough medics to help them.

Whoever was pushing her laughed. "Thought you'd get away from us," he said, leaning close to her ear.

Kerrie balled her fist and thrust it over her shoulder, striking him in the face. Blood burst forth from his nose, spattering the shoulder of her white hospital gown. Then, with all the strength she could muster, she lifted herself from the chair and moved as fast as her wobbly legs would carry her. She managed to reach a male nurse and grab his arm to prevent herself from falling. When she turned to look back, her assailant had disappeared into the cloud of dust.

"Some terrorists blew up the hospital," she gasped. "My friend is an FBI agent." She pointed at Roger through the smoky haze.

"My mother's injured. Please help her." She indicated the area where Dana still lay.

The nurse rushed to get her wheelchair. Folding it, he carried it back to where she was sitting on the pavement. Lifting her into the chair, he managed to maneuver it to Roger's gurney and the protection of his fellow FBI agent. He then took off running to help Dana.

When Kerrie told the agent about the man who tried to kidnap her, he radioed other agents in the area, telling them to search for him as well as the other terrorists.

Kerrie pleaded with the agent to take her to her mother, but he wouldn't leave Roger alone. After some discussion with other agents on his radio, he commandeered an ambulance that had just returned from taking a patient to another hospital. The attendants loaded both Roger and Kerrie inside. They then drove back out to the road and made their way to the area where Dana was still prone on the pavement, with the nurse hovering over her.

Roger refused to be taken to another hospital, so both he and Kerrie were unloaded onto the parking lot and the ambulance left to recover other patients. By the time Kerrie reached her mother's side, Dana had her eyes open and was protesting that she wasn't seriously hurt. A large lump had swelled on her forehead but no bleeding was visible.

Sarah stood close by wiping tears from her dusty cheeks. When Kerrie's wheelchair approached, Sarah rushed over to hug her. "You mom's going to be fine. She was hurrying over to get you when she fell."

Kerrie curled her lip and cried.

"The nurse thinks she may have a mild concussion but it's nothing to worry about."

Dana sat up with the nurse's help and managed to smile at her daughter. "We're survivors," she said, before telling the nurse to see to other patients. There were plenty of them in worse shape than she was.

Ambulances from other hospitals were ferrying the most seriously injured patients from the triage area as firemen continued to put out blazes in the hospital. A dump truck and backhoe pulled into the parking lot to rid the area of debris and aid emergency vehicles in their rescue efforts. Someone very efficient was obviously in charge of cleanup.

***

Their planned escape route was blocked by a fire truck that had pulled up to the back entrance of the hospital. The only thing they could do was to retrace their steps and leave by a side entrance. Smoke was now so thick that they could only find their way by placing their hands on the walls. No one but firemen must be left in the building. When they reached the first intersecting corridor, a large man in hazmat gear grabbed the arm of the first faux orderly and told him to leave the building.

"We're looking for patients who might still be inside," the lead man said.

"Everybody's out of the building. You need to leave too."

"But—"

"Out," the fireman demanded. "Leave now by the back entrance."

When the man refused to move, the fireman forcibly turned him around and gave him a more than gentle shove. He then discovered the others. "Outside," he repeated, "or I'll see that you're all arrested. Nobody's getting in the pharmacy."

"We're not after the drugs," one of the masked men said. "We just need to look for—"

The fireman herded them to the back entrance and opened the door. In the light of day he looked like someone from Star Wars with a gas mask that made him sound like Darth Vader. He stood and watched as they scurried off around the building carrying their black medical bags.

When they reached the corner of the building they were stopped by three tall men in gray suits who demanded to see their hospital I.D.s. The men in scrubs all protested that their badges were in their street clothes in the surgery wing. One of them nervously glanced at his watch.

Told to remove their masks and open their medical bags, they hesitantly did as they were told. In the process, the smallest of the men dropped his bag and ran. He was chased down and subsequently handcuffed. The remaining agents drew their guns and demanded that they empty the contents of their bags on the ground. It didn't take the officers long to identify the remnants of bomb making.

Threatening to take them back inside if they didn't confess that another bomb was due to detonate, one of the men told them where to look. A bomb expert was hurriedly called in and made his way to the alleged area.

***

Danny Saunders had been with the Denver police for six years and had a wife and two small sons. He had been in ordinance disposal during his navy career, so when he joined the PD he was a natural for the bomb squad. His partner was out sick and this was a hurry-up job, so he decided to tackle it alone. The gift shop had been trashed and it took him several minutes to find the homemade bomb. The terrorists hadn't made it easy for him, but he thought he had time to disable it.

***

Another explosion rocked the building, leveling the entire right wing. The air was again polluted with blinding smoke and rubble. A large chunk of concrete landed on an ambulance, crushing it as attendants were loading a patient. Those standing nearby were injured to varying degrees as smaller chunks fell around them. There was a rush to clear the entire area and patients were carried or pushed across the street to the city park. The grass was littered with the dying and injured who had not yet been taken to other hospitals.

Dana pushed her daughter across the street to the park and returned with Sarah to move Roger's gurney and IV stand. Police had blocked off the streets around the hospital and everyone who could was helping those who were unable to help themselves. Dana wondered if this was how the 9/11 disaster had happened— on a smaller scale. She hoped no one had jumped from a hospital window. There must have been a number of people killed in the explosions who were still inside the hospital.

She could hear babies crying somewhere in the park. When she reached Kerrie's wheelchair she discovered an infant in her daughter's arms.

"I want one of these for Christmas," Kerrie said and turned to smile at Roger.

Whoa, daughter, you're moving much too fast.

He returned her smile and protested when his FBI friend arrived with several EMTs to load him in an ambulance.

"Boss's orders, my friend," the agent said. "We've got to get you back on your feet."

The agent handed Kerrie a yellow slip of paper. On it was written the name of the hospital where Roger was going to be taken as well as his room number." Come visit him when you're able," he said and left.

Kerrie suppressed a sob as she waved to him with her free hand. When the ambulance pulled away, she said, "Roger was in x-ray when the first explosion happened in the wing where his room was located. He would have been killed if it had happened earlier."

Dana nodded sadly.

"Good thing the second blast was delayed or the three of us would have been blown into the next world."

So Kerrie knew.

"Someone up there's looking after us, dear."

"Or maybe your ESP was working overtime. If you hadn't disconnected my IV and got me in the wheelchair, we'd have all died in my room or the elevator."

"It was pure instinct and a mother's desperate attempt to save her only child."

Kerrie smiled. "I overheard Roger's partner say that they caught the bombers as they were leaving the hospital."

"I wonder why they didn't arrest them *before* they planted the bombs."

"They were all dressed in hospital scrubs and carrying medical bags."

"Then how did the police know—?"

Kerrie lifted the baby to her shoulder. "They stopped people who left the hospital to check for I.D.'s"

"But they didn't know about the bombs until they went off?"

"They found wires and a detonator in one of the bags but they weren't sure where the bombs were planted."

"I hope none of the agents were killed in the blasts."

Kerrie's lower lip quivered. "They discovered one dead police officer so far. He was trying to defuse the third bomb when it went off in the gift shop."

"But why the hospital?"

"Who knows, Mom. Maybe they thought it was a likely first target."

These terrorists were much better organized than those they had dealt with earlier. Hopefully, they thought they'd accomplished their mission. Dana scanned the parking lot from the park, searching for anyone who looked familiar. Or suspicious. It was still total chaos with additional fire trucks moving in and medics rushing to treat victims of the latest blast.

A broadcast truck pulled into the parking lot and added to the confusion.

"Our guardian angels were looking after us, dear."

"I don't know about the angels, Mom. Roger said that the bureau has been guarding the three of us since the shooting–at a distance."

"Using us as bait for the terrorists?"

"I hope not but that's how it seems."

Dana was too relieved to be angry they'd been used as decoys. She hoped the others involved in the terrorist plot had been captured. Recalling the Internet videos of known terrorists photographed by hidden cameras sneaking across the border with Mexican nationals, she knew there could be thousands of them spread out across the country waiting for orders to commit more acts of terror.

As she had watched hospital patients pouring from the building, she wondered whether she was responsible for all this death and destruction. If only she hadn't insisted on pursuing the investigation of Lori Murphy's death. It had nearly cost her own daughter's life.

Sarah reached to hug her when Dana hung her head and cried.

"Dana, two police officers are heading this way," Sarah warned.

"They'll have to take *me* to jail if they want Kerrie."

"Oh, Mom, I can handle it."

A uniformed officer with graying hair approached, his partner standing back. He appeared embarrassed when he said, "Kerrie Compton?"

"You're looking at her."

"Lieutenant McGregor sends his apologies and invites you to join him at the station."

Invite her to the station? Dana thought bitterly. What a nice way to say she was going to jail.

Kerrie laughed. "Tell the lieutenant I accept his apology but decline his invitation. But I'll take a rain check." He seemed surprised. "Are you sure, Miss Compton? I thought you'd want to get away from this mess. Your mother and her friend are welcome to join you."

"I'm sure. There are injured people here who need our undivided attention."

The office nodded and turned on his heel.

"That was gutsy, my dear," Dana said.

"I may need some information from the police for a story someday. It never hurts to have someone in authority that I can contact."

"Are you planning to stay in Denver at the magazine."

"That depends."

"On what?"

"Roger's due for a transfer."

"To where?"

"Cheyenne."

"How did you talk him into that? On such short notice?"

"We're soul mates, Mom."

"I remember another young officer you fell in love with on a first date."

"That was different. I've grown up since then."

"I certainly hope so. It would be wonderful to have you living within driving distance in Wyoming."

"But won't you miss working for the magazine?" Sarah said.

"Not really. Besides, there's a newspaper in Cheyenne that may need an ace reporter. Then again, I might even follow in my Aunt Georgi's keystrokes."

"Meaning?"

"I just might write a mystery series featuring two sassy senior sleuths who can't seem to stay out of trouble."

#

ABOUT THE AUTHOR:

Jean Henry Mead has published 14 books, six of them mystery-suspense and historical Western novels. An award-winning photojournalist, her magazine articles have been published domestically as well as abroad. She also served as a news reporter and news, magazine and small press editor. A native southern Californian, she currently lives in Wyoming with her husband and Australian Shepherd.

The fourth novel in her Logan & Cafferty mystery/suspense series will be released in 2012.

Her website: www.jeanhenrymead.com.